PRAISE FOR MATT DUNN

'Matt Dunn's writing makes you laugh out loud'
– Sophie Kinsella

'Witty, astute, and tender too' – Freya North

'Funny, moving, and a guaranteed page-turner. Brilliant!'
– Mike Gayle

'Frighteningly funny' – Chris Manby

A DAY AT THE OFFICE

A DAY AT THE OFFICE

Matt Dunn

LAKE UNION
PUBLISHING

Text copyright © 2013 Matt Dunn
All rights reserved.

Published by Lake Union Publishing

www.apub.com

ISBN-13: 9781612184555
ISBN-10: 1612184553

Cover design by Inkd

Library of Congress Control Number: 2013915261

Printed in the United States of America

For my goddaughter, Anna Davison

CONTENTS

1

Sophie Jones clutched her Oyster card tightly in one hand, adjusting her scarf with the other as she made her way automatically along Devonshire Road and towards Harrow-On-The-Hill tube station. She'd made the forty-minute journey to and from her office so often now she felt she could almost do it with her eyes shut, and had actually tried that once, thanks to one cocktail too many with the girls after work one day, until a loud honking from the number 340 bus had warned her she'd strayed off the pavement by mistake.

She sighed to herself as she walked, her breath forming clouds in the crisp February morning air, and contemplated another day at the office. So far, her job as a marketing assistant wasn't quite living up to the lofty ambitions she'd set herself back when she'd graduated. And while she wasn't naïve enough to believe a 2:2 in Business Studies meant it was only a matter of time before she'd be declaring herself 'out' from behind a pile of money on *Dragon's Den*, back then, she'd truly believed that if she worked hard enough, anything was possible.

Sophie smiled wryly as she strode into the station. Perhaps she simply hadn't worked hard enough. Still, she reminded herself as she swiped her way through the barrier, she was only twenty-eight. The world was still her oyster. She even had the card to prove it.

It wasn't just her career that was getting her down. Since moving to London, she'd been lonely. Not because of a lack of friends—her colleagues in the office were pleasant enough, and her new boss Julie was, well, if not a friend, at least she was friendly—but because of the lack of a boyfriend. The relationship with Darren, her college sweetheart (whom she'd abandoned when she'd moved from Eastbourne to Harrow) had been okay, but not what she'd wanted, and while she might not have known what it actually was she'd wanted, Sophie had been pretty sure she didn't want Darren and the traditional stay-at-home-and-be-a-housewife plans he'd had for her.

Which was why two years ago, more than a little surprised to have landed the first job she'd applied for, she'd handed him the keys to their shared bed-sit just off the sea-front, upped sticks from the sticks, and rented a room in a flat-share here on Devonshire Road. Harrow had sounded exotic to her—well, more exotic than the Costa Geriatrica, as her friends referred to Eastbourne—and it was London, and multicultural, and on the Tube, and full of young people, and next to Harrow-On-The-Hill, the home of Harrow School, and therefore (Sophie had assumed) a little bit posh.

In reality, it was a little noisier than she'd have liked, and quite a way from the centre of the city, plus her part of Harrow was a bit less salubrious than even the Eastbourne street where she and Darren had lived. And although the recent opening of the 24-hour Tesco Metro on Pinner Road had injected a whole new level of joy into her life, especially the excitement of not knowing what delights would be waiting for her to choose from in the 'reduced' section when she called in on her way home every night, there were times she missed the gentility of the seaside. More worryingly, Sophie realised as she joined the crowds of commuters on the platform—most of whom seemed to be whispering hurriedly into their mobile phones before the Underground journey cut them off from the outside world, or staring fixedly at the 'arrivals' board in the hope this might somehow speed up the appearance of the next tube—there were even times she missed Darren.

Her train arrived, and—more concerned with finding a gap than minding one—Sophie squeezed herself on board. Even this near to the beginning of the line the tube was packed, and her chances of getting a seat were pretty poor at the best of times, but today for some reason her carriage seemed fuller than normal. With a loud 'excuse me,' followed by a sarcastic 'thank you' when nobody moved, she pushed in between a young Asian woman typing a text message on her phone quicker than Sophie could speak and a grey-suited man carrying a huge bouquet of roses, and wedged herself against the window. She glared crossly through the stems, trying not to prick herself on the rose thorns, wondering what kind of idiot carried a huge bunch of flowers on the tube during the morning rush-hour (and more importantly, what he'd done wrong to have needed to buy such an extravagant bouquet) until she realised with a start what was going on. Today was Valentine's Day.

She picked up a discarded copy of *Metro* and checked the date, then peered up and down the carriage. Every third or fourth seat seemed to be occupied by someone carrying flowers, from single red roses to huge bunches of ... Well, she didn't know what they were called, but they were beautiful, and Sophie supposed she should be grateful that for a change the train smelled of something other than sweaty armpits and garlic breath. Other people were clasping gift-wrapped or heart-shaped boxes of chocolates, and she briefly allowed herself to imagine how it would feel to receive such a gift when she got to the office until the reality of her situation hit her, and she swallowed so hard the sound made the woman next to her look up from her phone. The only thing the postman had brought this morning was her credit card statement, and while that had made Sophie's heart skip a beat, that was simply because her January sales shopping spree had pushed the balance scarily close to her credit limit.

Sophie almost wanted to cry. A city of some seven million people, and not one of them had sent her a Valentine's card. Not even Nathan Field, the dreamy guy who ran the technical support desk at her office, though Sophie knew she shouldn't be surprised. London was full of prettier girls than her. Girls who probably wouldn't make fools of themselves in front of him like she had.

She blushed at the memory of her first week at work; she'd been having email issues and hadn't been able to believe her eyes when someone who looked like that guy from the Diet Coke adverts had come to fix them, and there and then she'd decided to invent some technical problem at least once a week. When he'd told her she had problems with her Outlook, she'd bitten her bottom lip suggestively and—Sophie hadn't known what had come over her—told him that wasn't the case from where she was sitting, and for a second or two, she'd thought they were having a 'moment'. Trouble was, the moment had evidently passed Nathan by, as he'd simply mumbled something innuendo-free about needing to reboot her system, and Sophie had felt like curling up and hiding under her desk. From that day forward she'd been too embarrassed to ask for technical support again, relying instead on the well-thumbed (and appropriately titled, Sophie often thought) copy of 'Windows for Dummies' she kept in her desk drawer. Still, she reminded herself, it hadn't been a complete disaster. At least now she could add 'familiarity with Microsoft' to her CV. Even though getting familiar with Nathan was what she'd really wanted.

She turned and stared out of the window, trying to ignore the carriage's loved-up air, knowing it was her own fault she was single. It had been her decision to finish with Darren, and since then she'd justified her lack of a love life by telling herself her career came first. Trouble was, she hadn't been doing so well at that either, and after what had felt like a very long couple of years, Sophie feared her behaviour was becoming desperate; she sometimes tailed good-looking guys round the supermarket to check whether the contents of their shopping baskets included meals-for-one like hers did, or practised signing emails with the surnames of men she barely knew simply to see how it looked, and kept a bottle of Chardonnay permanently in her fridge for 'emotional emergencies,' which turned out to mean most nights when she came home alone. The other day, she'd even considered getting a kitten.

It wasn't that she didn't get her fair share of offers. She wasn't unattractive, and had even been told she looked a bit like Kate Winslet, though the person who'd said that had then proceeded to say he'd hated *Titanic*, which had taken a bit of the gloss off the compliment, and not only because *Titanic* was one of Sophie's favourite films. No, she was just being picky, and besides, it would have to be someone pretty special to divert her from the path of world domination she'd hoped the move to London would set her off on. And while she'd perhaps only gone a couple of steps along that path, Sophie loved where she worked, at a software company in trendy Soho, with her own business cards with her name on them—and not a hand-written-in-black-Biro addition, either. And although she still didn't quite understand what the software did or how it did it, she knew she was working at the cutting edge, for a dot-com, and a search engine too. 'Just like Google!' her dad would boast proudly in front of his friends from the golf club on the occasional weekends she went home to visit her parents, and Sophie would smile and nod, even though exactly how Seek Software was like Google she wasn't sure.

Still, the office was near the bright lights of the West End, and (more importantly to Sophie) the shops along the not inconsiderable length of Oxford Street, which were where most of her salary went in an attempt to keep up with the oh-so-trendy girls she'd eye enviously in the pubs and bars she walked past on her way home. And while she might have preferred to live in Clerkenwell, or Islington, or even Stoke Newington—any of the London areas that regularly appeared in the Sunday supplements as the *latest* latest place to be—Harrow was still London. And that, after all, was the only thing that really mattered.

In actual fact, she'd chosen it at random—the advert on Gumtree had sounded appealing, Meg, the girl she shared with (though hardly ever saw) was nice enough, and most importantly, it was cheap. But as far as Sophie was concerned, moving to anywhere in London would have been a step up. Just to be within even a clanking, stop-start, packed-like-sardines-tube-journey's reach of the centre of the capital—the centre of the world, in Sophie's eyes—made even a miserable commute like hers worth it, and even though she'd swapped the sea, the beach, a pier, and the magnificent beauty of the South Downs for, well, a school and a hill, Sophie swore the only time she'd go anywhere near Beachy Head again would be to throw herself off it.

Her train stopped at Baker Street, and by some miracle, a nearby seat became vacant. Sophie fought her way single-mindedly towards it, and was just about to claim it triumphantly when she noticed a pregnant woman about to do the same. With a sigh, Sophie stood aside, and the woman sat down gratefully. This, she reflected as the tube rattled on, summed up her life since moving here. The attempted flirt with Nathan had been summarily ignored—or not even noticed. The promotion she'd been hoping for had been thwarted by her new boss Julie's arrival in the office just before Christmas. Even the Gucci handbag she'd wanted in the Selfridges sale had been snatched, literally before her very eyes, by a Chinese girl with very sharp elbows. On top of all that, she suddenly realised, for the first time since she'd dumped Darren, the usual unsigned Valentine's card in an envelope bearing an Eastbourne postmark had failed to materialise through her letterbox earlier.

For the second time that morning, Sophie felt her lip trembling, and she tried to prevent the tears coming by conjuring up a brief daydream about Nathan appearing at her desk later with a huge box of chocolates, then decided there was probably more chance of Leonardo DiCaprio getting on at the next stop. She sniffed loudly, and a fat man clutching a bunch of lilies that had seen better days caught her eye from the other side of the carriage.

'Cheer up, love,' he said, grinning at her. 'It might never happen.'

Sophie stared back at him. That, she knew, was her biggest fear. And while normally the thought would have depressed her even further, for some reason, surrounded by all these soon-to-be-delivered or gratefully received declarations of love, of hope, of optimism, she felt strangely energised instead. This year, she resolved there and then, things were going to be different. The world was her oyster, and she was going to grab it by the scruff of the neck, and ... She stopped herself, unsure whether oysters had necks. But Nathan Field certainly did, and a very kissable one, she'd noticed, as he'd leant over her desk that day and she'd caught a whiff of an aftershave that had certainly been an intoxicating step or two up from Darren's Lynx body spray.

The recollection made Sophie's mind up for her. Excitedly, she jumped off the train at Charing Cross and, instead of heading straight for her office, strode purposefully through the station, checked that no-one she knew could see her, and ducked into Smiths.

❦

South of the river, Calum Irwin was ironing his shirt, attending to the collar and cuffs last (a tip he'd picked up thanks to his recent subscription to *GQ Magazine*) to ensure he wouldn't end up creasing them as he ironed the rest of it. He was pretty sure he wouldn't be removing his jacket (or any other items of clothing) this evening, so he supposed he could have gotten away with just doing the visible parts like he normally did, but you never knew, which was why he was also wearing a brand new pair of Calvin Klein 'hipster' underpants—a radical departure from his normal ASDA three-pairs-for-£5 briefs. He'd ironed those as well, and while he'd been slightly disappointed to find out that he appeared not to have any discernible hips (or at least nothing like those of the washboard-stomached model in the photograph on the front of the packet), when he'd pulled the still-warm pants on a few minutes earlier, Calum had consoled himself with the fact that at least the branding on the waistband drew the eye away from the spare tyre above it.

He hung the shirt carefully on the back of a chair, then hunted under his bed for his tallest-heeled pair of shoes, wondering whether he should pick up a pair of insoles on his way to work, or perhaps just wear two pairs of his thickest socks instead. Emma was expecting him to be six foot one, whereas Calum was actually only five ten-and-a-quarter in his stockinged feet.

He smiled to himself at the phrase. He'd written it on his profile when he'd first joined LondonDate, and had received almost a dozen responses (along with some very interesting photographs) straight away from fetishists who'd misinterpreted his description of his height as some sort of code meaning he liked to wear women's underwear. Responses he'd been too scared to follow up, of course.

Valentine's Day had been the goal he'd set himself at Christmas, when, sick at the prospect of another lonely year, Calum had decided to do something about his single status and had signed up for what he'd heard people in the office describe as 'this internet dating lark'—although it hadn't been much of a lark up until he'd heard from Emma, and if anything, the lack of appropriate interest his profile had been getting had made him feel even worse. But today, Calum had a feeling things were about to change.

He considered ironing a spare shirt to take in to work, but quickly dismissed the idea, partly because he hated ironing, but mainly because his job—telesales executive for a software company in central London—meant he didn't have to leave the office, so as long as he watched what he ate and drank over the course of the day, he'd be unlikely to get in a mess.

Calum loved his job. He was good at it, too. And it suited him down to the ground—he was great at cold calling, had an excellent rapport with customers, and most importantly, always seemed to know exactly what to say and when to close the deal. It was ironic, he knew, how he was a good salesman, yet useless at selling himself, though according to all the courses he'd been on, you had to believe in the product, and maybe the issue was simply that he didn't believe in himself—not in person, at least. In front of people—well, women, to be precise—he felt awkward. Started perspiring. Stammered, even. And certainly didn't demonstrate the confidence he exuded on the phone.

Which was why he'd believed internet dating would be the answer. He could do everything over email, or 'live chat'—which was even better than the phone, as far as he was concerned, as the women he'd attempt to (live) chat up couldn't hear any nervousness in his voice. And while at some point Calum knew he'd have to meet them and risk turning back into his sweaty, stuttering self, he'd decided he'd cross that bridge when he came to it.

Besides, he didn't have much choice. Speed dating certainly wasn't for him—he was the kind of person you had to take time to get to know, and three minutes certainly wasn't long enough for that—and at twenty-nine, he'd learned years ago that simply approaching a woman in a bar or a club was asking to be humiliated. No, the more he'd thought about it, the more internet dating had appeared to be the answer. A chance to put himself out there without actually physically having to go out there. And of the hundreds of sites that had come up when he'd typed the words 'internet' and 'dating' into Seek's search engine, LondonDate had appealed over the rest for two simple reasons: Calum lived in London, and he wanted a date.

He'd logged on as a woman first of all to check out his competition, and what he'd seen had horrified him: the men were all buff model-types, or had the same bronzed surfer-dude look as Brad Pitt (one had even appeared to *be* Brad Pitt from his profile picture), and what was worse, they'd posted pictures of various body parts— their ripped abs, or even (in a couple of instances) a few inches beneath them—in order to stand out from the crowd. Some had been standing out more than was decent, and Calum had been appalled, but even worse than that had been the descriptions. How could he ever hope to compete with this bunch of bungee-jumping, Ferrari-driving entrepreneurs?

In the end, he'd decided not to try. 'Just be yourself' had been the advice on LondonDate's website, and Calum had decided to take it, so he'd been honest up front when filling in his profile, telling anyone reading it that if they were expecting some hunky, gorgeous outdoors type then they were going to be disappointed. Trouble was, Calum being himself had only led to a series of disastrous dates, and despite reassurance on LondonDate's forums that it was more about chemistry than looks, Calum had learned that in actual fact, for most people, chemistry was down to looks. And that was where he fell flat on his slightly-less-chiselled-than-he'd-have-liked face.

It wasn't that he was ugly; rather, he was ordinary, and in the super-competitive world of internet dating, where the judging was so superficial, someone who'd never been super anything didn't stand a chance. So with his self-imposed deadline inching ever closer, Calum had taken the radical decision to become, well, 'Calum.' Six foot one. Athletic build—though in truth, and despite the effort he'd been putting in at the gym recently, more of a shot-putter than, say, a hundred-metre runner. At least 'a software professional' was true (he'd thought it sounded better than saying he worked in telesales)—Calum did work for a software company, and he had been told he was very professional (he wouldn't have been made the office fire safety 'responsible person' if he wasn't), so putting the two together wasn't exactly a lie. Whereas 'into adventure sports' was. The closest thing to an adventure sport Calum had ever done was when he'd taken a wrong turn and accidentally jogged through the estate round the corner from the flat in Balham where he lived, and been chased by a scarily fast group of pre-teen hoodies. He'd just about escaped with his iPod. If not his dignity.

He shook his head at the memory as he pulled his shoes on, and made a mental note to do some research when he had a quiet moment in the office, just in case Emma decided to quiz him on the finer points of bungee-jumping or white-water rafting later, though, thinking about it, he could probably just make stuff up.

She was more into long walks in the country, and *Mad Men*, and roaring log fires and dogs—although when he'd quizzed her, she didn't actually live in the country, or have a dog, or a log fire, so he guessed that made them kind of even. Still (and unlike almost all the other single women his age he'd ever met) at least Emma had said she much preferred dogs to cats. And given Calum's cat allergy, he couldn't help seeing that as a sign.

He'd met her within five minutes of changing his profile—well, 'met' in the online sense—but tonight they were actually meeting. In the flesh. Quite a lot of it, on Calum's side. And while it seemed a little strange to him to have their first date on Valentine's Day, Emma had insisted on it, telling him that the fact he could spend this evening with her would prove he was single—unlike most of the other men she'd met on the site, apparently. And even though he'd been initially (and unreasonably) jealous at the thought of her dating anyone else before him, strangely Calum had taken heart from this. If she'd gone out with a number of other men, he reasoned, then she must be a looker. Not that he knew, though, seeing as there hadn't been a photograph on her profile, and she'd refused to send him one. When he'd asked her why, she'd told him looks weren't important, insisting it was what was inside that counted, and while Calum knew he could have taken that as a clue that maybe she was no oil painting, he'd been more worried she was referring to him. Then again, he'd reminded himself, she'd been the one who'd made the first contact, and he'd had a photo up, and it had actually been of him, and of his face, so she must have liked what she'd seen. Though Calum still found that hard to believe.

They'd been corresponding for about two weeks, some nights live-chatting into the small hours like old friends (which by then, Calum felt, they almost were) when Emma suggested they meet up, and he'd leapt at the chance. While she still hadn't sent him a picture, she had assured him he wouldn't be disappointed. And given how excited he was that they were finally meeting, Calum had been more than happy to take her word for it. He'd offered to book the restaurant, and had known just the place—Old Amsterdam, on Charlotte Street. He walked past it every day on his way to work, and though he'd never eaten there, in a moment of inspiration he'd chosen it because Emma had insisted on 'going Dutch,' and while he was well aware that wasn't quite what the phrase meant, at least it would give him an ice-breaker. Start the evening off on a lighter note. Maybe divert her attention away from any inconsistencies she might notice from his profile.

He slipped his shirt on carefully, then checked his watch, his stomach already in knots even though there were ten or so hours to go, but despite his feelings of anxiety, Calum couldn't keep the grin off his face. He had a date. A proper, hundred percent bona fide actual real night out with an actual real live woman, and on Valentine's Day to boot! And while he would have preferred not to have gone straight from the office, he didn't have much choice—Emma had insisted on meeting at six, and on neutral ground, which (since she lived in Archway) seemed to point to central London. Though meeting in the centre of town had its advantages—if they found they had nothing in common, then there'd be no harm done, no awkward 'how do I get out of this?' moments, or tricky share-a-cab situations. They could simply bid each other good night, jump on the bus, and head off in opposite directions, hopefully getting home before the streets became too chock-a-block with loved-up couples, then they'd make for the safety of their computers, delete each other from their 'favourites,' and do their best to forget the evening had ever happened.

Though Calum hoped that wouldn't be the case. He'd had enough of not having a girlfriend, and however bad tonight was, he knew it was better than the alternative. If you were on your own, Valentine's Day was the worst day of the year, given it was impossible to avoid having your single status rammed down your throat. Normally, he'd go to the annual office Anti-Valentine's event that Nathan Field organised (ten-pin bowling this year, so Nathan's email circular had informed him), but for the first time, Calum realised proudly, he'd be able to tell the guys at work he had a date. More importantly, he'd be able to tell himself that. He finished dressing, popped his glasses on, and after a final glance in the mirror, made his way into the kitchen.

'I'm off, then.'

His mother looked up from the large bowl of Special K she was working her way through and made a long-suffering face, and Calum regarded the half-empty box suspiciously. Given how she seemed to be working her way through a large bowl of Special K no matter what time he appeared in the kitchen in the morning, he suspected it wasn't the only one she consumed each day, yet he didn't dare suggest that was the reason the diet her doctor had put her on didn't seem to be working. Either that, or she'd secretly refilled the box with Frosties.

'Without shaving?'

'I'll have a shave at work. So I'll be, you know…'

'As smooth as a baby's bottom for your hot date?' His mother laughed. 'You should think about growing a beard. Your father had a beard.'

'Did he?'

'When we first met, he did. With that bright red hair of his, he was quite a sight, I can tell you. As you would be if you grew one.'

'Mum, no-one has a beard nowadays. Not anyone my age, at least. And for the millionth time, my hair's not red. It's...'

'Strawberry blond. I know. Still, whatever colour you want to call it, you look very smart today,' she said, and Calum blushed.

'Thanks.'

'Come and give me a hug.'

'Mum, I'm twenty-nine...'

'Yes, but, I might not see you later.'

'It's a first date. We're not eloping.'

'Even so. You're leaving here my little boy, and you might be coming back...' She put her spoon down, and regarded him levelly. 'A man.'

'Mum, please.'

'Your dad would have been proud of you. You know that?'

'For what?'

'Well, for looking after me for all these years when you could have been off sowing your wild oats, for one thing.'

Calum rolled his eyes. 'Chance would have been a fine thing.'

She patted the chair next to her, and Calum sat down obediently. 'Now, I know you were too young for him to ever have a little chat with you. So if there's anything you want to ask...'

'About what?'

She lowered her voice. 'S-E-X.'

Calum almost leapt out of his chair. 'Mum!'

'I'm just saying. I wouldn't want you to get in trouble. Or get some poor innocent girl in trouble.'

'Emma's hardly some poor innocent girl, mum.' He grinned. 'At least, I hope she isn't.'

'Well, as long as one of you knows what you're doing.' She reached up and briefly stroked his cheek with her hand, her eyes

15

searching his face, and for a moment, Calum was transported back to the time when he was ten years old, and she'd woken him up with the same gesture to tell him about the car crash that had killed his dad. 'Hold on,' she said, rummaging in her handbag and producing a small gift-wrapped box. 'I've got something for you.'

'You shouldn't have.' Calum took the present and tore off the paper. 'Seriously, you shouldn't have,' he said again, staring in disbelief at the packet of condoms in his hand, and his mother laughed.

'If you think this is embarrassing, imagine how I felt buying them. At my age.'

Calum fought to keep the colour from his cheeks, then looked at the clock on the kitchen wall, and wondered idly whether he should wait in for the postman, but what would be the point? Emma wouldn't have sent him a Valentine's card—she didn't have his home address, just like he didn't have hers, as per another recommendation on LondonDate—and if previous years were anything to go by, his chances of receiving one from anybody other than his mother were pretty slim. Not wishing to appear ungrateful, he slipped the condoms into his inside jacket pocket, then picked up his keys from the kitchen table.

'Don't forget to take your tablets,' he said, sliding the ever-present pill box towards her.

'Yes, dear.'

'Call me if you need anything.'

'I will.'

'And don't wait up.'

'I won't. You have fun, you hear?' His mother smiled. 'And don't do anything I wouldn't do.'

'Mum!'

'I'm just saying,' she said again, before turning her attention back to her breakfast.

Calum smiled as he shut the kitchen door behind him, then caught sight of his reflection in the hallway mirror. Worried his current pallor made him look like an extra from the *Twilight* films, he considered whether he had time to fit in a tanning session at the gym, but it was February, and he didn't want to look unnaturally bronzed this evening. Besides, knowing his luck (and his Irish heritage) his face would only end up as red as his hair.

He checked his breath in his cupped hand, his wallet for cash, and his briefcase for the foil-wrapped red rose he'd bought on the way home the previous day. With a final run-through of his mental checklist, he picked up his gym bag from its usual spot by the front door, hurried out of the flat, and made his way excitedly towards the bus stop.

∽

Meanwhile, in the kitchen of his Bayswater flat, Nathan Field peeled today's cartoon from the front of his Dilbert calendar—an ironic (he hoped) present he'd received in the office Secret Santa exchange at Christmas—double-checked the date on his iPhone, then balled the cartoon up without reading it and tossed it angrily into the bin. To tell the truth, he normally found Dilbert amusing, but as far as Nathan was concerned, there was nothing funny about Valentine's Day.

Not that he had a problem with the concept. Nathan was all for celebrating love. What he didn't want to celebrate was Ellie dumping him. And today, as he'd painfully remembered as soon as he'd woken up from a fitful night's sleep, was the third anniversary of that.

Nathan shuddered as he thought back to that fateful night. It hadn't been an ordinary dumping—despite the date, he could have coped with that. This one had been played out loudly in public, surrounded by loved-up couples at his and Ellie's favourite Italian restaurant in Notting Hill, and the end of a two-year, five-month, and fourteen-day relationship. Though that hadn't been the worst of it: Nathan had been down on one knee at the time.

He still had the ring—it had been his grandmother's—hidden inside a pair of reindeer-patterned novelty socks (the previous year's Secret Santa gift) in his underwear drawer, though he doubted he'd ever propose with it again. Not that there was anything wrong with it, but Ellie's refusal had somehow tainted the thing, although for a few, desperate moments, he had thought she simply hadn't liked the antique silver-and-diamond combination, before he'd realised something that had been a much harder thing to swallow than the oysters he'd impulsively ordered as a starter: she actually hadn't liked *him*.

Afterwards, when shock had turned into disbelief, then anger, then tears, Ellie had confessed she'd been planning to leave him for weeks, though if the admission was supposed to make him feel better, it hadn't. Why she'd waited until Valentine's Day of all days was still a mystery to him. As was how she'd found the time to meet the 'someone else' she was leaving him for.

Nathan still didn't know what had gone wrong, though he supposed his job hadn't helped. Ellie worked in the glamorous world of PR—each week she'd have some trendy new nightclub, glitzy restaurant, or swanky cocktail bar to promote, whereas 'glamorous' was the last word you'd use to describe his profession. Everyone thought people who worked in technical support were geeks. Nerds. That they probably still lived with their mothers, and spent their evenings satisfying an Angry Birds addiction, or on Facebook, or playing some strange sword-and-sorcery computer game into the small hours in the company of their virtual friends because they didn't have any real ones. Maybe Ellie had simply been ashamed of him. Embarrassed, perhaps, by the prospect of spending the rest of her life explaining to people that her husband was a techie.

Though Nathan had never fitted the typical profile of one. He was tall, for a start, his hair wasn't greasy, and the only glasses he ever wore were a vintage pair of aviator-style Ray-Bans. He played football twice a week—in person, not Championship Manager on his Xbox—had his own flat in the almost-Notting-Hill part of Bayswater, rode a Vespa, and had even been described as a 'cool hunter' by his friend Mark Webster at the office. Though Mark was an accountant, so Nathan had taken that particular compliment with a pinch of salt.

No, Nathan just happened to have an affinity with computers, something he'd discovered when he was at school, so when it had been time to choose a career, technical support had been the obvious choice. Besides the money was good, especially since he'd been promoted to Technical Support Manager (though since he was the only one working in technical support in the Seek Software office, it was more of an honorary title), plus Nathan liked helping people. He just didn't seem to be a very good judge of them. Or (unlike the latest operating systems or software program) able to suss out how they worked.

He still found that strange. Very few things in life flummoxed Nathan like Ellie had. He could deal with the trickiest of technical problems, was good with engines, and even cooking (assuming he had a recipe to follow) held no fear for him. And yet, Ellie's barely audible 'no' that night in that restaurant had knocked his understanding of the opposite sex for six. And ruined every subsequent Valentine's Day for him, too.

He knew he could just play it safe. Take the day off and stay at home. Maybe download a couple of mindless martial arts films, order in a takeaway, get drunk on his favourite bottled Mexican lager, and write February 14th off as easily as he'd just thrown away the page from his calendar. But that wasn't in his nature, and besides, people were relying on him today—and not just to fix their computers.

Nathan smiled to himself. That first year, when he'd come up with the idea of an 'Anti-Valentine's' night and arranged an impromptu evening for all the singletons at the office, just two people—Calum Irwin and Mark Webster—had responded to the email he'd circulated. Since then, he'd been surprised how popular it had become; last year, they'd nearly reached double figures, and he'd already had nearly a dozen responses for tonight. Including himself, almost half of the twenty-six people who worked at Seek's UK office were single. Though Nathan found that statistic both reassuring and depressing.

And while he suspected many of them were only going this evening on the off-chance they might cop off with some other similarly damaged, disillusioned, lonely (or even just drunk) person, for the rest (if previous years were anything to go by) it would be a pretty fun night, aided by the fact he'd managed to get the bowling alley (obviously grateful for the business on an evening when no-one in their right mind would surprise their date with a romantic ten-pin tryst) to throw in a free cocktail for everyone. And he'd enjoy himself too, he knew, as long as there was no mention of love, or no reminder of money wasted on themed dinners in over-priced restaurants, or on expensive bunches of flowers that began to shrivel up and die as soon as they were presented—just like Nathan's hopes and dreams of a future with Ellie had when he'd presented them to her.

Besides, Anti-Valentine's had become a tradition now. This year, people had been asking him about it almost straight after the office Christmas party. In fact, Nathan had even felt a little pressure to top the previous one, but that hadn't been a bad thing. If anything, it had taken his mind off the actual reason he'd begun organising the event in the first place.

Briefly.

He checked the app he'd used to send invites out for the event on his shiny new iPhone—the management team at Seek had all been given one the previous week—and scrolled through the list of tonight's attendees. Many of them had come last year, but there were a few new names, maybe the victims of recent break-ups, not wanting to spend another night alone at home, stuck in front of the television. And no wonder, he thought, scanning through his phone's menu to check tonight's TV listings—sure enough, the channels were full of romantic comedies, or romantic 'comedies,' to be precise. Because if you were single, there was absolutely nothing funny at all about sitting alone at home on Valentine's night watching a film about other people in love.

An email pinged into his inbox—Paul from legal, asking if it'd be okay to bring passport photos of his ex to stick on the bowling pins. Nathan laughed, and replied with a 'sure,' wondering whether he should do the same, then he remembered he'd deleted all the photos he'd taken of Ellie when it became clear she wasn't coming back, and that she'd actually been seeing whatever-his-name-was behind Nathan's back for a good few months.

He'd found that out when he'd hacked into her Facebook account to read her messages in an attempt to understand why she'd said 'no,' and though he'd got some satisfaction from changing her status update to 'Ellie Robertson has been cheating on her boyfriend' then changing her password so she couldn't delete it, recently he'd begun to feel a little ashamed of his actions. Which was progress, he supposed.

Though it was the only progress he had made. While Nathan knew that after three years he should be ready to date again, he simply hadn't felt like it. And while he told himself that was partly because he hadn't met anyone who measured up to Ellie, in reality, he hadn't allowed himself to meet anyone at all. At some point, he realised, he'd have to bite the bullet and start asking women out, and (like going through the foot-bath at the swimming pool as a kid) it would be unpleasant but necessary if he wanted to dip his toe in the water, let alone manage a few lengths, but exactly when that point would come, Nathan wasn't sure. In the meantime, he had to get today—and tonight—over with first.

With a sigh, he slipped his phone into his pocket, collected his crash helmet from the hall table, slung his bag over his shoulder, and headed out into the street.

∾

Across town, Mark Webster was squinting out of the window of his Bermondsey flat, his thoughts not on how unusually sunny it was for a February morning, or on the impressive City skyline, or even on what he was going to pick up for breakfast from the bakery on Borough High Street on his way to work, but (as his thoughts were quite often nowadays) on Seek's marketing manager, Julie Marshall. He wondered what she was doing right now; probably getting ready for work, like him. Maybe she was just about to step into the shower, perhaps perspiring lightly after her morning run, her chest heaving as she peeled off her skin-tight running shorts... He shook his head to get rid of the rather delicious image that had just popped into it, and took another sip of orange juice.

Mark was in love with Julie. He had been for months, especially since they'd kissed in the taxi they'd shared after the office

Christmas party, though he knew if he were being completely honest he should really say he loved her. Being 'in' love suggested some degree of reciprocity, and as far as he could tell, Julie didn't even remember the kiss. She certainly hadn't mentioned it the next day, and while Mark could have taken that as a bad sign, Julie had said she couldn't remember much about the entire night. Hadn't even referred to the 'pass-the-balloon' game in the pub he suspected had led to them locking lips in the back of the cab later. Although she'd seemed relatively sober when they'd played that.

He could still remember the soft, warm, overwhelmingly delicious sensation of their lips touching, the taste of her, even. And while that taste had been primarily cranberry juice, thanks to the half-a-dozen Cosmopolitan cocktails Julie had reportedly drunk that evening, it was one he'd been keen to revisit at the earliest opportunity. Only there hadn't been an opportunity, and Mark had been too much of a coward to engineer one, particularly since a part of him worried she might be pretending to not remember anything just to spare his feelings.

In actual fact, she'd so not mentioned it that Mark had begun to doubt that the kiss had actually happened. He certainly wasn't confident enough in his recollection to have brought it up himself, or told anyone else at the office—not even his best friend there, Nathan Field. But that was all about to change. Today was the day he was going to lay his cards on the table, remind Julie what had (hopefully) happened between the two of them, and—assuming she didn't recoil in horror, or accuse him of sexual harassment—ask her out.

Probably.

Mark worried that opening up to her was a risky strategy. They had to work together, after all, and if Julie rejected him...Well, he'd just have to deal with that. But the alternative was to spend the rest of his days wondering what might have been, and besides, faint heart never won fair lady, or even brunette one in Julie's case. One thing he knew was that he didn't want to miss his chance, then run the risk of perhaps watching her meet, go out with, and even fall in love with someone else. And if there was a better day than Valentine's Day to tell her how he felt, Mark didn't know when that was.

Besides, he had to say something today, if only because the last seven weeks had been torture, mainly because Mark couldn't work out why Julie hadn't said anything. He didn't think she had a boyfriend (or a girlfriend, especially given the way she'd pounced on him on the cab's back seat that night) but he couldn't be sure. Julie always seemed pretty guarded in the office. Not one for idle chat. All he actually knew about her was that at thirty (he'd checked her payroll records for her date of birth) she was three years older than him; that she lived in Chiswick in a large, red-brick building (because that was where the cab had dropped her, and because he'd revisited her house using Google Street View several times since that night); and (thanks to the time he'd 'accidentally' bumped into her coming out of the Nike store at Oxford Circus carrying a new pair of Air Pegasus running shoes) that she was training for the forthcoming London Marathon. It wasn't much to base true love on, perhaps. But in a way, that mysteriousness just added to her allure.

For the hundredth time that morning, he checked that the Valentine's card he'd bought her was still safely hidden inside his briefcase, as if worried someone might have sneaked into his flat while he was shaving earlier and stolen it. He'd spent ages on Saturday choosing one, hanging around in Clinton's for so long the staff had begun to give him funny looks. One—and she must have been his mother's age—had even come and asked if he needed any help, and Mark had blushed, told her about the 'pass the balloon' game, explained what had happened in the taxi afterwards, then mumbled something about needing a card that conveyed 'fancying' rather than 'love.' The woman had backed away slowly and looked at him as if he was mad.

He'd ended up in Smiths, where things hadn't been any clearer. All the cards either had dedications of eternal devotion on the front (which was probably a bit forward under the circumstances) or some jokey cartoon-type design involving soppy-looking teddy bears, which Mark thought was inappropriate, as he didn't want Julie to think he wasn't serious about her—or twelve years old. In the end, he'd settled for one with a classic design of a single red rose on the front, and 'blank, for your own inscription' inside—though what on earth that inscription was going to be had turned out to be another problem. He'd already decided he wasn't going to sign it, and he couldn't refer to the kiss—not if Julie didn't remember it or, even worse, was trying to forget it—so in the end, Mark had decided to keep it simple, and fortunately, the name of the company they both worked for, Seek Software, had come to his rescue. In fact, the more he thought about it, the more 'From your Seek-ret admirer' had seemed like a stroke of genius, conveying both a clandestine thrill and that it had come from someone in the office.

He'd tried signing it with his left hand to disguise his handwriting, but had made such a hash of it he'd had to Tipp-Ex the words out, and then worried it had looked as if he was re-addressing a Valentine's card someone else had sent to him, so he'd had to go back to Smiths and spend another £2.45 on another one. Not that he'd minded that much—Julie was worth it—but this time he'd taken no chances, and signed it using his proper hand. So what if she recognised his handwriting? That was the point, wasn't it—that the person you'd 'anonymously' sent the card to actually knew who it was from? Otherwise he might as well have just left the money on her desk.

Mark had considered adding another little clue, too, wondering whether some reference to their taxi ride to Chiswick—or the big tip she'd left the driver—might jog her memory, but he'd worried mentioning where she lived might make her suspect he was some kind of stalker, plus any reference to 'big tips' could make him sound like a pervert, and he knew he had to give himself a back-out option in case she was offended, or (even worse) uninterested. 'Plausible deniability' was the American term—although given how intoxicated Mark was with her, if Julie did confront him angrily, or accuse him of taking advantage when she'd been drunk, he wasn't sure how plausible he'd be able to appear.

He'd been sober, that night, or rather, sober-ish. Certainly not too drunk to remember every detail about the kiss, or where Julie lived, or how she'd called him a gentleman when he'd offered her the first taxi that had come along, and then, when she'd suggested she could drop him off on the way, he'd insisted on seeing her home safely instead, and at that, he thought he'd seen something flicker in her eyes. He hadn't dared to hope for an invitation in 'for coffee,' which had been just as well, but the goodnight kiss Julie had given him had electrified his senses like the strongest of espressos, and before he'd recovered, she'd stuffed some money into his hand for the fare to Chiswick, and bolted from the taxi through the rain to her door. The cabbie's 'where to now, Guv?' had jolted him back to reality, as had the discovery he didn't have enough money to pay the driver to take him home. Mark had ended up begging to be dropped off back in Soho, and while the subsequent two-mile walk back to his flat in the rain had ruined his suit, it certainly hadn't ruined his evening. Though Julie's reaction (or lack of it) at work the following morning had ruined every day since then.

Initially, he'd suspected she was just playing it cool, but as the weeks had progressed, Julie had become something approaching sub-zero, and Mark just couldn't work out why. He wasn't a bad kisser—her reaction in the back of the cab had proved that—so had she simply been drunk? Well, so what? Mark believed the old adage that drink brought out your true personality, and if it had made her want to kiss him, he had to take that as an encouraging sign. He also knew there was one way to test out that particular theory, and tonight's Anti-Valentine's party, with its free cocktails, could be the perfect opportunity.

He finished the last of his orange juice and stood up purposefully. If Julie told him she couldn't date someone at work, well, he'd just have to resign himself to the fact. Or resign. That would show her he was serious.

Or crazy.

Mark smiled to himself as he rinsed his glass out and placed it in the dishwasher, suspecting he might be a bit of both. For the final time that morning, he made sure Julie's card was in his case, then he walked out of his flat, closed his front door carefully behind him, double-checked that it was double-locked, and made his way towards the station.

❧

Over in Chiswick, Julie Marshall had been in the shower, but right now, as she did every day since she'd hit the big three-oh last September, Julie was examining her reflection in the bathroom mirror. She wasn't in bad shape for her age, she knew. Nothing was drooping, sagging, or, as far as she could tell in the morning light, going grey. Which she was grateful for, under the circumstances.

A noise from the letterbox startled her, so she padded along the hallway and picked up what looked like a credit card statement and a copy of the Boden catalogue from where they'd just dropped onto the doormat. No Valentine's card this year, she noted. Though Julie supposed she shouldn't be surprised.

She'd already been out for her run—with the London Marathon only two months away, Julie knew she couldn't afford to miss any sessions—and while she suspected the mileage she was putting in wouldn't be quite enough to get her round the course without the occasional rest stop, the training was at least benefiting her in other ways, not in the least the half stone she'd lost since she'd first begun some six months ago. Stepping on the scales after her shower just about made up for having to drag herself out of bed at six-thirty, but then again, she had nothing else to lie in for, and in truth, she was pleased to have another excuse to spend some time out of the house. Besides, it made her usual mid-morning muffin from the Pret A Manger across the street from the Seek Software office all the more guilt-free, and Julie reckoned she could do with a few guilt-free pleasures nowadays.

She'd been puzzled on her run today. It had been a typical freezing February morning, so cold it had almost hurt to breathe, and yet as she'd concentrated on putting one foot in front of the other while trying to avoid stepping in anything, she'd noticed the Chiswick streets had been unusually busy. It was only when the third Interflora van driver had honked his horn and leered at her that Julie had twigged the reason for this pre-work frenzy of activity, and she'd almost laughed out loud at the futility of it all.

For the rest of her run, she'd fought an insane urge to tell everyone she passed on the pavement that Valentine's Day was a complete waste of time. Far from being the most romantic day of the year, it was simply a marketing event, and the people it really made happy were greetings card manufacturers, florists, confectioners, and restaurant owners, but given how she worked in marketing, Julie knew she couldn't be too critical. And in actual fact, she was more angry about how all it really did was promote the myth that this was the day where men could make one desultory gesture which excused them from being romantic for the rest of the year, as if a hurriedly bought bouquet of half-wilted carnations from the local BP garage on their way home could excuse a history of indiscretions, or a lifetime of forgotten birthdays and anniversaries, or even a lack of simple chivalry. And in her experience, discreet, thoughtful, chivalrous men were few and far between. If you didn't count Mark Webster, that was.

Not for the first time, Julie found herself thinking about the office Christmas party. She hadn't wanted to go in the first place, but an already-tipsy (thanks to the bottle of champagne they'd been sent by their design agency) Sophie Jones—her number two in Seek's marketing department—had cajoled her into it by quizzing her as to whether she had something better to go home to. And when Julie had thought about it, the answer had been 'no.'

She hadn't been that drunk. Sure, she'd had a couple of Cosmopolitans, but Julie's Scottish ancestry meant she could hold her drink. And then, when someone had suggested that ridiculous balloon game...She smiled, and shook her head at the memory. The things grown adults got up to after a few drinks. And passing a balloon from one end of a line of people to the other without using your hands was just, well, childish. But Julie had been the new girl, and she hadn't wanted to get a reputation for being stand-offish, so when her turn had come to take the balloon from where it was lodged between Aisleen-from-personnel's thighs, she'd dutifully

29

knelt down and, to much whooping, grabbed it under her chin. Standing up triumphantly, she'd turned around to see who she should pass it on to. And there, standing right in front of her, was Mark Webster.

They'd stared into each other's eyes for the briefest of moments, then Mark had moved towards her and—she felt a little frisson of excitement at the recollection—slowly lowered himself until his face was level with her chest, then he'd gently taken the knotted end of the balloon between his teeth, all the while keeping his eyes firmly fixed on hers. Julie had found it incredibly erotic, and knew there and then they'd kiss. Although not, of course, in front of everyone.

But then he'd had to pass the balloon on to Mary from admin, who'd subsequently burst it—on her stubble, someone had said a little too loudly from the back of the room (and rather cruelly, Julie had thought, although her nickname of 'hairy Mary' in the office wasn't without foundation)—which had sent Mary running out of the pub in tears, and of course had meant the end of the game. And just as the balloon had burst, so too had Julie's bubble, and all thoughts of kissing Mark had vanished.

Until later, that was, when they'd found themselves outside, waiting for a taxi in the rain, and Mark had insisted she take the next one, and she'd insisted they share it, even though she lived in Chiswick, and he... Well, it hadn't seemed to matter to him—or her—where he lived.

Julie had been sure they'd flagged down a black cab, but the driver must have thought they were in some kind of racing car, or perhaps he'd simply been keen to get back to the centre of town and another lucrative fare—Christmas party season meant for rich pickings, after all. In any case, a particularly violent cornering manoeuvre at Marble Arch had thrown her almost into Mark's lap, and that was when it happened. One of those kisses. Tentative at first, before building in delicious intensity into something that could potentially have lasted the rest of the night.

Almost immediately Julie had feared it wasn't a good idea, though that hadn't been enough to make her break away, but fortunately when they'd eventually come up for air somewhere around Shepherd's Bush, Mark had seemed almost bewildered, and from then onwards, it had been easier to pretend to be drunk. Not that it had been easy for her to resist kissing him again, but she'd known that would have been a mistake. Once she could have written off as an accident, but twice? That suggested intent. A promise of things to come.

Afterwards, watching West London whiz by through the taxi's steamed-up window while trying her best to act as if the kiss had never happened, she'd almost had to sit on her hands to stop herself from grabbing Mark again. She was a great believer in kissing. Too few people were good at it. Most of the men she'd known seemed to count it as foreplay, and therefore something to get out of the way rather than as a pleasure in itself. But Mark? He'd seemed in no rush whatsoever. Julie would have been happy kissing him for hours. And she'd suspected he felt the same way.

When the taxi had reached the end of her road, Julie had been tempted to tell the driver to carry on to Mark's place, but at the last moment, she'd chickened out—after all, she wasn't that kind of girl, or at least, was pretty sure she wasn't. And so she'd quickly kissed Mark goodnight, forced herself to ignore the alluring smell of his skin and the enticing, manly feel of his stubble against her cheek, then she'd stuffed a handful of notes into his hand for her share of the fare and sprinted out of the cab. And though it had been raining hard, in truth, the cold shower had been welcome. The following day, more than a little embarrassed, Julie had decided to play it cool—after all, she knew nothing about Mark—so when he'd 'accidentally' bumped into her at the photocopier and awkwardly asked whether she'd had fun the previous night, she'd claimed alcoholic amnesia. To his credit, Mark had almost managed to keep a straight face, but Julie could tell he was crestfallen, and she'd felt terribly guilty.

She'd wanted to tell him he was a great kisser. To let him know that, under different circumstances, she might have encouraged him further. And maybe if he'd have pressed her, perhaps even asked her out, she'd have found out if he was as good at the rest of 'it'— God knows, she'd spent the whole night after the party lying awake wondering exactly that—but since then, Mark hadn't said anything further and, as far as Julie knew, hadn't mentioned it to anyone else, which (she'd reluctantly concluded) was probably for the best. She certainly didn't want that kind of reputation at the office.

Speaking of which, she didn't want a reputation for being late either, and unless she left in the next ten minutes, she'd miss her usual tube. She finished dressing, checked her watch, and then— careful not to wake Philip, her husband, who was snoring loudly in the next room—Julie let herself quietly out of her front door, walked down the steps to the pavement, and made her way towards Gunnersbury station.

2

Sophie Jones clutched her bag tightly as she hurried along Frith Street, though more to protect its precious cargo of the Valentine's card she'd bought for Nathan than because she feared getting mugged. She loved being in this part of town; not simply the West End, but Soho. Her mum had been concerned when she'd told her parents where she'd be working, and although her dad had raised his eyebrows too, she'd managed to reassure them that the area didn't deserve that reputation anymore. Well, not as much as it used to, she thought, as she nodded hello to the shivering, scantily dressed girls having a cigarette outside Spank-o-rama, the hostess club (or 'titty-bar,' to give it its proper title, at least as far as the guys in the office were concerned) round the corner from the office.

She turned into Bateman Street, passed the pub on the corner, and made her way towards number sixteen. Seek Software had the lease on a grey, three-story building on the short stretch between Frith Street and Greek Street, and while it was a little cramped for the twenty-six employees who worked there, and the air-conditioning couldn't cope on the one or two days a year London actually had anything resembling a summer, no-one could moan about the location.

She retrieved her key card from her purse and swiped her way inside, then crept quietly down the stairs and peered into the tech support room on the lower ground floor. Nathan wasn't in yet, and

Sophie wondered if he had some last-minute organisation to do for tonight's Anti-Valentine's event, which she'd resisted signing up for, mainly because she didn't want anyone in the office to think she was that desperate. In truth, she was a little disappointed not to see him, but she supposed it was better this way. It gave her a few precious minutes to come up with something witty to write in his card.

For a moment, she started to doubt the wisdom of what she was doing, sending a Valentine's card to the man who organised an evening that was anti the whole concept, but then it occurred to her that the fact he did would suggest he was single, and looking for a reason not to be alone on Valentine's night. And if that was the case, then Sophie would do her best to give him one.

She blushed at the phrase, and decided not to write that in the card. Nor, she realised, should she make any reference to what he did for a living, particularly with the words 'hardware' and 'software.' And while she was used to writing short, snappy pieces of copy for the company's marketing material, the computing clichés that kept popping into her head were sadly inappropriate where romance was concerned.

Or were they? Maybe Nathan might appreciate some clever technological reference, perhaps a poem that rhymed 'heart' with, say, 're-start,' or 'cute' with 'reboot,' or 'USB' with 'you and me.' Trouble was, no matter how hard she thought about it, Sophie couldn't come up with one that didn't sound either particularly lame or overly suggestive, and mentioning anything about a hard disk would just be asking for trouble.

The sound of the front door opening startled her, and Sophie sprinted back up the stairs, relieved when she saw it was just Mia-Rose, Seek's receptionist, barrelling in through the doorway, a Starbucks cup in one hand, and a Krispy Kreme bag in the other.

'Morning, Sophie,' said Mia-Rose, through a mouthful of donut.

'Hi, Mia.' Sophie nodded towards the bag of donuts. 'Miss breakfast this morning?'

'No. Why?' Mia-Rose set the cup down on her desk. 'Though I'm thinking of making these my breakfast every morning. They're delish!' She broke into a broad grin, and Sophie couldn't help but do the same She liked Mia-Rose—a beautiful Nigerian girl with the most infectious laugh, and though she was somewhat full-figured, Mia-Rose didn't seem to be at all hung up about her weight. Unlike most of the other girls in the office, Sophie included.

'Want one?' said Mia-Rose, offering her a donut, but Sophie shook her head.

'I'd better not.'

'Watching your figure?'

'Not really. I'm just...'

'Hoping someone else is?'

Sophie blushed, and tried to think of an appropriate answer, but fortunately the postman chose that moment to arrive, so she just smiled, then made her way out of reception. The office was starting to fill up, and she realised she needed a bit of privacy to write Nathan's card. Taking the stairs to the first floor two at a time, Sophie nipped into her office, grabbed a pen from her desk, and made her way into the toilets.

༄

Nathan Field piloted his Vespa along Oxford Street, gritting his teeth against the cold air that was turning the tip of his nose numb. Sure, he was a little exposed to the elements on the bike, but at least he didn't get stuck in traffic jams, or have to cram himself onto the tube along with the millions of commuters that had to make a miserable, stuffy subterranean journey into town every day. On his bike he was king of the road, able to dodge through gaps, accelerate round taxis, leave buses trailing in his... A figure darted out in front of him, and he slammed his brakes on and screeched to a halt, cursing under his breath as he fought to keep from somersaulting over the handlebars. Why didn't people look when they crossed the road? He beeped his horn and pointed to his eyes, indicating the offending pedestrian should consider using theirs, but when he looked closer and saw it was Julie Marshall, Nathan changed the gesture into a friendly wave instead.

'Good Morning,' he said cheerily, pulling his bike over to where she was standing on the pavement.

Julie took a mouthful of coffee from the Starbucks cup she was clutching. 'What's so good about it?'

'Er...'

Nathan shrugged, and she smiled apologetically. 'Sorry,' she said, stepping back to let a delivery man carrying a huge bouquet of roses pass. 'It's just, you know...'

Nathan rolled his eyes. He did know. 'Will we be seeing you later?'

'Later?'

'Anti-Valentine's.'

Julie frowned. 'What on earth is that?'

'Sorry, I forgot you were the new girl.' He grinned. 'It's kind of become an office tradition. A night out. Tonight.'

'What sort of night out?'

'One for anyone who doesn't fancy spending tonight in.' Nathan nodded towards the heart-shaped-balloon-filled shop window behind them. 'And about as far away from all this rubbish as you can get.'

Julie turned to look at the gaudy window display and then shook her head. 'I'm not sure. What does it involve, exactly?'

'We're going bowling.'

'Bowling?' She raised the back of her hand to her forehead melodramatically. 'Be still my beating heart.'

'And there'll be cocktails. Which I seem to remember you being quite partial to at the Christmas party.'

Julie fought hard to stop herself from blushing—hopefully that was the only thing Nathan knew she'd been partial to that night—though she was surprised to find her next reaction was to ask whether Mark would be going, and she fought hard to stop herself doing that as well. 'I don't know…'

'Come on,' said Nathan. 'It'll be a laugh.'

Julie stared at the window display as she considered her alternative—another night at home ignoring Philip's efforts to ignore her—and realised that, actually, a laugh was something she could really do with. 'Okay. You've talked me into it.'

'Great. Cheers.' Nathan grinned again, then nosed the Vespa's front wheel back out into the traffic. 'I'll mail you the details,' he said, accelerating out just in front of a taxi before she could change her mind.

He watched Julie in his rear-view mirror as he thrummed towards Oxford Circus, wondering why she'd seemed so negative. Maybe he'd just caught her off guard. More likely, he guessed, and probably like so many people this morning, her Valentine's Day hadn't quite started the way she wanted. But it was hard to tell with Julie. She was a bit of a dark horse, and nobody at the office really knew that much about her—though she had only been working for Seek for a few months. And while there had been some rumours going round about her going home with someone Nathan suspected might have been Mark after the Christmas party, he didn't think there was any truth in them, especially since Mark hadn't mentioned anything about it, and because he and Julie had virtually ignored each other since then. Mind you, Nathan reconsidered, as he rode into Soho Square, maybe that was the proof.

She was 'fit,' he had to concede, and in both senses of the word—he'd seen her out running once or twice after work, and Nathan suspected he'd have struggled to keep up—even on his bike. He'd overheard the girls in the office say she was training for the marathon, but fortunately, Julie didn't seem to be one of those people who shove a sponsorship form under your nose for some obscure charity that's probably just their holiday fund, or direct you to a Just Giving page with a picture of some emaciated rescue animal on it. No, she appeared to be running the marathon for herself. Which Nathan thought probably said an awful lot about her.

He steered his bike into a nearby parking space and hauled it up onto its stand, then carefully secured the lock, just in case he had to leave it there overnight. He was bound to have a few drinks later, and depending on how soon Ellie came up in conversation, it could well be a fair few. Nathan wasn't the type to drink and drive—in fact, he wasn't the type to do anything that meant he might lose control. Not anymore, anyway.

He strolled down Greek Street, then called in as usual at Poles Apart, the Polish café on the corner, and ordered himself a latte to go from the pretty girl behind the counter, skimming through the new messages on his phone while he waited for her to make it. He wondered whether he should text Mark to tell him Julie would be going this evening, but Nathan decided he'd keep that particular snippet of information for when he saw him. That kind of good news was best delivered in person.

'Here you go.'

The heavily accented words told Nathan his latte was ready. 'Thanks', he said distractedly, still staring at his phone.

The girl handed him his coffee, and as she clicked a plastic lid onto his cup, he noticed she'd drawn a little heart in the froth on the top, and when he looked up in surprise, their eyes met. Instinctively he averted his gaze. Why did this kind of thing make him feel guilty? Nathan knew the answer to that, of course. Had Ellie said 'yes,' they'd have been married by now, and this kind of behaviour would have been, well, if not illegal, then certainly frowned upon.

But Ellie hadn't said yes, so surely he was free to smile at whoever he wanted? Flirt, even. Ask them out, if he fancied. And he'd have to be blind not to fancy... Kasia. That was it. At least, that was what he'd heard some of the other regulars call her, and he'd made a point of trying to remember it. Kasia the Cashier. Okay, so that wasn't strictly her job, but Nathan wasn't very good at remembering names, and the one tip he'd been given that seemed to make a difference was to associate them with what the person did. So Kasia the Cashier she'd become.

For a second, and to his surprise, he toyed with the idea of asking Kasia out. Maybe she was free this evening? She could come along to Anti-Valentine's, and... He stopped himself, wondering who he was trying to kid. A girl as attractive as her probably had a boyfriend, and anyway, inviting someone along to an event like that on a first date probably wasn't the best idea. Besides, all he knew about Kasia was her name, that she was from Poland, and what she did for a living, and while he liked her—and coffee—who knew if they'd even be the slightest bit compatible?

And that, Nathan understood, was his problem. He'd gone out with Ellie for the best part of three years before he'd popped the question, and thought he'd known every little thing about her, from her favourite song to her first pet's name, her Facebook password (luckily for him, those last two things had been the same), and her favourite sexual position—although that had actually turned out to be underneath someone else. But there were so many elements that made up a person, was so much you had to learn or know or understand about them, and then even when you thought you knew it all, the fact that all that effort could still suddenly come to nothing... For Nathan, it made starting again with someone new just so, well, hard.

With a sigh, he paid for his coffee, mumbled an embarrassed 'thanks,' and made his way out through the door.

∾

Calum Irwin sat on the bus and stared anxiously at his mobile, unsure how to play things from here on in. Under the circumstances, he didn't know what the etiquette was for sending Valentine's Day greetings to someone you hadn't actually met.

He glanced into his briefcase, checking that his rose hadn't been squashed in the crush when he'd changed buses at Clapham Common. Hopefully Emma would appreciate the low-key gesture—he'd feared a whole bouquet of flowers might be over the top, and buying her a box of chocolates would have been a risky strategy, as he was so nervous he was likely to eat them himself over the course of the day. Calum hadn't known what else might be appropriate—certainly not lingerie, as he didn't know her size—and to try and guess opened up a whole world of potential pitfalls. Besides, he didn't want her to think he was making assumptions.

Of course, as well as wishing Emma a happy Valentine's Day, Calum had an ulterior motive for getting in touch: to check whether she was still planning to turn up this evening. He had her email address, her contact details on LondonDate, and her mobile number, which she'd sent him last night just in case he was running late this evening (though Calum had assured her there was absolutely no chance of that), and was tempted to use all three just to make sure she got his message, but he didn't want to appear desperate. Even though that was exactly how he was feeling.

He began composing a quick text, then hit 'delete,' telling himself to relax. Maybe he'd just send her an email from the office when he got there. Besides, he reminded himself, Emma had made the first move, and suggested they meet up this evening, so in actual fact, she should be more worried that *he* wouldn't turn up.

Calum let out a short laugh, the words 'yeah' and 'right' forming a sentence in his head, and, as the woman he was sitting next to edged away from him, mumbled an embarrassed apology. It was a funny concept, this internet dating, he thought. That you could get to know someone, find out all about them, have long, late-night 'conversations' online before actually having physically met them, struck him as odd. It was the opposite of what would happen in a pub or a club. There it was all about attraction, or alcohol, and Calum wasn't good at either of those things—especially the alcohol. Ironically, given his size, just a few pints could transform him into a drooling wreck, and in fact, the pub was the only place he'd ever heard himself described as a 'lightweight'—something he'd have found funny if he weren't so sensitive about his waistline.

He'd already made a mental note not to drink this evening, knowing that had been part of his problem in the past. Girls always wanted to go out for a drink, and he'd often get to the bar early, then be unable to stop himself having one or two before they'd arrive just to calm his nerves. Trouble was, Calum's nerves took a lot of calming, which usually resulted in him having three or four, then getting drunk and embarrassing himself, meaning any first date had almost always been the last date too.

But he hadn't embarrassed himself with Emma—not yet, and not on LondonDate, at least. There, he could string a sentence together, had been told he was funny—'quick-witted,' in fact—though that was perhaps because his combination of good grammar and an ability to touch-type meant his responses pinged back faster and more coherently than the text-speaking LOL-ers he was up against. But that kind of thing counted in your favour when you were trying to romance someone via the medium of live chat.

Live chat. It sounded seedy to him, like a premium-rate phone service you'd see advertised on one of those cards that were stuck up in almost every telephone box around Soho, featuring photos of topless, huge-breasted women with bright yellow stars Photoshopped over their nipples. 'Live typing' would be better—and more accurate. Let your fingers do the talking. Calum just hoped Emma wouldn't set eyes on him later and show him two—or one—of hers.

He wiped the condensation from the inside of the bus window and peered out through the gap, still feeling guilty about lying about his height. It wasn't that he was short, but most women seemed to insist on a six-foot minimum, and Calum had feared that if he'd been honest, he'd have been dismissed out of hand. Not that he could ever understand why that 72-inch cut-off was so important—in his experience, women averaged around five foot three; even allowing for heels, they'd still only come up to his shoulder. Was kissing fun when it gave you a crick in the neck, or was that what women meant when they said they wanted a man they could look up to? Calum didn't have a clue.

It had occurred to him that maybe Emma was some sort of giantess. That would be just his luck. But even if she was, he could always just tell her that people were all the same height lying down... Or perhaps he wouldn't. That was maybe a bit too suggestive. Too forward. And he didn't think that Emma was the suggestive type.

He'd done a quick search for her on Facebook, but not knowing her surname, it had been impossible to work out which one—or if one—of the seventy-three London-based Emmas that had turned up was her. Twenty-four of them had private profiles, and while he'd spent a couple of evenings skimming through the photos (and some of the friends' photos) on the rest looking for clues, or references to Archway, or pictures of dogs, or log fires, or the clincher—dogs in front of log fires in Archway—he still couldn't be sure if she'd been one of them. At least none of those Emmas had looked tall, though of course he couldn't even be sure of that. They could just have tall friends.

But Calum had persevered with his detective work. He'd even made notes. Though while he'd had had his hopes raised when he'd stumbled upon a series of photos of a fit-looking north London Emma in a bikini on a girls' holiday in Ibiza last year and could hardly wait to work the subject into their next conversation, it had turned out to be nothing. 'His' Emma had never been to Ibiza—unless she'd been playing a double-bluff... He smiled to himself. That was the trouble with the internet. Like some of the more graphic responses he'd had on LondonDate, too much information.

He suspected Emma had probably done the same to him, from what he'd gleaned from the cackling covens the women in the office formed around their computers from time to time. Girls, he'd found out, were big-time Googlers when it came to the opposite sex, and the day he'd learned that, Calum had gone through his own Facebook profile and deleted anything unflattering. Which, on reflection, had turned out to be most of his photos.

Eventually, worried that there was a fine line between stalking and simply doing some background research, he'd decided to stop. Besides, the surprise was part of the fun. It added excitement. And although he'd practised his deadpan Oscar-losing face in the mirror just so he wouldn't look too disappointed if she did turn out to be aesthetically challenged, Calum was determined to approach tonight with an open mind. Stay till the end. Do his best to enjoy himself—and make sure Emma had a good time too—whatever she looked like.

He stared out of the window as he recalled his last two internet-sourced dates. The first, with a girl called Clare, had started out well enough. Despite the initial look of disappointment on her face, she'd let him buy her a drink—though when she'd downed it within ten seconds of him putting it on the table in front of her, Calum had simply assumed she must be as nervous as he was. He'd waited for a couple of minutes to see if she'd offer to buy him one back, but when she hadn't, he'd just sat there awkwardly, sipping at his pint, wondering what to do next, before asking if she'd like another. She'd refused, and instead, excused herself to go to the ladies, leaving Calum anxiously tapping his fingers on the table for five, ten, fifteen minutes... Until he was sure of what he'd initially feared: she wasn't coming back.

Perhaps he should have suspected something when she didn't take off her coat despite the pub being quite warm, but he'd never expected she'd do something so rude. And what was worse was when he'd got home and sent Clare an email to check whether she was OK—a part of him had worried about her, after all—he'd found out she'd 'blocked' him. And it had made him feel awful.

The incident had taken Calum a couple of weeks to get over. He was surprised someone could be so thoughtless, and while he'd never be so cruel, he considered he'd had a lucky escape—after all, who'd want to go out with someone like that? So he'd logged back on to LondonDate and tried again, striking up a conversation with a girl called Annie who Calum had been pleased to find came from the same part of Ireland that he did. But when she'd pinged him back to say she hadn't moved all the way to London to go out with 'an eejit from back home,' he hadn't quite known how to take that.

So he'd blocked her—childish, he knew, but it had made him feel better—and searched on, widening his criteria to include the 30 to 39 age group, and almost immediately he'd received a message from a woman called Ruth. While she'd been at the upper end of Calum's age limit, she'd looked good in her photo, and they'd got on in their initial few live chats, so when she suggested a meeting, he'd leapt at the chance—despite the ten-year age gap. Trouble was, when they'd actually met, Calum had suspected there was also a ten-year age gap between the photo on Ruth's profile and the woman sitting in front of him. While he wasn't rude enough to use the phrase 'old enough to be my mother,' he'd had to call her on it, and yet, the amazing thing was, Ruth wasn't at all apologetic. She'd even challenged him for being ageist. He'd said he was sorry, and that one of the things he looked for in a woman was honesty, but Ruth had just laughed, and said 'good luck with that.'

He'd felt a bit sorry for her, so he'd stayed for a drink—a drink that, of course, he'd paid for—while wondering how he could let her down gently. He tried the 'I want to have kids one day' line, and she'd laughed, and said he could have hers—all five of them. Calum hadn't found that funny, so he'd gone with 'I just don't think we'd be compatible,' and Ruth had pointed out that men and women weren't anyway. Which she knew from experience—she'd been divorced twice.

In the end, it was Ruth who'd made her excuses—she'd had to get home to relieve the baby sitter—and Calum was relieved himself, until she'd tried to kiss him, and not just on the cheek, as if some last-minute lunge might demonstrate how passionate she was, and leave him wanting more, though the only thing the unexpected presence of her nicotine-flavoured tongue in his mouth had left him wanting was a sick bucket. He'd finally managed to break away, though not before wondering whether that was how the guy in the *Alien* film must have felt when that thing had attached itself to his face and forced god-knows-what down his throat. And when Ruth had asked him if he thought she was a 'MILF,' Calum had nodded politely—he knew what the letters stood for, but had wanted to change the 'f' to 'flee'—so he'd done just that, then gone straight home, rinsed with almost half a bottle of mouthwash, and changed his LondonDate settings back to his original age range.

And it was then Calum realised that although it had initially seemed he was a child in a sweet-shop, in actual fact, internet dating made him feel more like a blind person trying to navigate his way through a minefield. Far from providing him with an endless succession of dates from which he could pick and choose his ideal partner, the reality was he could be wasting years on a series of one-night... Well, not even 'stands.' Interviews, perhaps, and interviews where he had to buy the interviewer a drink. And this, he knew, was one of the reasons he was so looking forward to tonight. He'd already gone past the interview stage with Emma. And aside from her asking him for references, the job—that of being her boyfriend—was his to lose.

As his bus stop-started along Oxford Street, Calum stared anxiously back down at his phone, and then an idea popped into his head, so he quickly composed a text and pressed 'send' before he lost his nerve. 'It'll be lovely to see you later,' was what he'd written. And that, he realised, was doubly true.

❧

Mark Webster exchanged 'good mornings' with Mia-Rose as she watered the huge rubber plant in reception, then he walked into his office, sat down at his desk, and—with a loud sigh—switched his laptop on. For the past seven weeks, he'd been trying—and failing—to come up with imaginative ways to break the ice with Julie, and although he thought he'd finally found one, it had occurred to him on the tube this morning that sending her an anonymous Valentine's card wasn't necessarily going to help him do that. If anything, he feared it might make him more nervous about talking to her, and given that he'd been little more than a mumbling fool in her presence since the night they'd kissed, that probably wasn't a good thing.

He could always forget the card, he realised, and try the sideways approach instead. Collar her about something work-related, bring up the subject of Valentine's Day, then cleverly steer the conversation on to the two of them. But talk about what? Mark was Seek's UK Financial Director, Julie was their Marketing Manager. The only reason they'd actually have to talk about anything today would be if he was questioning the expenses claim she'd filed last week, and you'd have to be a genius to turn a conversation about the receipt she'd presented him with for a dozen Krispy Kreme donuts for the last sales meeting into 'will you go out with me?'

He opened his briefcase and stared at the bright red envelope. He'd have to drop it off in her pigeonhole soon if he wanted to be sure she got it first thing, or else risk trying to sneak it onto her desk when she popped out for her usual mid-morning muffin from the Pret A Manger across the street. He hadn't seen Julie come in yet, so perhaps dropping it off now was the safer option, but then Sophie might see him, and the last thing Mark wanted was for a rumour to start. Especially if that was all it was ever going to be.

Suddenly aware of a figure looming in his doorway, he shut his briefcase hurriedly and pretended to be interested on something on the screen in front of him.

'Wotcha!' said Nathan, breezily.

Mark breathed a sigh of relief. 'Surprised to see you here so early.'

'Huh?'

'I thought you'd have trouble climbing over that pile of cards on your doormat.'

'Yeah, yeah. Very funny,' said Nathan sarcastically. He and Mark were good friends, so good he'd even told him about Ellie, then politely resisted his continued attempts to help him get 'back in the saddle.' In return, he'd managed to get Mark drunk one night before Christmas, when he'd learned about his 'thing' for Julie, though Mark had made Nathan swear on pain of never having his expenses approved again that he wouldn't tell anyone. Especially her. He pulled his phone out of his pocket and swiped the screen to wake it. 'Just wanted to check you were still on for this evening?'

Mark nodded. 'I suppose so.'

'Try not to sound too enthusiastic.'

'Sorry. It's just... I don't suppose she's going, is she?'

'Who?' said Nathan, as innocently as he could, and Mark reddened.

'You know exactly who.'

Nathan made a show of searching through the list on his phone. 'When I checked last night she wasn't,' he said, and Mark's face fell. 'Lucky for you I talked her into it when I bumped into her on the way in this morning. And I almost did bump into her. She ran right out in front of...'

'Does she know I'll be there?'

Nathan shrugged. 'I didn't tell her. Which reminds me...' He tapped at the keyboard, and Mark peered at him anxiously.

'What are you doing?'

'Relax. I'm just mailing her the details.'

'Oh. Right.'

'Sorted.' Nathan slipped his phone away. 'You said anything to her yet?'

'Don't be ridiculous.'

'Like me to?'

'No!' said Mark, sharply. 'Sorry. No, thanks.' He lowered his voice to a whisper. 'Though I have got her a Valentine's card.'

Nathan raised both eyebrows. 'Good on you.'

Mark tapped the briefcase at his feet. 'I thought I'd better, you know...'

'Why are you showing me your briefcase?'

'Because that's where the card is.'

'And is Julie in there too? Or d'you mean you're actually going to give it to her, rather than have one in there to give her, which isn't necessarily the same thing?'

'Of course I'm going to give it to her. I just need to pick my moment.'

'Well, given that you've probably got around five minutes before she gets here, you'd better pick one quickly.'

'What?' Mark leapt to his feet, a panicked expression on his face. 'But...'

'Relax.' Nathan put a hand on his friend's shoulder. 'I've got to go past her office. I'll drop it on her desk if you want?'

'Really?'

'Really.'

'Well, if you're sure?' Mark reached into his briefcase, checked that no-one was walking past his doorway—being seen giving a Valentine's card to Nathan would be one piece of gossip both of them could do without—then removed the envelope and handed it over. 'Thanks.'

'No worries.' Nathan pulled a copy of *Computer Weekly* out of his bag and slipped the card inside. 'So, back to tonight. Five-thirty, SuperBowl on Queensway.'

Mark gave him the thumbs-up. 'It's a date.'

Nathan nudged him with his elbow. 'You just make sure that's what it turns into,' he said, heading for the stairs.

❧

The sound of a polite cough made Sophie look up from where she'd been bending over the printer trying to free a paper jam, and while the unexpected sight of Nathan silhouetted in her doorway made her heart skip a beat, she feared presenting her not-quite-Kylie-esque bottom to him like this perhaps wasn't the best way to begin her Valentine's campaign.

'Morning!' he said, an awkward grin on his face, and Sophie stood up quickly, wondering what he was doing here. As far as she knew, there were no outstanding issues with either her or Julie's laptops that would require a visit from technical support, so unless Nathan had seen her sneakily drop her card onto his desk a few minutes ago, or had worked out who'd sent it from her clever computing puns, he'd have no reason to visit.

'Morning yourself.' Sophie frowned at the printer as she pulled hard at the stuck sheet of A4. 'What's your...'

'Nathan.'

'What? Oh, you thought I didn't...No, I was frowning because I couldn't...I mean, when I said "what's your...," I was actually speaking to the printer.'

'Speaking to the printer?'

'Yes. You know, asking it what its problem was.' She blushed. 'Well, not asking it in that I was expecting it to actually tell me.' She let out an embarrassed laugh. 'I knew your name was Nathan, obviously. Well, not obviously...' Sophie stopped talking. To freely admit she knew his name might give him a clue that she'd sent that card, but then again, of course she knew his name, and besides, that was what she wanted, wasn't it? Suddenly she wasn't so sure. What had she been thinking? He was gorgeous, fit, funny, trendy, clever, and she...Well, she wasn't sure she was any of those things, though to her shame, Sophie knew she'd have taken the 'gorgeous' tag at the expense of all the others.

He nodded at the printer. 'Problem?'

With a desperate tug, Sophie triumphantly freed the offending document, then shook her head. 'Not anymore,' she said.

'Great.'

She glared at the machine, which was sitting there inanimately, then struck it lightly on the side. 'Come on,' she whispered.

'You sure?'

'Just waiting for my prints to come...' Sophie suddenly realised how that phrase could be misconstrued—today of all days—and blushed. 'I mean, for it to print.'

Nathan walked over, reached past her, and pressed the power button, and the machine whirred into life. 'You just needed to, you know...'

Sophie swallowed hard and tried to ignore the musky scent of his aftershave. 'Turn it on?'

'Exactly.' He took a step backwards. 'Your boss around?'

'Julie?' Sophie tried to perch casually on the corner of her desk, only realising after the third attempt that it was too high for her, then worried it looked like she'd been trying to scratch her backside against it, like a bear might on a tree. 'Er, no. Not yet.'

'Excellent.'

Nathan winked conspiratorially at her, and Sophie felt herself go weak at the knees. 'Anything I can, um, you know…' She wanted to slap herself. Of all the basic life skills, Sophie thought she'd mastered 'talking' years ago, but apparently not—or at least, not when Nathan was around. She cleared her throat. '…do for you?'

'That's okay.' Nathan smiled again, and briefly patted her upper arm, and Sophie fought not to reach up and touch the spot where his hand had been. 'Just got to drop something off. Probably best for all concerned if I do it when she's not here.'

He pulled a red envelope out from between the pages of the magazine he was carrying, and Sophie couldn't believe her luck. Nathan surely wouldn't have had the time to open her card, work out who'd sent it, then go out and buy one for her, so unless he had a supply of cards in his desk drawer for such eventualities—though she wouldn't have been surprised—he must have been thinking the same way as she was, and had bought it for her beforehand.

Sophie wanted to punch the air, and shout 'yes' at the top of her voice—she knew they'd had a connection that day—but she told herself to be cool and let him make the first move. Though unfortunately, as she held her breath in anticipation, the move Nathan seemed to be making was to walk straight past her to place the card slap-bang in the middle of Julie's desk.

It was all she could do to stop her jaw dropping open, and for the third time that morning she almost felt like crying. How could he? Especially when there was a card from her sitting on his... Suddenly, she noticed Nathan still had his coat on, and his bag over his shoulder, which could only mean one thing—he hadn't been down to his office yet. And if that was the case, then he wouldn't have seen it.

She had a sudden impulse to run down and get her card back, but there would probably be other people milling around downstairs by now, and she'd have a hard time explaining her actions. Besides, she knew that would be a bit defeatist—just because Nathan was giving Julie a card, it didn't necessarily mean he wouldn't be open to offers from elsewhere. Plus, if Julie wasn't in yet, then logically he couldn't think the card he'd shortly be finding on his desk was from Julie, which meant he'd know he had an admirer somewhere else in the office. And anyway, Sophie decided, even if her boss was going to be her rival for Nathan's affections, she could deal with that, especially after she'd seen what had appeared to be her going home with Mark Webster after the Christmas party.

She became aware Nathan was looking at her strangely—possibly because she was staring off into space with a dreamy expression on her face. She struggled to control the blush she could feel building up, then smiled up at him.

'Sorry. Miles away.'

Nathan nodded back towards where he'd just deposited the card. 'As I probably should be too. Don't want to get caught red-handed.'

'Or red-carded.'

'What?'

She pointed to Julie's desk. 'The card. It's in a... Well, the envelope's red. I mean, the card might not be, but...' She swallowed loudly. 'You know, a red card? Like in football?'

'Oh yeah.' Nathan flashed her a white-toothed smile. 'Good one.'

'Thanks.'

'And Soph?'

Soph. Normally she hated it when anyone shortened her name, but coming from Nathan's lips, and in his almost East-end accent, it was... Well, *sexy* would be pushing it. But it still made her feel tingly.

'Yes?'

'Do us a favour, will you? Promise you won't tell?'

Sophie nodded eagerly. Even though she was disappointed, she knew she'd have promised Nathan anything.

∽

Julie Marshall nodded a brief hello to Mia-Rose at reception, raised her eyebrows at Nathan as he barrelled past her and disappeared downstairs and into the technical support room, then walked towards the stairs that led up to her first-floor office. While her route took her past Mark's doorway, and she'd usually glance in on the off-chance they could exchange a casual-yet-friendly greeting, today she kept her eyes firmly fixed on the floor in front of her. Recently she'd suspected he'd been pretending not to see her. Which, she knew, was probably fair enough.

She felt pretty rotten about how she'd behaved, but then again, Julie could argue she'd had a reason for that. Besides, the alternative was to have started a conversation she didn't really want to get into, or even to start something else that she might not be able to finish, and neither of those options particularly appealed to her. But then again, divorce wasn't either, and she was thinking seriously about going through with that.

Instinctively, she glanced down at her left hand. She'd seen taking off her wedding ring as the beginning of the end, though in truth, the end had begun a long time before that. She and Philip hadn't had sex for the best part of a year—well, he had, but not with Julie, which was what had started off these whole proceedings—and she often wondered whether, had he not slept with that woman he'd met at the book festival, things might have been different. But she doubted it.

Julie shook her head as she walked up the stairs. Why did she have to marry a writer? Actually, she took that back. She hadn't married a writer. She'd married a lawyer. And then, when he'd had some sort of early mid-life crisis two years ago and given 'it' all up to try and become the next John Grisham... Well, that was when things had begun to change. She'd supported him for the first eighteen months, and then had needed to change her job simply so they (or rather, she) could keep paying the mortgage on their Chiswick flat. The flat that he'd refused to move out of, even when she'd confronted him about the affair.

Which was fair enough, she supposed. Philip had paid most of the deposit and both of their names were on the deeds; besides, he had nowhere else to go (or no way of paying for it), and at least he'd moved into the spare bedroom. And while the other option was for them both to move out, trying to sell the flat at the moment wasn't a good idea, given what was happening with the housing market; while they'd surely get a good price for it, neither of them could subsequently afford to buy somewhere else, or even buy the other out. And all they'd invested—in the flat, and the marriage—would have been for nothing.

Julie almost smiled. As depressed as she was, it was evident the housing market wasn't, and while normally that would be a cause for celebration, she hated being in this strange, limbo-like state, unable to move on because neither of them could afford to move. Not able to get on with her life, because Philip wasn't getting on with his, and all the while, neither of them getting on with each other.

She'd read some of Philip's stuff once. It had been...Well, she'd thought she could probably have done better herself. And despite—what was it now?—twenty-seven rejections from most of the leading publishing houses and agents in the UK, Philip had refused to believe it was his writing that was the problem. Just like he'd refused to believe his behaviour was the problem in their marriage. And that had been the final straw for Julie. She'd always suspected he was a little selfish (though nowadays, she'd describe it as pig-headed), but she'd never realised how selfish until he'd informed her she was the selfish one for not allowing him to follow his dream. He'd even accused her of driving him into the arms of that woman—though Julie couldn't see how, unless the fact that she'd given him a lift to the festival was what he'd been referring to. When she'd found out, and told him she thought the two of them needed some space, he'd gone ballistic and said she was giving up on their marriage. Julie had replied that there were some things that you just had to give up on, and she'd also meant his writing, though he'd chosen to ignore her on both counts.

But while the constant rejections from publishers hadn't seemed to dent his confidence, being rejected by Julie had sent him into a downward spiral, which was why, nowadays, he hardly ever left the spare bedroom—or his laptop, though given that the combination of a new job and her marathon training left her without the energy to deal with Philip every night, that had suited Julie just fine. Or at least it had suited her, up until the Christmas party. How she'd have loved to have invited Mark in. To have been able to wave the taxi away and spend some time with some-one who seemed to be interested in her, rather than simply his MacBook.

She glanced back down the stairs at Mark's firmly shut door, fearing she'd well and truly blown that now. With a sigh, she helped herself to a drink from the water cooler on the upstairs landing, then walked towards her office, forcing herself to smile as she came in through the doorway.

'Morning.'

'Hello,' replied Sophie, brightly.

Julie dumped her bag on the floor and eyed Sophie suspiciously. Normally, getting anything more than a sleepy grunt out of her before midday was impossible. 'Anything happening?' she asked, shrugging her coat off.

'You tell me,' said Sophie, her eyes flicking towards Julie's desk, where she'd propped the envelope up against the telephone to make sure she wouldn't miss it.

'What's that?'

Sophie shrugged. 'Well, unless it's a rather unusually presented quote for those brochures we asked for, I'd say it's a Valentine's card.'

'Really? You shouldn't have.'

'What? It's not from...'

'I'm teasing you, Sophie.' Julie hung her coat on the rack in the corner of the office, then stared at the card from a distance, reluc-tant to touch it, as if that meant she'd be somehow obliged to the sender—whoever that was. Eventually she picked it up, then held it up to the window, and Sophie laughed.

'Traditionally, opening the envelope is the best way to see who it's from.'

'And this was here when you arrived, was it?'

'I couldn't say,' said Sophie, as innocently as she could muster.

'I see.' After a moment's consideration, Julie slit the envelope open with her thumbnail and hesitantly removed the card, and Sophie found herself willing it to be unsigned—the last thing she wanted was for Julie to know Nathan had a thing for her. She was sure she'd get a chance to check later when Julie took her usual trip across the road to Pret, but when her boss simply glanced at the message, slipped the card back into its envelope, then into her desk drawer, Sophie couldn't help but ask.

'Well?'

After the briefest of hesitations, Julie retrieved the card, and handed it to Sophie. 'It's sweet, I suppose.'

'And do you have any idea who your 'Seek-ret admirer' might be?' she asked, feeling a surge of jealousy as she repeated the inscription. Why hadn't she come up with something that good?

Julie made a face, though it was hard for Sophie to read. 'Maybe.'

'And?'

'And don't you have some work to do?' Julie took the card back, and Sophie gave a mock salute.

'Yes, boss. Sorry. Point taken.'

Julie half-smiled as she put the card back in her drawer and wondered what her next move should be. She assumed it must have come from Mark, which she supposed was a good thing—at least she hadn't pissed him off completely—though what she was going to do about it, she wasn't sure. Unless...

She sat down at her computer, scrolled through her inbox, and found the email Nathan had sent her about tonight's event, pleased to see Mark was on the list of attendees.

'Tell me something, Sophie. Are you going to that...thing... that Nathan's organising tonight?'

Sophie looked up sharply. She'd been considering it, for the simple reason that Nathan would be there, but given the size of this morning's credit card bill, and the fact that it was two weeks till pay day, she'd doubted she could afford to go. But then again, if Julie was going, she couldn't afford not to.

'Anti-Valentine's? I was thinking I might. Why?'

'Oh,' said Julie. 'Right. I thought I might, too.'

And as Julie composed a message to Nathan confirming her attendance, Sophie hurriedly clicked on her Outlook icon, found the email Nathan had sent her, and did exactly the same thing.

3

Calum had been sitting at his desk for the best part of an hour, alternating between staring at his mobile and hitting 'refresh' on his Hotmail account. He knew messages would come in automatically, but it was nudging ten o'clock, and seeing as he'd heard nothing at all from Emma, he was starting to worry that his phone—or even the internet—might be broken.

Perhaps he'd been too flippant earlier. Maybe his text had been a bit, well, unromantic—after all, today was supposed to be the most romantic day of the year. He began to fear he was being stupid, going out for a first date on Valentine's Day, and wished he'd insisted on a different night—that way, he'd have avoided all this pressure. But it had been Emma who'd suggested they meet this evening, and Calum had been too worried about putting her off to say no.

He took a deep breath, and reminded himself it was just a date—both today, and tonight. At least he had a date, and more importantly, as far as his office cred was concerned, he didn't have to go to Anti-Valentine's for the third year running. As much as he enjoyed bowling (one of the few 'sports' he was good at), Calum didn't want the reputation of being a regular fixture there. Which reminded him...

He got up from his desk and walked downstairs. Mia-Rose was juggling the usual first-thing-in-the-morning influx of phone calls on reception while trying to sort the mail, and as he passed her desk she rolled her eyes at him and he smiled coyly back. Calum liked Mia-Rose, but since she'd joined the company last September, he'd been too shy to say more than a simple hello or goodbye to her whenever he walked through reception. He'd even stood in the queue behind her in Pret A Manger once, trying—and failing—to pluck up the courage to start a conversation, and had ended up thinking his soup choice of 'chicken' when he'd reached the counter had been pretty appropriate.

'Nice suit,' she mouthed, and he blushed and mouthed an embarrassed 'thank you' back, then headed down into the basement and popped his head round the doorway of the technical support room. Nathan was on a call, so Calum waited until he'd heard the usual 'have you tried turning it off and on again?' followed by 'you're welcome,' and then cleared his throat.

'Morning.'

Nathan looked up, frowned, then checked his watch. 'Surprised to see Sales in before midday,' he said, replacing the phone receiver on its cradle. 'And dressed like a grown-up, too.'

Calum grinned at him. 'Well, someone has to make some money for the company.'

'So what's with the suit? Due in court later?'

'No!'

'Got an interview, then?'

'Something like that,' said Calum, awkwardly.

'Well, as long as you're back for half-five. I don't want to be the only drooling drunk this evening.'

'I... Um... Well, that's what I wanted to talk to you about.'

'Oh yeah?'

'I can't make it.' Calum could feel his chest swelling with pride. 'Tonight.'

Nathan raised one eyebrow. 'Why not? Don't tell me you've got a hot date?'

'Well, yes, actually.'

'You're kidding?'

'Thanks a lot!'

Nathan made a guilty face. 'Sorry, mate. Didn't mean it like that.'

'That's okay. Although I'm not sure if she's hot or not. I mean...' Calum stopped talking, mainly because Nathan's expression suggested he'd need to explain himself. He walked further into the room, then pushed the door shut behind him. 'We met online.'

'Really? You kept that quiet.' Nathan sat back in his chair and folded his arms. 'So, who is this mystery woman?'

'She's called Emma.'

'Nice name. And does the rest of her measure up?'

Calum perched on the corner of the adjacent desk. 'Well, we've not actually, you know...'

'And tonight's the night?'

He nodded. 'Yup.'

'So, where are you going? Your place? Hers? A hotel?'

'No, I mean we haven't actually met. Not the other. Although of course we haven't done that, either.'

Nathan shook his head. 'You sly old dog. Why didn't you say anything?'

'Well, you know. Internet dating, and all that.'

'Calum, I don't know if you've noticed, but you work for an internet company. People do everything online nowadays. There's no shame in meeting a woman that way.'

'Yes, but...' He jabbed a thumb towards the door. 'I didn't really want anyone here to think I'd been, you know, looking. For a woman.'

'Why not? I'm sure they look for a lot worse. In fact, I know they do. I've seen what's on their hard drives.'

'Maybe.' Calum sighed. 'But there's still a stigma if you can't find a partner the normal way, isn't there?'

Nathan shrugged. 'Why? There are still bookshops, but it's not as if anyone laughs at you for ordering stuff from Amazon. And isn't this really just the same kind of thing?'

'Well, not quite...'

'Still, what are you worried about?'

'It's just...' Calum sighed. 'I don't know what she looks like. And so I'm worried she might look, you know, better than me. And if that's the case she...' He stopped talking. Nathan had raised both eyebrows this time, as well as both palms in a 'stop' gesture.

'You don't know what she looks like?'

'No. She contacted me. And she didn't have a photo up. But we got chatting, and it turns out we have a lot in common, and so tonight we're...'

Nathan was shaking his head incredulously. 'I'm sorry. You don't know what she looks like?'

'Er, no.'

'And you're still going out with her?'

'It's not all about looks, you know?'

Nathan opened his mouth to say something, and then shut it again.

'And besides,' continued Calum. 'I'm hardly, you know...'

'What?'

'Brad Pitt.'

Nathan laughed. 'You're not exactly arm pit either. I take it you had a photo on there.'

'Yup.'

'Of you?'

'Of course.'

'In colour?'

'Why wouldn't it be?'

Nathan grinned. 'You being a ginger, and all that…'

'Nathan, for the millionth time, my hair's…'

'Strawberry blond. So you've said. And I'm just kidding, so what are you worried about?'

'That she might be out of my league, and therefore doesn't fancy me.'

Nathan shrugged again. 'Why wouldn't she? Besides, by the sound of things, she does already. She wouldn't be meeting you otherwise, would she? And certainly not tonight.'

'Maybe.' Calum's eyes flicked around the room. 'But there's one thing…'

'Which is?'

'I may have lied a little about my…' He coughed awkwardly. 'Physical dimensions.'

'Christ, Calum. What kind of dating site was it?'

'Not that. My height.'

'How much did you lie, exactly?'

Calum held his palm a couple of inches above the top of his head. 'About this much.'

'What on earth for?'

'Because you had to fill it in on your profile. And women like men over six feet tall.'

Nathan rolled his eyes. 'This is internet dating, not Alton Towers. You don't have to be a certain height to, you know, go on the rides.'

'You'd be surprised. Plus everyone else on there spends their weekends water-skiing or bungee-jumping except for me, so I worried if they thought I was short as well…'

'Yeah, right,' said Nathan. 'They say that, but in reality, each of them is probably a sad loser who still lives at home with his mum, so I wouldn't... What's the matter?'

'I still live with my mum,' said Calum, quietly.

'What?'

'Since my dad died. She's not been well, and she's got no-one else, and...' He stared miserably down at his feet. 'Thanks, Nathan. That's something else I haven't been honest about. Now I feel even worse.'

'But that's different. You're looking after your mum, by the sound of it, not the other way round. And that's a good thing.'

'You think?'

Nathan smiled reassuringly. 'I wouldn't worry about it. She's on a dating site, and she hasn't even put up a photo, so I'd say you're allowed a few exaggerations or exclusions yourself.' His computer pinged at the arrival of an email, and he glanced briefly at the screen before hitting 'minimize.' 'Though why do you think she hasn't?'

'I don't know. Maybe she's shy?'

'Doesn't sound like it. She contacted you, after all.'

'Maybe she's...'

'Disfigured? Only got one leg?'

Calum laughed—briefly. 'I was going to say 'famous,' but your suggestions are probably more likely. Though she said I wouldn't be disappointed when we met.'

'Okay. So she's good looking, but she hasn't put up a photo. Which might suggest something else.'

'Which is?'

'You already know her. Or at least, she knows you.'

'I don't know anyone named Emma. Or that many girls, full stop, come to think of it.'

'You might have yourself a stalker!'

'That's not funny. Or likely, really.'

'You never know.' Nathan grinned. 'So, where are you meeting her?'

'Old Amsterdam. Six o'clock.'

Nathan nodded approvingly. 'Well, we'll miss you this evening. But remember, if it doesn't work out, you can always come along afterwards. And if it does, you still can. Just make sure you bring her too. So us jealous single blokes can check her out.'

'Yeah, right.'

As Nathan turned his attention back to his laptop, Calum hopped off the end of the desk and walked back out into the corridor. If tonight did work out—and he was going to do his best to make sure it did—then the last thing he wanted to do was jeopardise his chances by introducing Emma to his good-looking friend. Besides, he was sure there'd be other opportunities to show her off. At their wedding, maybe... He smiled to himself as he took the stairs back up to his office two at a time. Their wedding! Best not to get ahead of himself—though 'Emma Irwin' did have a nice ring to it...

Slightly out of breath, Calum sat back down at his computer, trying—and failing—not to check his phone for texts and his email for messages before his backside had even made contact with his chair.

⁓

Sophie had been pretending to work for the past half hour, though in actual fact, she'd secretly been studying Julie over the top of her laptop screen instead, and she could see why Nathan might have a thing for her. Julie was attractive, after all, and she had that annoying (to other women, at least, thought Sophie, glancing down at her own more womanly curves) combination of large breasts and a slim figure, but physical attributes aside, surely she wasn't Nathan's type? He was outgoing, and fun, and—apart from when Sophie had seen her reluctantly joining in with pass-the-balloon at the Christmas party—Julie wasn't exactly the life and soul of the office.

They got on well enough, she supposed, which was probably just as well with only the two of them in the marketing department. And while Julie had never been overly friendly, Sophie reasoned that was because she was her boss, and who was ever best friends with their boss? Although there was no reason why that couldn't change, and in fact, Sophie decided, it had to. She needed to know her competition, or at least, know if Julie was her competition, and that meant finding out if she was interested in Nathan. An idea suddenly occurred to her, so she leaned back in her chair, stretched exaggeratedly, then stood up.

'Coffee?'

Julie looked up distractedly from the report she'd been editing. 'Huh?'

'I thought I'd nip out and pick us up a coffee. Well, a couple of coffees. Proper ones, from Pret. Not that instant rubbish in the kitchen.' Sophie realised she was babbling. 'If you'd like one, that is?'

Julie glanced at her watch, then shrugged. 'Sure. Thanks. A latte, please. Oh, and a...'

'Chocolate muffin?'

'Am I that predictable?'

'Not predictable. Just...' Sophie hunted for the right words. *Set in your ways* perhaps wasn't the kindest description of Julie's love of routine. 'Well, maybe just a little.'

Julie shot her a look, then reached for her bag. 'Let me give you some money.'

'That's okay.' Sophie smiled sweetly. 'My treat,' she said, making for the door.

She hurried down the stairs, resisted the temptation to go down another flight to Nathan's office just to see whether he had her card displayed on his desk, then ran outside and across the road to the Pret A Manger on the opposite corner. Five minutes later (and nearly ten pounds worse off, Sophie was shocked to find out), she was back.

'So,' she said, breathlessly placing a latte and a muffin down on Julie's desk. 'Valentine's Day, eh?'

Julie made a weary face as she pulled the lid off her cup. 'Tell me about it.'

For a second, Sophie wondered whether Julie actually wanted her to, before deciding she probably didn't, though her boss was a tough person to read, so she just rolled her eyes in what she thought was a 'sisters together' kind of way and leant against the edge of her desk. 'Looking forward to this evening?' she said, tipping a sachet of sweetener into her cappuccino.

'The bowling? Not really.' Julie blew on her coffee, then took a tentative sip. 'You?'

Sophie frowned. Her interrogation technique didn't seem to be working. 'What's wrong with bowling?'

'Besides having to put on a pair of shoes that a thousand other people have already worn?'

'Fair point.' Sophie smiled, then stirred her coffee as she wondered what to say next. After an awkward silence, 'Funny, though,' was the best she could come up with.

'What is?'

'Nathan.'

'What about him?'

'Organising Anti-Valentine's.'

'Funny ha ha, or funny peculiar?' asked Julie, breaking the muffin in half. She held out a piece, but Sophie reluctantly waved it away.

'Funny peculiar,' said Sophie. 'In that he's single. A good-looking guy like him.'

'You think?'

Sophie frowned at her, trying not to salivate as Julie took a bite from her muffin. This was harder than she'd anticipated. Was Julie asking whether she thought Nathan was good-looking, or whether she thought it was funny that he was single? 'I mean, it's strange, isn't it?' she continued. 'You work with someone, see them every day, but you don't have a clue what they're like. What their... situation is.' She took a mouthful of cappuccino, then realised it was still ridiculously hot, and had to pant-hoot like a monkey to cool the liquid down before she could even think about swallowing it.

'Maybe he's gay.'

Sophie almost spat the still-too-hot coffee out of her mouth in surprise at the prospect. 'Nathan? No, he can't be!'

'Why not?'

Sophie didn't like to say *Because he wouldn't be interested in you if he was.* 'He just... No, I can't believe it. I mean, you can tell, can't you?'

Julie raised one eyebrow. 'Can you? In my experience, it's pretty hard sometimes.'

'Well, I'm pretty sure he's interested in women.'

'Why?'

'I've just... Seen stuff.'

Julie swallowed another piece of muffin. 'Stuff?' she said, licking chocolate crumbs from her fingers.

'Stuff that makes me think he wants a girlfriend.'

'He'd hardly be likely to organise this Anti-Valentine's night if he was after a girlfriend, would he?'

'Unless it's a clever double-bluff.' Sophie tapped the side of her nose conspiratorially and was mortified to find a blob of chocolaty froth on the end of it.

Julie passed her a tissue from the box on her desk. 'Maybe.'

'Do you think he's gay?' Sophie asked, wiping her nose, then tossing the tissue into the waste bin in the corner.

Julie contemplated the question for a moment. 'Like I said. It can be hard to tell.' She took another sip of coffee. 'But I don't think so.'

'Right.' Sophie felt suddenly encouraged, and then her heart sank, and she wanted to ask why Julie didn't think so, whether she had first-hand knowledge. Perhaps she'd made a mistake, and it had been Nathan she'd seen take Julie home after the Christmas party, not Mark, and maybe Nathan's card was some acknowledgement of that, but she held her tongue, worried that to probe any deeper would be overstepping the mark. 'So what do you think Nathan's problem is?'

Julie frowned. 'Problem?'

'You know—why he doesn't have a girlfriend. If, you know, he isn't...' She cleared her throat. 'Gay.'

Julie put her coffee down on her desk and popped the last of the muffin into her mouth. 'Search me,' she said, in between chews. 'Maybe there's something in his past. Maybe he's simply got his eye on someone.'

'Unrequited love?' Sophie sighed. 'How romantic,' she said, before realising that if that was the case, and the object of his affections was the person sitting opposite, her job this evening would be even harder.

Julie smiled, and shook her head slowly. 'Whatever it is, Sophie, I wouldn't waste my time trying to get to the bottom of it.'

'No?' Sophie wondered whether she was trying to warn her off. 'Why not?'

'Because relationships can be…' Julie took a huge gulp of coffee. 'Complicated,' she said cryptically.

Sophie noticed her boss had almost finished her latte now and, worried the opportunity for their little chat might be coming to an end, decided to try a more direct approach. 'What would you do if it was him who'd sent you that card?'

There. She'd said it. And while she hoped Julie would treat the question as hypothetical, at the same time, she really wanted to know her answer.

'Nathan? Well…' Julie stuck her lower lip out contemplatively. 'Like you said, he is very good looking. But an office romance… Do they ever work?'

She stared at Sophie for a second or two, then turned back to her report, indicating the conversation was over, and Sophie felt slightly encouraged. Even if Nathan did fancy Julie, by the sound of things she'd rebuff any approach he made, leaving her in the perfect position to swoop in and pick up the pieces.

But later, as she replayed their conversation in her head, Sophie's smugness suddenly evaporated as she realised something. Despite Julie's earlier vagueness, and for all her rhetoric, her last statement had actually sounded like a genuine question.

❦

Nathan waited until he was sure Calum had gone back upstairs, then opened his drawer and stared at the envelope. He was pretty sure what must be inside, and also knew not opening it wouldn't make it go away. But even so, he couldn't quite bring himself to do the inevitable.

It was funny, he knew, how he'd been happy enough to deliver Mark's card to Julie, but the moment the focus had shifted onto him, he'd begun to feel uneasy—scared, even—when he should have been feeling flattered. So someone in the office liked him—big deal. And yet, it *was* a big deal.

He did a quick run-through of all the single women who worked at Seek, wondering who it might be, though to be honest, he felt it could have been any of them. And that wasn't being conceited—Nathan just couldn't tell if anyone was flirting with him nowadays. The whole Ellie experience had made him unable (though maybe 'unwilling' was a better description) to identify the signs, so he'd simply decided to close himself off emotionally. It had just been easier that way.

He knew what his problem was: the futility of it all. He'd spent three years with Ellie, trying to please her, getting to know her intimately, and yet it turned out he'd hardly known her at all, and Nathan didn't think he had the energy to go through all that again with someone new. Especially if he was only going to end up with the same result.

It wasn't that he hadn't been lonely. Of course he wanted a girlfriend—a wife, even—or at least some companionship, and sex, although he'd shied away from the couple of offers of one-night stands he'd had in the past few years. Because the trouble was, what did you do when you thought you'd found perfection—your soul mate—only to realise you couldn't have got it more wrong? And if Nathan couldn't trust his judgement about someone after two-and-a-half years, how, he wondered, could he possibly do it after five minutes?

Despite his cynicism, he'd been struck by how excited and apprehensive Calum had seemed about his date this evening, and as for Mark's nervousness where Julie was concerned—well, he'd teased him about it, of course, but in reality, he'd found that quite touching. And while at the same time Nathan had fought a wild urge to warn them they might be wasting their time, equally, ironically, he knew that was the only way love had a chance to develop: by wasting your time with someone else who maybe might like to waste theirs with you. And while he'd tried to spare himself the hurt he felt whenever he thought about Ellie by not allowing himself to even consider life with someone else, he knew that was short-sighted. Pathetic, too. Even Calum, who Nathan suspected would be crushed if this evening didn't work out, was prepared to put himself through potential heartbreak and humiliation in public, tonight of all nights, in search of happiness. And that last thought made him feel ashamed.

Then, to his surprise, and perhaps thanks to Calum and Mark's optimism, Nathan realised something: he needed to get a grip, if for no other reason than if he didn't, Ellie might spoil things for him forever. Once, a taxi had knocked him off his Vespa, and he'd known he had to get straight back on—otherwise he might never have been able to ride it again. And although Nathan knew you could hardly describe an abstinence of three years as 'getting straight back on,' there was no time like the present.

He took a deep breath, removed the envelope from his drawer, and tore it open.

❧

On the floor above, Mark Webster was staring intently at the Excel spreadsheet on his screen, and while the columns would normally make perfect sense to him, today the numbers were all a bit of a blur. He knew that was probably down to the constant self-inflicted interruptions he'd suffered, which had so far come to nothing: Julie hadn't been in the kitchen any of the five times he'd gone and made himself a cup of coffee he had no intention of drinking, nor had she walked past the photocopier when he'd been pretending to stock it with paper, visited the water cooler, gone to the toilet, or even been walking up and down the stairs during one of the numerous occasions he'd made his various journeys. She'd even failed to go out to buy her mid-morning muffin—an event he could usually set his watch by—and so far, his plan to casually bump into her and ask whether she'd had any Valentine's deliveries was failing.

He supposed he shouldn't be surprised. After all, what had he been expecting—that she'd somehow decipher his cryptic message, come down to his office, clear his desk with one sweep of a well-toned arm, and demand he take her there and then? He leant back in his chair and rubbed his eyes wearily, then got up and paced around the room. Why hadn't he just written his name in the card? That way, at least he'd have known where he stood, rather than had to suffer this interminable waiting of—what had it been now? He looked at his watch. Two hours.

Mark knew his other option would have been to have referred to that fateful night directly, but seeing as Julie could be pretending not to remember it, that might not have been such a great plan. And if she really didn't, it may even have got him in trouble.

Maybe he'd got Valentine's Day all wrong. Perhaps, he mused, it was more of an event for existing couples, rather than for trying to 'woo' someone, though he almost laughed out loud at the word. How old did using it make him sound? And anyway, Mark wondered, maybe his plan to woo her was stupid—after all, he'd hardly wooed Julie before. She'd been drunk, jumped on him, and they'd kissed. That hardly ranked him up there alongside the great romantics.

It occurred to him that he could try that tactic again tonight. Engineer the seat next to her at Anti-Valentine's, offer her a couple of bowling pointers, and most importantly, buy her a couple of drinks. But on reflection, Mark decided getting Julie drunk wasn't such a great plan either. She hadn't remembered what had happened between them the last time she'd had a drink, so even if he did manage to kiss her, he'd be back to square one the next day. Though possibly even more frustrated.

No, Mark realised, this time he had to try romancing her. See whether throughout the course of today he could get Julie to start thinking about him in a different way, or even remind her about the Christmas party. That way, she'd be primed and ready at tonight's 'do,' and then, if he did manage to pluck up the courage to ask her out, it wouldn't come as a complete surprise.

He sat back down and stared out of the window, trying to work out what it was they had in common, or which gesture or gift might jog her memory, and thought about sending something to her house, but that might be inappropriate—and she might be angry that he'd gotten her home address from the payroll file. Plus, he needed to do it today, or at least before tonight.

But do what? Everything else Mark had tried since Christmas in order to make contact had failed up until now, from trying to mimic the events of that night by simply hanging around outside in the hope they might be heading in the same direction for lunch, to approving some rather spurious expenses for the last trade show she'd attended. Nothing had provoked more than a cursory nod or a brief thank you. And he was beginning to run out of ideas.

Mark knew he was being silly. He was twenty-seven years old, and head-over-heels about someone who seemed not to have the slightest idea how he felt about her. It was no way for a sensible adult to behave, and he was certainly a sensible adult—it was one of the things accountants were known for. He also knew he had to consider that perhaps Julie simply wasn't interested. Maybe she had been drunk, and even if she could remember what happened, she might simply be trying to forget the kiss. Perhaps she was embarrassed or, even worse, didn't fancy him, but Mark doubted that. He'd felt a real spark between the two of them, a sense of urgency in her kiss, as if she hadn't been kissed like that for a long, long time.

One thing he was sure of was that he didn't want to feel like this for much longer. The last seven weeks had been torture for him, and it had made work rather awkward too. He worried that everyone in the office could tell what was going on from the way he looked at her. Everyone except Julie, that was.

He knew that Nathan thought he was being pathetic. He'd only told him he liked her because he'd wanted to enlist his help, or at least get his opinion as to what he should do, even though Nathan perhaps wasn't the best person to ask for advice where matters of the heart were concerned. But Mark had been desperate, and while Nathan had been happy to listen—and even happier to help—when Mark had asked for his point of view, Nathan had just shrugged. 'Who knows what women want?' he'd said, and then he'd changed the subject.

But that was fine. Mark could probably guess what women wanted. They wanted to be romanced, as if every day was Valentine's Day, and romance was cards, and presents, and chocolates, and perhaps even a bit of mystery. Though seeing as his card hadn't worked, Mark knew he had to make that mystery a bit more obvious.

He peered around his office, searching for inspiration, then his gaze alighted on the stationery cupboard in the corner, and an idea suddenly struck him. Mark had the only key (oh, the responsibility!), and while yesterday's office supplies audit hadn't been the most exciting afternoon he'd ever spent, he had discovered a few items that had somehow found their way in there after the Christmas party.

Before he could lose his nerve, he took an envelope out of his desk drawer, wrote Julie's name on the front in capital letters, then walked over to the cupboard and unlocked the door. With a smile on his face, he retrieved what he was looking for, slipped them inside the envelope, and then—once he was sure the coast was clear—he darted into the hallway, crept up the stairs, and slotted the envelope into her pigeonhole.

～

Julie Marshall was in a quandary. She wanted to find out whether Mark had sent her the card, and yet she couldn't afford to raise his hopes—or her own, for that matter. As she'd almost confessed to Sophie, her relationship was complicated, and getting involved with Mark could only confuse things even further. Besides, she didn't have a clue what to say to him.

She knew he deserved some sort of explanation for her behaviour since the night of the Christmas party—and especially for her behaviour *on* the night of the Christmas party—yet at the same time, Julie felt Mark was the last person she could tell about her home life. Despite her current living arrangements, she was a married woman, and yet she'd kissed him. What would Mark think of her if he found that out?

Julie wasn't particularly proud of herself, and wanted him to understand, and yet she feared telling him might drive him away. And while she hadn't had a night out in ages, and the idea of going out for a few drinks with Mark and the office crowd tonight was actually rather appealing (especially when the alternative was a moody evening at her flat with a sulky Philip staking out his half of the sofa), she also knew she couldn't afford to get drunk and leap on Mark like she had at Christmas. The irony was, Julie felt like she needed a drink. She'd been feeling that more and more recently, and while she knew it was perhaps understandable given her situation at home, it wasn't a particularly healthy way to be.

She looked up from her laptop to see Sophie staring at her, then got up from her desk and peered out of the window, down at the huddle of smokers that had already assembled outside the pub on the corner. As one of them—an old man with no teeth—leered up at her, she stepped back from the window hurriedly and made her way into the hallway, absentmindedly removed the brown Manila envelope she'd spotted poking out of her pigeonhole, and walked back into her office.

'Not another one?'

'Pardon?'

'That.' Sophie nodded towards the envelope. 'Another Valentine's card?'

'Huh?' Julie followed Sophie's gaze, then did a double take. The handwriting on the front did seem familiar, although it didn't feel like there was a card inside. 'No, this is...' She tore the envelope open and peered inside, almost dropping it in shock until she realised it didn't contain, as she'd first thought, a bag of multicoloured condoms—albeit for someone with an incredibly deformed penis—but in fact a packet of assorted balloons.

Julie smiled to herself, aware Sophie was watching her closely from the other side of the room. The card this morning—now these. Unless the balloons were from Dave in personnel—and she doubted that, as she'd met Dave's boyfriend a few weeks ago—it had to be Mark.

She could see what he was doing, trying to remind her of the events of that evening, and considered sending him an email to say it was okay, she actually remembered everything, but to be honest, Julie was intrigued to see what he might do next. And, she realised, she was enjoying the attention. It had been a long time since someone had tried to romance her, or sent her anything like this.

For a second, Julie decided she shouldn't feel guilty about her home situation. Mark might even understand. In fact, she was sure there were probably thousands of people in the same boat as her, unable to sell up and go their separate ways. At least she and Philip were living separate lives, and while they were still married on paper, surely that was only a matter of time. But the fact that she'd taken her ring off, not said anything to anyone, and still kissed Mark... Well, she could see how that might appear a little duplicitous. She pulled the bag out of the envelope, and Sophie's laugh snapped her back to reality.

'Something amusing you?'

'No, it's just... Balloons?'

Julie smiled. 'Romantic, eh?'

'Do you know who they're from?'

'I've got an idea.'

'And?'

'And what?'

'Sorry.' Sophie turned back to her computer screen. 'I understand if you don't want to tell me.'

'No, it's nothing like that. It's just... It might be... complicated,' said Julie, aware she was in danger of over-using that word today. 'How about you, Sophie? Get any cards yourself?'

'I don't know.' Sophie fixed her eyes on the email she was typing and readied the lie she'd been rehearsing all morning. 'I left before the postman came this morning.'

'And did you send any?'

Sophie's fingers froze above her keyboard. 'Just the one.'

'And did Nathan like it?'

Sophie blushed. 'How did you...'

'Just a wild guess, based on the fact that your tongue virtually hits the floor whenever you see him.'

'Is it that obvious?'

'To me, yes. To him? Hard to say. But...'

Sophie looked up anxiously. 'What?'

'Are you sure he's not gay?'

'Yes I'm sure,' said Sophie, indignantly, though she realised the only evidence she had was the fact she'd seen him delivering Julie's card earlier. And she certainly wasn't going to give up that particular piece of information.

'Suit yourself,' said Julie. 'Although...'

'Although what?'

'Well, Nathan is very good-looking, and yet, have you ever heard him mention a partner—of any kind?'

Sophie wondered whether Julie realised people could say the same about her. 'Well, no, but...'

'Don't you think you ought to find out, before you make...'

'A fool of myself?'

'Any declarations of love, I was going to say. Though if you're wrong, the end result would be the same.'

'Okay.' Sophie propelled her wheelie chair over to her boss's desk with her feet. 'So how do I do that?'

'You could ask him.'

'I'm not so sure I like that as a plan.'

'Okay.' Julie smiled. 'I could ask him for you.'

Sophie shook her head quickly. If Nathan did indeed fancy Julie, the last thing she wanted was for the two of them to have a cosy little tête-à-tête—even if it was on her behalf. 'Bit too direct, isn't it? Besides, how would you go about it, exactly?'

Julie thought for a moment. 'Good point.'

An idea occurred to her, and Sophie sat bolt upright. 'You could ask Mark Webster.'

'Mark Webster?'

Sophie nodded enthusiastically. 'He and Nathan are good friends. And so he's bound to know.'

'Ah.'

'What's "ah"?'

'That might be a little...' Julie stopped talking. While she didn't want Sophie to know anything about her and Mark, she did want an excuse to talk to him. 'No, you're right,' she said, standing up suddenly. 'That does sound like the best way. I'll give it a go.'

'You're going to ask him now?' said Sophie nervously.

'Like I'm going to get any work out of you today if I don't.'

Julie grabbed the back of Sophie's chair and wheeled her back to her desk, then strode purposefully out of the office. This, she realised, gave her the perfect excuse to bring up the subject of Valentine's Day. Mark was bound to crack, and if so, well, maybe now was the time to start being a bit more adult about what had happened.

Maybe.

She nipped to the toilet and quickly checked her make-up in the mirror above the sink, then headed downstairs, took a deep breath, and knocked on Mark's door.

4

Calum was feeling extremely anxious. It was approaching midday, and the fact that he'd still heard nothing from Emma was beginning to worry him. Maybe she was testing him, but he feared it was more likely she'd simply got cold feet, and the last thing he wanted—tonight of all nights—was to be sitting on his own in a restaurant, hanging around waiting for someone who was never going to show up.

Perhaps she'd simply been playing him. After all, it was possible she'd been communicating with loads of guys on the site, and could have arranged half a dozen dates this evening, perhaps planning to pick the best of them on the day and go to that one, leaving the others to wait for her in vain. And if that was the case, Calum was sure he'd be one of the others.

It occurred to him his choice of a mid-range Netherlands-themed restaurant hadn't quite cut it, especially if Emma had some other wealthy suitor who'd offered to take her to one of those posh places they were always going on about in *GQ*, like The Ivy, or Nobu, or that restaurant where the chef swore at everyone. Then again, maybe she was ill, or she'd had an accident, and he wondered whether he should phone around the local hospitals just to see, but then Calum remembered he didn't know Emma's surname, so that might prove a little tricky. Alternatively, of course, and perhaps the simplest option—he could simply call her.

Calum picked his phone up for the hundredth time and scrolled through to where he'd programmed in her number, and then—for the hundredth time—put it straight back down without dialling. Instead, he got up from his desk and took a few deep breaths, telling himself to relax, worried that if he was this nervous now, he was bound to be a complete wreck this evening. Suddenly, Nathan's Anti-Valentine's night was looking like a much better option.

He walked out of his office, navigated his way through the maze of desks where the admin team sat, and was hovering by the kitchen, wondering whether his usual late-morning black coffee was a good idea given his white shirt, when he bumped into Sophie. Calum liked Sophie, and under different circumstances—if they didn't work together, and more importantly, if he weighed a stone or two less and had about a hundred times more self-confidence—he might have asked her out.

'Hey, Calum,' she said, pleasantly. 'You're looking smart today.'

Calum blushed. 'Thanks. You too. Not that I don't think you look smart every day. Well, maybe "smart" isn't the right word...'

He'd begun to sweat, so Sophie changed the subject in an attempt to put him out of his misery. 'Will we be seeing you tonight?'

'I hope not,' he said, then he felt guilty for his lack of faith in Emma. 'I mean, no.'

'Hot date?'

Calum blushed again. 'Well, yes, actually.'

Sophie's eyes widened. 'Ooh. Good for you. You kept that quiet.'

'Well, we've only just met, and...' Calum lowered his voice. 'To be honest, Sophie, I'd appreciate a woman's advice, if you've got a minute?'

Sophie peered down the stairs towards Mark's door and realised Julie must still be in there. While she was slightly worried her boss had been making a serious point when she'd joked about not getting any work out of her today, she could probably spare Calum a few minutes. 'Sure,' she said, sitting down on the sofa by the window and patting the seat next to her.

Calum glanced anxiously round the office. The middle of the first floor was open-plan, and he didn't want to be overheard by one of the gossip-happy admin team, or by Mia-Rose, who'd just appeared in the kitchen. 'Not here,' he whispered, leading Sophie through the double doors by the top of the stairs and onto the office's roof terrace, where the half-dozen or so smokers who worked at Seek would occasionally disappear for a crafty cigarette.

'It's just…' Calum pushed the doors firmly shut behind them. 'We met online, and we've been chatting for a couple of weeks, and tonight's the first time we're actually meeting…'

'Tonight's the first time you're meeting?' Sophie tried not to look shocked. 'On Valentine's Day?'

'I know, I know. So I was wondering. What do women look for in a man?'

Sophie puffed her cheeks out, trying to ignore the description of Nathan that had just popped into her head. 'Blimey, Calum. That's a big question. I mean, there's obviously attraction, but I suppose you also want someone who's kind, who makes you laugh, who's honest…'

'Honest?' Calum swallowed hard. Why hadn't he told Emma he lived with his mum? 'Okay. But what if the attraction thing isn't necessarily there? I mean, what if you like someone, and you get on well, but there's no, you know, spark?'

'Hmm.' Sophie leant against the iron railings overlooking the courtyard behind Spank-o-rama then recoiled quickly at the cold-ness of the metal. 'As far as I'm concerned, there's got to be a spark. Don't you think?'

'Yeah. I suppose.'

'Is that what you're worried about? That you don't feel a spark with this... What's her name?'

'Emma. And no. I think she's perfect. I'm more afraid it'll be the other way round.'

Sophie rested a hand on Calum's arm, and he had to stop himself from flinching at the unfamiliarity of a woman's touch. 'Calum, how can there not be? She's agreed to go out with you, and on Valentine's Day. She wouldn't be doing that just because there's nothing good on TV this evening.'

'Maybe. But it might simply be because she doesn't want to be alone tonight.'

'That's hardly likely. Trust me, we girls know it's better to be on our own than with the wrong person, so if she wants to be with someone tonight of all nights, the most special day of the year for lovers, then she must think you're pretty special. And pretty special to have asked her.'

He coughed awkwardly. 'She, um, asked me, actually.'

'I'm impressed. And there you go. She sounds dead keen.'

'So why hasn't she contacted me this morning?'

As if on cue, his mobile bleeped, and Calum was in such a hurry to get it out of his pocket he nearly dropped it off the roof. He made a face at Sophie, then nervously peered at the screen.

'Well?'

'It's a text,' he said. 'From Emma.'

'Well, there you go, again!' Sophie smiled reassuringly. 'Aren't you going to read it?'

He turned his attention back to his phone. He almost didn't want to know what it said, convinced by now it was bound to be bad news, and yet, even though it said 'me too,' and was signed off with a smiley face, he didn't feel much better. The message was hardly dripping with enthusiasm, and while Emma had told him it was difficult for her to text at work, he couldn't help feeling disappointed at what was hardly the most exciting of emoticons.

Calum tried not to feel depressed. On the plus side, she was still coming, and even if she was turning up begrudgingly, he still had a date, and on Valentine's Day, and he hadn't been able to say that for a long, long time. Besides, a smiley face was better than a miserable one, surely? And certainly better than nothing at all.

He stared at the message again, trying to work out exactly what it meant. He was so hoping everything would go well tonight, and that this would therefore be the end of this internet dating lark. The process hadn't been fun, but then again, neither was having your offer to buy drinks for random women in bars turned down, or smiling at any girl who caught your eye on the tube only to have them look at you like you belonged in a care-in-the-community scheme, or picking the exercise bike next to someone attractive in the gym then watching them get straight off theirs because you'd forgotten to spray yourself with deodor-ant that morning, or trying to make eye contact with women on Tottenham Court Road without bumping into someone com-ing the other way. But Emma…Everything about her had felt different, so much so he'd been sure she was the one who could put him out of his misery. He'd waited so, so long to get to this evening's date—so long, in fact, that he didn't want the slight-est thing to go wrong. And this? While it wasn't perhaps wrong, something about it didn't feel quite right.

Calum stood there and thought about what he knew about her. Emma was the same age as him—at least, she'd said she was, though having been burnt before, Calum had tried to check that, and had been reassured that at least her cultural references had seemed the same as his: she loved *The Office* and Coldplay, and while anyone could of course have said that, you had to be his age to know who Lana Del Rey was, or find *The Inbetweeners* funny, and Emma had passed both those tests. She read *Heat* magazine, and liked *The X Factor*, and despite one misunderstanding, where he'd thought she'd told him she loved curry, but it turned out she'd said 'Corrie,' they actually seemed to have a lot in common.

Though perhaps he'd come across as too desperate. Given his behaviour before he'd met her, he may as well have been walking around wearing a sandwich board like those men on Oxford Street with the ones that advertised golf equipment sales, except his would have said 'please go out with me.' And maybe Emma's muted response today was simply a reaction to that. Perhaps she was trying to tone him down a little, or to get him to lower his expectations.

The idea of sandwich boards had made him feel hungry, so he tried to think about something else. Suddenly, he heard a loud throat-clearing, and he looked up to see Sophie hopping from foot to foot.

'Calum, it's cold out here...'

'Sorry.' He realised he'd been so preoccupied he'd forgotten she'd had been standing there. 'What does it mean?' he asked, handing her his phone.

Sophie studied the message. 'Well, what did you send her, exactly?'

'This.' Calum reached across and scrolled up to his earlier message, and Sophie frowned at the screen.

'Well, I'm no expert, but I think it means she's looking forward to seeing you later too.'

'Yes, but...' He stared at her helplessly. 'It means more than that, really, doesn't it?'

Sophie smiled. 'Calum, it's normally we girls who pore over every detail, every subtle nuance in messages like these. Not you men. You're just supposed to take them at face value.' She nudged him. 'Or smiley face value.'

Calum smiled weakly at her joke. 'Come on, Sophie. You're in marketing. You should understand that this internet dating is like a shop window, only it's like there's just one of everything, so if you see something you like, well, until you've actually got your hands on it…'

'So to speak.'

'Sorry. But you know what I mean. And maybe I'm putting too much pressure on tonight, but Emma's the one person I've met who seems to like me for me. And who doesn't expect me to play second fiddle to their cat.'

Sophie laughed, though she felt a little sick at the same time. 'It looks like it's worked for you.'

'One potentially decent date, Sophie. In six weeks. And even then, I had to lie about my height to get it.'

'You lied? What for?'

'Because everyone else does it,' said Calum, even though he knew it was like the excuses those sprinters used as to why they took drugs—that it was the only way to level the playing field. 'And when I say "lied," I only exaggerated a little. But so what? Say I was in a bar or a club, a woman's not going to be there with her tape measure, is she?'

Sophie nodded towards Spank-o-rama. 'Depends on the type of club.'

'But my point is, you need to meet them to give yourself a chance to wow them. Tell the truth about yourself online, and you don't get to meet them. It's how it works in sales, too. Get the meeting. The face time. And tell me something—what's so important about being six foot tall anyway?'

Sophie opened her mouth to answer, and for the second time, a vision of Nathan looking down on her popped into her head. 'I suppose height's not really that important. As long as they're not shorter than you.'

'But why does that matter? It's not as if it's the caveman days anymore, and we're expected to fight off others for your honour.'

'Isn't it?' said Sophie, thinking of the one time she'd been speed dating. There had been a few cavemen there—and not in a good way. 'Calum, it's not like some identity parade where she'd pick the tallest one, and you're not that short anyway, so what are you so worried about?'

'That she won't turn up.'

'I'd say from that text that you can be sure she will.'

'Well, what if she takes one look at me, then turns round and leaves?'

'Why on earth would she do something like that? You two have been spending the last few weeks getting to know each other virtually, so she'd be silly if she didn't give you a chance in the flesh. Even if you didn't turn out to be exactly what she was expecting.'

'Really?'

'Really. And anyway, she's picked you because she liked your thumbnail, right?'

Calum glanced down at his hand. 'My thumbnail?'

'Thumbnail photo, Calum. On the site.'

'Oh. Right. I suppose so.'

'So let me have a look.'

'What for?'

'Well, the only way she's going to be disappointed is if you don't look like your photo. So let me see it, and I'll tell you if you do or not.'

Calum shrugged. 'Sure.' He flicked through to the 'pictures' section on his mobile, selected the one he'd used on his profile—

the same one that was on Seek's website—and handed Sophie the phone. To be honest, it hadn't been hard to choose that one—he wasn't particularly photogenic, and most other pictures of him looked like something you'd see on *Crimewatch*.

'Yup.' Sophie held the phone up, peered closely at the photo, then at Calum. 'I'd say that's a pretty good likeness.'

'Really? It's not a bit of a McDonald's shot?'

'Huh?'

'Like when your burger arrives, and it doesn't quite look like the photo above the counter.'

Sophie smiled as she handed him back the phone. 'You still eat it, though, don't you? And in your case, I'd say WYSIWYG.'

'It's not a wig. I'm a natural strawberry blond.'

She laughed. 'No—it's an acronym. It stands for "what you see is what you get." And what I see is what she's actually getting. So how can she possibly be disappointed?'

'Really?'

'Really.'

Calum puffed air out of his cheeks in relief. 'Thanks, Sophie.'

'Don't mention it.' She smiled reassuringly at him, then shivered. 'And just remember—always think positive. Unless, of course, you're waiting for a girl to take a pregnancy test.'

Calum laughed, and Sophie clapped him on the shoulder. 'That's the spirit. Now, can we go back inside? It's freezing!'

Calum nodded, then followed her back through the door. He had to hope Sophie was right, though deep down, he couldn't shake the feeling Emma was bound to be disappointed when she met him.

Mainly because every other woman he'd ever gone out with had been.

෨

Mark Webster was feeling pleased with himself. After a bit of internet research (using the company's own software, of course), he'd found out the American sweet shop in Covent Garden stocked a brand of confectionery called Hershey's Chocolate Kisses, and thanks to the phone call he'd just made (and a not inconsiderable addition to his credit card bill), a packet was due to be delivered to Julie later this morning. Short of booking a taxi to take the two of them home from the bowling, there was little else he could do, but Mark hoped the combination of his card, the balloons, and the Kisses would do the trick. He'd been especially delighted when Nathan had told him Julie was going this evening. It would give him an additional three or four hours to work his magic on her, and despite his earlier concerns, he'd decided that if that 'magic' simply consisted of buying her a couple of cocktails and hoping for the best, then he'd try that too—but only as a last resort. He wanted Julie to remember this evening. Just like he wanted her to never forget today.

He supposed he ought to get back to work, and was scrolling through the company's end of year accounts when the sound of Julie's voice almost made him fall off his chair.

'Mark?'

'Hi,' he shouted, then said it again in his normal voice. Even dressed in what she probably thought was the plainest of grey business suits, Mark thought she looked...Well, 'as sexy as hell' just about covered it.

'Got a min?'

Mark nodded, biting off the 'the rest of my life, actually' response that had leapt to mind, then shifted uneasily in his seat as Julie shut the door behind her. 'What can I do for you?'

She wheeled his spare chair from the corner of the office over to the other side of his desk, and sat down. 'It's a little sensitive, actually.'

'Oh?' said Mark, though in his thoughts, he'd added the word 'no' afterwards. Was Julie here to confront him about the card, or maybe accuse him of sexual harassment like he'd feared? What had he been thinking, sending those balloons? He'd obviously meant to woo her over the course of the day, but on reflection, there was a fine line between romantic bombardment and stalking. 'Fire away,' he said, surreptitiously hiding the Hershey's receipt under a piece of paper on his desk, wondering whether it was too late to cancel the order.

'It's just…' Julie took a deep breath, and Mark braced himself. 'There's someone in this office who evidently likes someone else in this office.'

'Right.'

'And this person—not the one who's sent that someone else a Valentine's card but, you know, the someone else… Well, if they— the receiver—were gay, then that would make it all a bit of, well, a waste of time. Wouldn't it?'

Mark looked at Julie levelly, though his mind was racing. Was she trying to tell him she was gay? It would certainly explain her lack of response since their kiss—though it wouldn't quite explain why she'd kissed him in the first place, unless… Maybe she'd just been so drunk at Christmas she thought she'd try kissing a man, just to see what it was like. Perhaps she'd been questioning her sexuality, and that had been a good way to find out how she felt. Maybe he should be flattered she'd chosen him for her 'experiment,' though if that were the case, he felt depressed that he hadn't been good enough to 'turn' her. At the same time, Mark wondered how he could have got it so wrong. He'd been sure there'd been a spark between them, and surely that wouldn't exist if… Though thinking about it, he couldn't be sure either way—as far as he knew, Julie had never discussed her personal life with anyone here at Seek. And while Mark liked to think their office environment was pretty progressive (it couldn't not be, given their location near Old Compton Street, the gay heart of London), maybe Julie had experienced discrimination in the past. Or innuendo. Or even unwanted advances like his. Unless... Unless this was just a ruse. A way to let him down without hurting his feelings.

'I see,' he said, aware Julie was staring at him.

'So, what do you think?'

'Well, it's fine, of course. I mean, perhaps a bit disappointing, obviously, for the person concerned who sent the card. But that's the way of the world nowadays, and we should celebrate diversity, rather than...' Julie was frowning, so Mark stopped talking.

'So, is that a yes or a no?'

'Pardon?'

'I'm sorry to put you on the spot Mark, but you're his friend. You'd know, wouldn't you?'

'His friend?'

'Yes. Nathan.'

'What's Nathan got to do with anything?'

'He's the one who...' Julie made the speech marks sign in the air, '"someone" has sent a card to.'

Mark's jaw dropped. Was Julie referring to herself when she used the word 'someone,' and if so, did that mean she'd sent Nathan a card? Why on earth would she do that if she was gay? And if she wasn't, and he was...He scratched his head, wondering what on earth all of this had to do with, well, anything.

'I'm sorry, Julie. I'm a little lost.'

'Is Nathan gay?'

'Nathan?' Mark almost laughed. 'Why?'

She leant across the table towards him and lowered her voice, and Mark had to fight to stop himself staring at the rather delicious view of her cleavage this provided him. 'Because between you and me, someone in this office has taken rather a liking to him.'

'Ah. And just to be clear, this "someone" isn't gay.'

Julie sat back upright and folded her arms across her chest, much to his disappointment. 'Why on earth would you think that?'

'Sorry. Silly of me. Though of course if they were, it'd be okay. But...' Mark's voice caught in his throat. 'This "someone" has sent Nathan a Valentine's card?'

Julie nodded. 'That's right. And she doesn't want to be wasting her time, obviously. If he's, like I said...'

'Gay?'

'Exactly.'

Mark stared at her, still trying to compute what she'd said. Julie hadn't come in to accuse him of sexual harassment, plus she wasn't gay—which he supposed was good news on both fronts—but what wasn't such good news was that she seemed to be interested in Nathan, not him, which perhaps edged his mission into the 'impossible' category. He frowned, then scratched his head again, trying to come to terms with this bombshell, and realised the easiest thing to do would be to say that yes, Nathan was gay, thus heading Julie off at the pass. But that would be dishonest. And Mark wasn't the dishonest type.

'Can I just get this straight? You're asking me if Nathan is gay?'

'Yes.'

'Nathan in technical support?'

'That's right.'

'Nathan Field?'

'Is there another Nathan working here?'

'Well, no, but…' Mark shook his head. 'Can you think of anyone less gay?'

Julie shrugged. 'You can't always tell, can you? I mean, it's not as if people walk around with a badge on declaring their sexuality, is it?'

Mark felt even more confused. Was Julie referring to herself again? 'And you're asking because…'

Julie sighed. 'Because someone sent him a Valentine's card this morning. And she wants to know whether she's wasting her time.'

For the second time in as many minutes, Mark didn't quite know how to answer. Given Nathan's current emotional state, anyone interested in him was probably wasting their time. And while he didn't want to betray Nathan's complicated situation, he needed to know whether Julie had a thing for him. Not that he was worried—Mark was pretty sure Nathan wouldn't be interested in her, not just because of how he felt about things generally, but also out of loyalty to him—but he didn't want to be Julie's consolation prize.

Or did he? Maybe if he told Julie the truth about Nathan, and that he was off the market, he'd get her on the rebound, and while that perhaps wasn't the most honourable thing to do, he'd still get her. But Mark didn't want to do anything dishonourable. Not where the woman he loved was concerned.

'No,' he said, eventually. 'Nathan's not gay.'

'Great,' said Julie. She regarded him across the desk for a moment or two, opened her mouth as if to say something, then suddenly got up out of her chair and made for the door.

'Was there anything else?'

Julie paused in the doorway then she shook her head quickly. 'Just the, er, Nathan question. I'm pleased he's, you know...' She let out a nervous laugh. 'Not.'

Though as Mark watched her leave, and for purely selfish reasons, he suddenly found himself wishing the exact opposite.

༄

Sophie walked Calum back to his office, then leant against the radiator in the hallway for a minute or two, trying to get some feeling back in her fingers. It was touching to see how nervous he was, yet it depressed her that she couldn't remember the last time she'd felt like that. She and Darren had gotten together at college on one drunken night at the student's union, and since then... Well, the closest she'd come to breathless anticipation recently was running for the last tube home.

At the same time, Sophie knew she had a chance to feel like that again, and couldn't let a small thing like Nathan sending Julie a Valentine's card put her off. She also realised Calum was right—you had to do these things face-to-face, and the more face time she got with Nathan, the better. She popped briefly into the toilets to check her reflection, then made her way downstairs, and after a moment's hesitation, knocked on Nathan's open door.

'Hey, Soph.' He glanced up from his laptop and flashed her a smile, and Sophie suddenly felt the need to sit down.

'You busy?'

'One sec. Just dealing with a PICNIC.'

'Pardon?'

'It's a technical term. Problem In Chair, Not In Computer.' He grinned, jabbed at a couple of keys, then gave her his full attention. 'What can I do you for?'

'I was wondering. Tonight. If you...' She scanned his desk as she spoke, looking to see whether the card she'd sent him was on display, then hiding her disappointment when there was no sign of it. 'Did you get my email? About if there were any places left?'

'Sure,' said Nathan. 'The more the merrier.'

'Great.'

'No date tonight, then?'

Sophie tried hard to stop herself from blushing. 'Oh, you know. Johnny Depp called, but I told him I'd rather go bowling with the office crowd.'

Nathan laughed. 'Good call.'

'What about you? I'm surprised...I mean, how come you organise this?' she asked, then immediately regretted the question as Nathan's smile wavered. 'Not that I'm trying to pry, or anything.'

'Not at all. It's just...I know how Valentine's Day can be tough for some people.'

Sophie waited for him to continue, but when the awkward silence grew too much for her, she couldn't help but ask. 'How do you mean?'

'Well...Being on your own, instead of with someone you love.'

'But...Anti-Valentine's?'

Nathan made a face. 'Some people don't exactly regard it as their favourite day of the year.'

'What's not to like?'

Nathan shrugged. 'Come on, Soph. What about the disappointment of not getting any cards, for one thing?'

'I suppose so,' said Sophie, not daring to point out that wasn't something he could complain about this morning. 'But there's the excitement of sending them, surely?'

'Only to have your advances rejected?' Nathan suddenly seemed to be interested in something on the computer screen in front of him. 'There are lots of reasons.'

'There are lots of reasons to like it, too.'

'Such as?'

'The anticipation of starting a new relationship?' suggested Sophie.

Nathan's face darkened, and he opened his mouth as if to say something, then evidently thought better of it. 'Yes, you're right, Soph,' he said, with what looked like a forced smile. 'Who knows? Today might just be the beginning of something special.'

Sophie steeled herself to ask who between, but a noise— followed by a loud curse—from the top of the stairs startled them both. She rushed to the doorway, followed closely by Nathan, just in time to see her boss picking something up from the floor outside Mark's office.

'Sorry,' Julie called down to them.

'Did you drop something?' said Nathan.

Julie nodded. 'Phone.'

'I think you'll find it's pronounced "iPhone,"' said Sophie, desperate to make a joke to win back Nathan's attention.

Julie frowned down at her. 'Pardon?'

'The, er, "I" isn't, you know, silent.'

As she found herself wishing *she* had been, Sophie turned back round and found Nathan's chest centimetres from her face. As he took a hurried step backwards, he didn't seem able to meet her gaze.

'So, how many are there?' she said, desperate to fill the awkward silence. 'Tonight, I mean.'

'Including you and me?' said Nathan, and Sophie's heart leapt at being paired with him—even if it was just a figure of speech. 'Twelve, as it stands. That boss of yours is coming, right?'

'Julie?' Sophie's heart sank just as quickly. 'She said she was thinking about it.'

'Now she's someone who hates Valentine's Day.'

Sophie was puzzled. 'Really?'

'So it appeared when I bumped into her on the way in this morning.'

'Why?'

Before he could answer, Nathan's computer pinged, and he glanced at his screen. 'Sorry Soph. I have to respond to that.' He gave her one last brief smile. 'So, tonight. Five-thirty?'

Sophie nodded. 'Five-thirty it is. I'll see you there. I mean, then. And not just you, obviously...'

She cursed her tongue-tiedness again, and decided to leave it there, especially since Nathan was already intently typing an email, so she backed slowly out through the door, then almost skipped back up the stairs. If Nathan knew Julie hated Valentine's Day, and it didn't sound like he was too keen on the concept himself, then what on earth was he doing giving her a card? Unless...He'd been delivering it on behalf of someone. Or, maybe he didn't actually hate it, but instead, he might have been coming in to give the card to her, and when he'd seen Sophie was already at her desk, he'd been too embarrassed, so had pretended it was for Julie instead.

And even though that was pretty far-fetched, Sophie was pleased about one thing. Either of those scenarios meant Nathan probably didn't have a thing for Julie. And if that was the case, then surely there was no reason why he couldn't develop a thing for her.

⁦♋⁩

Nathan glanced up from his laptop and watched Sophie leave, then shook his head, wondering what was wrong with him. There was someone attractive, funny, clever, and single—all the things most normal people looked for in a woman—yet the minute she tried to talk about anything outside of office business, he found himself wanting to be anywhere but standing in front of her. That time when he'd gone to fix some problem she had with her email and she'd blurted out something flirtatious, he'd been more embarrassed than she had. To be honest, he was surprised she was still talking to him.

This morning in the coffee shop, he'd had the same feeling, and that, coupled with moments like the uncomfortable questioning Sophie had just subjected him to, reminded him he was a long way from being over Ellie. Why did he think he still owed her something, and more importantly, why did he feel he was being unfaithful if he so much as looked at another woman? Maybe because he still felt there was hope for the two of them. Not that Ellie had ever suggested getting back together—though of course, they'd have had to have spoken for that to have happened, and the closest he'd come to seeing her since they'd split up had been the occasional desperate drive past her office whenever he'd been feeling particularly lonely.

He finished typing his email, then hauled himself out of his chair, made his way up the stairs, and walked into Mark's office. Mark was engrossed in something on his computer screen, so Nathan tiptoed up to his desk, then leant down beside him.

'Any news?'

Mark looked from his laptop with a start. 'Jesus, Nathan. You might try knocking.'

'Whatcha up to?'

'Up to?' Mark held his hand horizontally at head height. 'About here, with the end of year report. And then I have to file our VAT return.'

'Living the dream, my friend. Living the dream.' Nathan grinned. 'Did I just see Julie leaving here?'

'You might have done.'

'And?'

Mark puffed air out of his cheeks. 'And nothing. We had some weird conversation about...Well, it doesn't really matter what it was about. But tell me something. Did someone send you a card?'

'When?'

'Christmas 1995.' Mark shook his head. 'Today, Nathan.'

'Um, yeah, seeing as you ask.'

Mark stared at him. 'And do you have any idea who sent it?' he said, hoping with all his might it wasn't Julie.

Nathan stuck his lower lip out and shook his head. 'Beats me. All they wrote was some poem with a rhyme about finding heaven and upgrading to Windows 7. Which was quite clever, if you think about it.'

'Isn't it?' said Mark, though he had no idea what Nathan was talking about. 'But no other clues as to where it came from?'

'Well, it had a Smiths label on the back, so I'm guessing there.'

'That's not what I meant!'

Mark had almost shouted that last sentence, and Nathan held both hands up to placate him. 'Keep your hair on. Only joking. What's up?'

'Sorry.' Mark got up and started pacing around his office. 'You don't think it could have come from...' He cleared his throat awkwardly. 'Julie?'

'Julie? Your Julie?'

'She's hardly...Yes. My Julie.'

'Whatever makes you think that?'

'I don't know,' said Mark, reluctant to admit Julie had virtually told him exactly that. 'Just a hunch.'

'Is this because she didn't say anything about your card?'

'No, it's just...'

'Did she?'

'Well, no, now you come to mention it. You sure you delivered it properly?'

'As opposed to improperly?' Nathan rolled his eyes. 'I put it right in the middle of her desk.'

'Julie's desk?'

'No, mate. Mary from admin's. Of course I put it on Julie's desk. Don't worry. And she can't have sent that one to me.'

'How can you be sure?'

'Because it was there when I got in this morning. And she wasn't.'

'Ah. Right. Good.' Mark stopped pacing, and sat back down at his desk. 'Sorry. So...'

'So?'

'So how are you doing, anyway?'

Nathan made a face. 'Trying not to think about what day it is. Which is proving a little difficult. Especially since—and thanks for reminding me—someone sent me a card.'

Mark smiled sympathetically. 'Come on, Nathan. It's been, what, three years?'

'To the day, funnily enough,' said Nathan, not looking like he found it funny at all. 'And you'd think it'd be getting easier by now, wouldn't you?'

Mark nodded exaggeratedly. 'Well, yes.'

'So why hasn't it?' Nathan slumped down in Julie's recently vacated chair and spun himself round.

'Well, as I've told you a hundred times, because you haven't moved on.'

'How can I?'

'Well, you can stop thinking she's coming back, for one thing. Or you can go out with someone else.'

Nathan stopped spinning abruptly. 'But what if she does? And I am?'

Mark smiled. 'What if she doesn't, and you're not? Who's going to suffer then?'

Nathan leant over and flicked at the Newton's Cradle on Mark's desk, then watched sullenly as the balls clicked against each other. 'Mark, if you've never done it, you wouldn't understand.'

'What are you trying to insinuate?'

'No, not that. I mean, get down on one knee.'

'God no. I mean, not yet, at any rate,' he said, trying not to think about doing exactly that with Julie. 'I've not been lucky enough to go out with someone I've wanted to do it with. Or rather, lucky enough yet.'

Nathan reached out a hand and stopped the balls from swinging. 'And that's the thing. Luck. I was lucky to meet Ellie. And no-one's that lucky twice.'

'Or that unlucky.'

Nathan looked up sharply. 'What do you mean by that?'

Mark cleared his throat. 'Well, she cheated on you, didn't she? So looking at it another way, you were unlucky to have met someone you fell head-over-heels for who'd do that to you.'

'No, I was lucky...'

'The only lucky bit was that you found out before you got married. And you'd have to be extremely unlucky for that to happen again.'

'Well, that's one way of looking at it,' said Nathan, thinking that it wasn't his way of looking at it.

Mark sighed. 'So how long are you going to completely ignore every other single attractive woman you meet?'

Nathan half-smiled. Put that way, it did sound a little ridiculous. 'Maybe until I can trust my judgement again.'

'Don't you think you're being a little hard on yourself?'

'Perhaps. But at least I won't get hurt that way.'

Mark's phone rang, and he put one hand on the receiver. 'Listen,' he said. 'Let me buy you lunch later. We'll talk about this some more.'

'I'm not sure,' said Nathan, hesitantly.

'What else are you going to do? Ride your bike past Ellie's office again just to see if you can spot her through the window?'

'That was a year ago.'

'And two years ago. So you better meet me here at one, otherwise it might become a habit.'

As Mark picked his phone up, Nathan stared at his friend, and nodded resignedly.

⁓

Julie snapped the battery cover onto her phone as she headed back up the stairs, her hands still shaking a little. It'd been the first time she'd been alone with Mark Webster since that fateful night, and she'd had to work hard to keep her cool, though at least he hadn't seen her drop her phone like a nervous schoolgirl as soon as she'd left his office.

While she'd been hoping her enquiry about the Valentine's card Sophie had sent Nathan might make Mark let something slip about the card and balloons she suspected he'd sent her, in truth, he'd seemed almost to make a point of not mentioning anything. Then again, she supposed, perhaps quizzing him about his friend's sexuality wasn't the best way to achieve that, and in any case, if it had been he who'd sent them, how would he have done it, apart from asking her directly whether she'd liked them? Given how he'd never even mentioned their kiss apart from his clumsy 'did you have fun' question the following morning, Julie didn't think he was the 'asking directly' type. And while she'd promised herself that if he didn't, then she'd bring it up herself, when the time had come, she'd lost her nerve.

Still, Julie thought, even if Mark hadn't quite been as straight with her as she'd have liked, at least Sophie would be pleased with the news that Nathan was. She headed back up to the office to tell her, popping into the kitchen on the way to get a drink, and almost bumped into Mary from admin, who was filling her 'I ♥ cats' mug up with hot water from the kettle.

'Not out of coffee, are we?' said Julie, nodding towards the mug of clear liquid.

'Oh, just hot water and lemon for me,' said Mary. She retrieved a plastic bag from the fridge labelled 'Mary's—hands off,' then removed a slice of lemon from the bag and dropped it into the cup. 'Helps keep my weight down.'

To what? Julie wondered, trying not to look surprised. Mary was almost as round as she was tall. *Fifteen stone?*

Mary waited as Julie made herself a coffee, updating her on the latest devastating issue the admin team were having to face, which as far as Julie could tell simply amounted to Benedict, the new intern, not being as 'hot' as the previous one, then the two of them walked back towards the admin area. 'So, Julie,' she continued, sitting down at her desk, where a huge card with a picture of a cat sitting on a heart-shaped cushion on the front dwarfed her computer monitor. 'Will you be joining us at the bowling this evening?'

'Well, I thought I...Someone's sent you a Valentine's card?' said Julie, trying desperately to keep the surprise out of her voice.

Mary was beaming up at her. 'Maybe.'

'May I?'

Mary nodded, so Julie picked the card up and read the inscription.

'Who's Mister Whiskers?'

'He's my cat.'

Julie tried to keep a straight face. Given her nickname in the office, Julie's first thought had been that Mister Whiskers was 'hairy' Mary's pet name for her husband, rather than just the name of her pet.

'Your...cat sent you a Valentine's card?'

'Oh yes. We exchange them every year.'

'Exchange?' Julie had to bite her lip to stop herself from laughing. 'And what about...' Julie thought hard. 'I mean, does your husband not send you one?'

Mary made a face. 'Why did you think I was married?'

'Because...' Julie wanted to remind Mary of the times she'd said she was going home to 'him indoors,' or even point out the ring she was wearing on her wedding finger, but if that turned out to have been a gift from Mister Whiskers, she wasn't sure she'd be able to hold herself together. Besides, Julie was married, but she wasn't wearing her ring. 'I just assumed...'

'Oh no,' interrupted Mary. 'Who needs a man, when you've got someone like Mister Whiskers waiting for you at home?'

'Well...'

'Men are unreliable,' continued Mary. 'And cruel. And selfish. At least, my ex-husband was. Whereas cats...They love you whatever.' She gazed adoringly at the framed photograph of a tortoiseshell cat behind her keyboard. 'You should get one. If you're not with anyone, that is.'

Julie just smiled politely. If this was her future, she was dreading it.

'So,' Mary leant in conspiratorially towards Julie, giving her a close-up of the sprouting growths on her chin that had earned her the nickname. 'You didn't answer my question.'

'What question?' said Julie, wondering just how long she could keep her home situation a secret.

'Whether you're going tonight. To Nathan's little thing.' Mary nudged her. 'Though from what I hear, Nathan's thing isn't that...'

'Yes,' said Julie, quickly. 'I am. I thought it might be...' She so wanted to use the word *fun*, but like she'd mentioned to Nathan earlier, it was bowling. 'An idea.'

'No-one at home waiting for you, then?'

Julie wanted to tell Mary to mind her own business, but she remembered how sensitive she could be, though of course, to have said 'no' wouldn't have been a lie. She was pretty sure the last thing Philip would be doing this evening was waiting for her. She took a large gulp of coffee. 'No one like Mister Whiskers.'

'Well, get a cat, then,' said Mary.

Julie sighed to herself. If only the answer to her problems was that easy. 'I'll think about it,' she said, and Mary beamed at her again.

'It's a shame about that Nathan, though.'

Julie raised both eyebrows. 'What is?'

'You don't know?'

Julie wondered whether this was the gay thing. Despite Mark's denial, she hoped she wouldn't have to disappoint Sophie. 'Know what?'

'Well, I don't like to gossip.'

Julie almost did a double-take. If there was one thing Mary liked to do—and it certainly didn't seem to be 'work'—it was gossip. 'But?'

'Let's just say there's a reason he organises these nights.'

'Really?'

'Something in his past.' Mary tapped the side of her nose with her index finger. 'Bit of a dark horse. Just like that Mark Webster.'

Julie caught her breath. 'Mark Webster?'

Mary nodded, and Julie felt suddenly nervous. 'Rumour has it...' She stopped talking as Paul from legal strode past, examining a piece of paper as intently as if it contained next week's winning lottery numbers.

'Go on.'

'You haven't heard?' Mary's face lit up at the prospect of sharing another bit of gossip. 'Well, you know how he usually acts so... What's the word?'

Julie didn't dare suggest one. 'I don't know.'

'Professional. That's it. Well, apparently, at the Christmas party, he was seen leaving with someone.'

Julie tried to keep her voice level. 'And?'

'With someone.' Mary raised and lowered her eyebrows like a ventriloquist's dummy. 'And he's an accountant!'

Julie wondered what that had to do with anything. 'And did anyone see... I mean, does anyone know who it was?'

Mary shrugged. 'Too dark to tell, unfortunately.' She nodded towards the filing cabinet in the corner, where a girl was rummaging around in one of the drawers. 'But Aisleen saw him. Or rather, him and some bimbo.'

'Really?' Julie peered at Aisleen, who she remembered had been so drunk that night she could hardly stand up. And given the standard of her work—due to the fact she refused to wear her glasses in the office 'because they made her look nerdy'—Julie was surprised she'd even recognised Mark.

Mary looked at her. 'You left about the same time, didn't you?'

Julie caught her breath. 'I can't remember. You know what it's like at those dos. A few too many Cosmopolitans...'

'So you didn't see anything?'

Julie shook her head, and Mary looked disappointed. She wasn't good at making office small talk, and in truth, she'd felt out of her comfort zone the moment Mary had started talking about Mister Whiskers. The important thing was that no-one seemed to suspect she was the bimbo who'd shared a cab with Mark that night. And though Julie didn't feel particularly proud of what she was about to do, there was one way to reinforce that.

'And you're sure it wasn't Aisleen that Mark left with? You know, she might be saying it was someone else as a cover story.'

Mary's eyes widened. 'Do you think?'

Julie shrugged. 'Like I said, I didn't see anything. But you never know.'

Mary considered this for a moment. 'But she's a married woman.'

Julie hoped Mary hadn't seen her flinch. 'But Mark's not married, is he?'

Mary shrugged. 'I suppose not.'

'And there's no proof that he...' She cleared her throat. 'Did anything with that woman. Whoever she was.'

Mary looked at her as if she was stupid. 'Come on, Julie. He's a man. They'd both been drinking. It was Christmas...It doesn't take a genius to know something must have happened.'

'Why?'

'Mark Webster. I would. Wouldn't you?'

'I suppose he is nice looking,' said Julie, trying not to shudder at the thought of Mary and Mark together. 'And what about you, Mary?' she continued, keen to move the conversation away from Mark. 'Anyone you've got your eye on this evening?'

Mary blushed. 'Oh no. I couldn't.'

Julie wondered if that was because of Mister Whiskers. 'Why not?'

Mary gave Aisleen a sideways glance, then turned her attention to her computer screen. 'I wouldn't want to get myself a reputation,' she said primly, indicating the conversation was over.

Julie gulped down the rest of her coffee, dropped her cup back in the kitchen, then made her way back to her office, thinking about Mary's last words. That, she knew, was the reason she ought to keep things on a professional level with Mark. It was different for a man— things like that didn't affect your standing in the office. Whereas for a woman, once people started talking about you...Well, she'd worked with people in the past who'd been hounded out of their jobs by vicious rumours, and the last thing she wanted was to be the subject of office gossip. Who knew what stories were circulating about her already? As far as she could tell, Mark didn't seem to have told anyone about what had happened that night, though Julie knew she could take that as a bad sign—perhaps he thought it wasn't worth telling anyone about. And besides, what if they did start something, and it all went pear-shaped? The office was too small for the two of them to avoid each other. She had to face it— her current relationship had gone wrong. What was to say her next one wouldn't either?

And yet, Julie knew that sometimes you had to take a risk. After all, what was the alternative? A lifetime ignoring hair that grew out of inappropriate places on your face, and the shame of sending yourself Valentine's cards 'signed' by your cat? If that was where she was headed, then Julie would gladly take being talked about behind her back. Trouble was, she knew she couldn't lead Mark on then let him down a second time; plus, how would Philip react if she came home late tonight, of all nights? Or didn't come home at all? Of course, she realised she was being a little presumptuous. After all, she had no way of being positive the card and the balloons were from Mark, and she had to admit he'd hardly been pursuing her with a vengeance since Christmas. But a woman could tell when someone was interested, and Julie hadn't had someone interested in her for so long she was doubly sure of it.

She knew she was possibly on the rebound, and didn't necessarily want Mark to be the person she left Philip for, only to work all her unresolved issues out on him. What did they call these—sorbet relationships? Something light to cleanse the palate after something, well, heavy? But if she did decide to go for it, she'd just have to take that chance, and besides, Julie felt that she could have something special with Mark. She believed in chemistry, a spark, and she'd certainly felt one that night. When she'd first joined Seek, and Mark had run her through the finer points of her contract, she'd remembered noticing how good-looking he was, but that had been all—she'd been too immersed in things with Philip back then to do anything about it. And besides, she hadn't suspected how good it could be between the two of them until they'd kissed.

She took a few seconds to compose herself, then walked back into her office. As Sophie looked up expectantly from her desk, Julie smiled reassuringly.

'You don't have to worry.'

'I don't?'

'Nathan's not gay.'

'Great. Thanks.' Sophie breathed a sigh of relief, then her face fell.

'What's the matter?'

'So why hasn't he responded to my card?'

'Does he know it was you who sent it?'

'Well, possibly not, no.'

Julie folded her arms. 'And what would happen if we sent a brochure out to someone without any contact details? Do you think we'd get a reply?'

'I suppose not.'

'And someone like Nathan, well, he's bound to have been sent a few cards today, right?'

Sophie tried not to entertain the possibility. And failed. 'Maybe,' she said, glumly.

'First rule of marketing, Sophie.'

Sophie stared at her boss, hoping her last statement wasn't a question. 'Is?'

Fortunately, it wasn't. 'Get yourself noticed.'

And as Julie sat down at her desk and tried to stop thinking about Mark Webster, Sophie stared out of the window and wondered exactly how she was going to do that.

5

Instead of spending the usual fifteen minutes out of her lunch hour working out the lowest-calorie combination of sandwich, drink, and snack from Boots' meal deal selection that still included some form of chocolate, Sophie was on a Central Line train heading west, cursing the fact she'd put on her oldest M&S underwear today. If everything went to plan this evening—and she had to believe it would—the last thing she wanted was for Nathan to see her wearing 'smalls' that didn't quite match the description. Besides, Julie had told her she needed to 'get herself noticed,' and what better way for Nathan to notice her than a flash of something exotic and lacy every time she bent over to pick up her bowling ball?

She'd popped into the Top Shop at Oxford Circus in the hope of finding something appropriate (and appropriately priced), but the only sexy bras there appeared to have been designed for Kate Moss's flatter-chested sister, and Sophie had soon realised she needed more of a big top shop, though when a woman she'd met in the changing rooms had suggested some range in Selfridges called 'Hanky Panky,' Sophie had felt her credit card do a back flip in shock.

Jumping off the tube at Bond Street, she made her way out of the station, dodging around the lunchtime shoppers as she crossed Oxford Street, feeling the usual buzz of anticipation as she entered the store. Sophie loved Selfridges. Everything about the place summed up the reason she'd come to London—it was stylish, cool, chic, and expensive, much like she aspired to be. Most Saturdays she'd come back into town and window-shop here, or try on dresses she could never afford, or treat herself to a free makeover from the vividly lipsticked girls that worked for MAC, or Bobbi Brown, or the other labels that, before she'd moved here, she'd only ever read about in magazines.

She rode the escalator up to the first floor, taking in the deep brown and cream décor, marvelling at the view of the seemingly endless number of designer brand concessions that occupied the whole of the street level. *So many things to buy, so little time*, she thought, before remembering her problem was more to do with having so little money.

Sophie stepped off the escalator and made her way over to the lingerie department, which was full of awkward-looking men buying last-minute Valentine's presents, and allowed herself to daydream that maybe next year Nathan would be one of them as she surveyed the various brand names. Of the ones she recognised—and could pronounce—'Triumph' would be strangely appropriate if she did get intimate with Nathan this evening, although Sophie couldn't help feeling that 'Dirty Pretty Things' might be more appropriate (after all, that was what they'd be tomorrow, if she got her way tonight). She bypassed the Spanx rail without giving it a second glance, then picked up a 'Barely There' pair of knickers from the 'Ell & Cee' range and nervously looked at the label. Forty-two pounds! The Zara suit she was wearing hadn't cost that much, and these...There was hardly anything to them.

In need of some assistance, she looked around the department, but all the staff seemed to be busy, so she carried the knickers over to the mirror and held them up to her hips, thinking she might as well wear nothing. As she studied her reflection, she caught sight of a black-clad male assistant walking past, so Sophie beckoned him over. He looked at her in surprise, then pointed at his chest, and Sophie nodded.

'Can I have some help?'

The man glanced around, hesitated for a moment, then walked over to where she was standing. 'Sure,' he said. 'What do you need?'

'Can I just check the price of these, please?'

The man looked at the label. 'Forty two pounds.'

'Even though they're pants?'

'I wouldn't say that.'

'Pardon?'

'I think they're quite nice.'

'No, I meant, well, not that they were *pants* pants. Just that there's not exactly a lot of material there. Given that they're, you know, pants.' She held them up again, shocked to see how transparent they were. 'Is there?'

The assistant smiled. 'Well, they say less is more.'

'Right.' Sophie smiled politely at his joke. 'And are they...' She stopped short of asking whether they were sexy. She didn't want a man she'd just met imagining her wearing them, even though she was hoping another man she hardly knew would be actually seeing her in them later, maybe even peeling them off with his teeth. 'What do you think of them? As a man, I mean.'

'They're very sexy,' he said, as if reading her mind. 'Why?'

'I'm just not sure they're me.'

The man peered at the knickers, then looked her up and down. 'Are you after something specific?'

'Hanky Panky,' said Sophie, then she giggled nervously at how that sounded. 'I mean, I'm looking for something from your Hanky

Panky range.' She carefully placed the hanger and its expensive cargo back on the rail. 'For...'

'Tonight?' suggested the man.

Sophie nodded.

'And what stage is the relationship at?'

Sophie opened her mouth, then shut it again. 'Well, it isn't really. We're going out tonight, and...'

'On a first date?' The man raised one eyebrow, and Sophie blushed.

'Well, strictly speaking, we're not really going out. There's a few of us. I just thought...I mean, I'm not planning to do anything. You know, it's just in case...'

'In case you have a car accident, you want to make sure you've got nice underwear on?' The man smiled again. 'Mother's advice?'

Sophie laughed. 'Yes! Well, not really, of course.'

'Say no more.' The man looked her up and down. 'I'd say you're about a, what, 32E?'

Sophie nodded, impressed he knew his stuff. 'You've got a good eye.'

'Thanks. So...' The man looked through the nearest rail and selected a black lace combination. 'What about this?'

'I'm not sure. Isn't black a bit...'

'Tarty?'

Sophie nodded. 'Something like that,' she said, though she realised that planning to flash her underwear at Nathan tonight might be considered tarty too.

The man shrugged. 'Only one way to find out,' he said, nodding towards the changing room.

'Haven't you got something a little bit less...I mean, a bit more me?' she asked. 'And perhaps a bit cheaper? Not that I'm, you know, cheap.'

'Hold on.' The man glanced around the shop floor, then led her over to a different rail. 'What about something like this?' he said, handing her a red bustier.

Sophie took the hanger and held the garment up against her, then studied her reflection in the mirror. 'But red's a bit...'

'Sexy?' The assistant nodded encouragingly. 'Isn't that the effect you're trying to achieve?'

'Well, yes, but perhaps not quite so...'

'Blatant?'

'Exactly.'

'Blatant isn't necessarily a bad thing. Remember, we men aren't all that sophisticated.'

'Even so. I'd like something to compare it to.'

'Okay,' said the man. 'Follow me.'

Between them, they scoured the rails until Sophie had a cross-section of all Selfridges had to offer. As she made her way to the changing room, the assistant followed her, and for a second, Sophie thought he was going to follow her inside.

'Thanks for all your help,' she said, pausing at the curtain.

The man shrugged. 'No problem. Let me know if you want a man's opinion once you've got them on.'

Sophie felt herself start to blush. 'I think I'll be fine.'

Drawing the curtain shut behind her, she checked both sides for gaps, and stepped out of her business suit. Despite the harsh light of the changing room, she wasn't too disappointed with her figure. She could only hope Nathan would feel the same way later.

She took the black bra-and-knickers set off their hanger and, trying to ignore the price, slipped them on over her existing underwear. As she'd feared, she looked like one of the Spank-o-rama girls—though they didn't have a pair of big pants on underneath, of course. She peeled them off and tried on the rest of the outfits in turn, only to get more frustrated with each one. Only the red bustier seemed to do the trick—the effect it had on her cleavage meant it lived up to its name—plus, Sophie realised, it just about covered her belly, which she knew wasn't quite the flat stomach the models she admired in the magazines she devoured every month all seemed to have. She looked at the label—a hundred and thirty pounds—and when she removed her credit card statement from her handbag to check her balance, Sophie was relieved to see she could just about afford it.

She stared at her reflection again and decided she had to buy the bustier. It did make her look, for want of a better word, sexy—the assistant had been right. And besides, you couldn't put a price on that, Sophie thought, until she realised that actually, you could, and that price was a hundred and thirty...

'How are you getting on?'

The voice from just outside the cubicle surprised her. 'Okay, I think,' she said, anxiously staring at the curtain, fearing the assistant was going to barge in any minute.

'Remember, if you want a second opinion...'

'I'm fine,' said Sophie quickly, then she stuck her head cautiously through the curtain. 'Although I was wondering whether you had anything like this, but...' She swallowed hard. 'Less expensive.'

'Like what?'

Sophie thought for a second. Surely all the male assistants in this section had to be gay, otherwise it'd just be too awkward. 'Like this,' she said, deciding to trust her instincts, before sweeping the curtain back to show the assistant what she was wearing.

'Wow!'

Sophie blushed for about the tenth time. 'Thanks. So do you?'

'Do I what?'

'Have anything like this, but cheaper?'

The assistant shrugged. 'You'd have to ask someone who actually works in this section.'

Sophie's mouth fell open. 'But...'

'I'm from the Hi-Fi department downstairs. I was just on my way to lunch.'

'Hey!' Sophie grabbed the curtain and pulled it tightly around her, then glared at him. 'Are you some kind of pervert?'

'You asked for my help, remember?'

'You could have said you didn't work here!'

'I do work here.' The man grinned sheepishly. 'Just not, you know, *here*.'

'Even so.' She peered crossly around the department, unable to spot another member of staff. 'Can you go and find me someone else?'

The man shrugged. 'Sure—if you want someone who'll try to sell you the most expensive thing in the shop. Or you can stick with me—someone who can give you a man's opinion, and tell you what looks nice on you instead.'

'Well...'

'What's it to be?'

Sophie rolled her eyes. 'The last thing, I guess.'

'Okay.' He smiled. 'Well, that last thing looks nice on you. It fits in all the right places. And whoever he is, he's a lucky man.' He glanced at his watch. 'So if you don't need me for anything else...'

'No.' Sophie glared at him again, but this time, with half a smile on her face. 'Thanks.'

'My pleasure.'

I'll bet, thought Sophie.

As the man left, she disappeared back behind the curtain and inspected her reflection one last time. Even though the episode had been a bit creepy, the assistant had been right. The bustier did fit in all the right places. And while she'd perhaps never seen herself as the kind of girl who'd wear something like this, she'd also never seen herself as the kind of girl who'd be with someone like Nathan—and things had to change. Carefully undoing the various fasteners that kept the bustier (and her) in place, she put it back on its hanger, then got dressed again, trying her best not to worry about the cost. Sure, it was expensive, but if it did the trick, Sophie suspected it might be the best money she'd ever spent.

She emerged from the changing room and made her way over to the cash desk, then stood in line behind a shifty-looking older man who was buying two different-sized but identical sets of underwear with the air of someone involved in a back-street drugs deal. When her turn came, she handed the bustier to the girl behind the till.

'Nice choice.'

'Thanks.'

'Just one thing,' said the girl, as she wrapped the lingerie in tissue paper, and placed it carefully in a yellow Selfridges bag. 'There's a "no returns" policy on all underwear once you've worn it. Just so you're aware,' she added, sweetly.

'No problem,' Sophie said. Hopefully, if she did get to the stage where Nathan saw her dressed in the bustier, then there'd be no going back for her either.

'That'll be a hundred and thirty pounds,' said the girl, and Sophie swallowed hard.

'Here,' she said, handing over her credit card, then punching her PIN into the terminal, and as she prayed under her breath it wouldn't get declined, Sophie almost laughed. She'd be hoping exactly that about herself later.

⁊

As Sophie was exercising her credit card in Selfridges, Calum was walking towards the other end of Oxford Street, his gym bag slung over his shoulder. He knew going for a quick lunchtime workout probably wouldn't make the difference between Emma falling for him or not later, but it certainly couldn't do any harm. Whereas the Big Mac Meal he'd spent the last hour dreaming of almost certainly would.

Swiping his way in through the gym turnstile, he found a dry spot in the changing rooms and changed self-consciously into his workout gear. Today's session shouldn't be too strenuous, he decided, carefully hanging his suit in his locker and setting the combination on his padlock. After all, he didn't want to tire himself out for this evening. Just in case.

He'd told Emma he worked out during live chat one evening, and had regretted the words as soon as he'd typed them, fearing she might expect him to be some muscle-man, and given the size of the weights he struggled to lift, Calum wasn't even as strong as that skinny Mr. Muscle man from the TV adverts. He'd even mentioned which gym he went to, and when Emma said she knew it, Calum hadn't gone for a week, just in case she was a member there and might see just how pathetically unfit he actually was, until the scary run he'd taken through the council estate had encouraged him to go back in.

He strolled through to the gym, nodded an embarrassed hello to the impossibly fit-looking girl on the desk, then chose an exercise bike in front of the TV. Calum loved watching TV, and found it ironic how he managed to combine one of his least-favourite activities with his most favourite, or rather, second-favourite—give him one of his mum's fry-ups and a can of lager and he'd be in heaven. But this was all about finding himself a different kind of heaven, he reminded himself, as he adjusted the saddle and the foot straps and climbed awkwardly on. With a final check that he was as comfortable as he could possibly get on a machine seemingly designed for torture, he set the bike's timer for twenty minutes, cranked the resistance down to six, and began pedalling.

Calum hated the gym. But he hated being single more, and that was why almost every day for the past six weeks he'd done some sort of exercise. Even if it was only going for a short run across Clapham Common and back when he got home, he'd locate the *Rocky* theme tune on his iPod Shuffle (the name of which pretty much described his running style), set it on 'repeat,' grit his teeth, and head off until he'd worked up a sweat. And while sometimes that happened before he'd even reached the end of his road, it was the only thing he did where he worked up a sweat. Which was motivation enough for him to do it.

He'd tried to avoid actual exercise at first, and instead had bought some of those 'Masai Barefoot Technology' trainers he'd read about on the bus one morning in a discarded copy of *Metro*. The moment he'd got in to work, he'd Googled 'Masai Warrior,' seen pictures of tall, skinny men, assumed the shoes would be the answer to his prayers, and had all but run to the shop that lunch-time. At a hundred and twenty-nine pounds a pair they'd seemed expensive, but the gym had been forty pounds a month, so Calum reasoned he could give them a go for three months first; if they didn't work, he'd simply join the gym then, and he'd have a pair of shoes into the bargain.

After a couple of weeks of walking about in them, and with no discernible difference in his weight, Calum had begun to believe he'd made a mistake. While the shoes had indeed made him taller, this had primarily been due to their extra-thick semi circular soles, which actually made them look like something prescribed for people with one leg shorter than the other—except on both feet. In addition, the rocking motion they'd made him walk with had made him feel a little seasick, not to mention ridiculous as he'd lurched along the street like a drunk. After a further frustrating week, he'd given up on them.

He'd been stupid, he realised afterwards, shelling out that kind of money for a pair of shoes to simulate walking barefoot, when for no money whatsoever he could have actually walked barefoot. And although the prospect of doing that across Clapham Common (with its ever-present spotting of dog-mess and the occasional broken beer bottle) didn't fill him with the greatest of pleasure, he'd also realised the fundamental flaw in the shoes' claims. All the videos he'd seen of the Masai on YouTube seemed to feature them jumping up and down on the spot for hours on end, and that— rather than endlessly walking around without any shoes on—was probably what kept them so thin (and made them so tall—though Calum conceded the 'height' thing might have been an optical illusion caused by the jumping). He'd stuck the trainers on eBay, hoping to get at least some of his money back, and had been sur- prised at the bidding war that had broken out. By the time the auction had ended, they'd sold for nearly a hundred pounds, which ironically, was what he'd had to spend on a pair of cross-trainers for the gym, but all in all, Calum wasn't too upset. There'd been no harm done, except perhaps to his pride, when he'd worn them on the bus one day and some tough-looking girls had shouted some- thing unpleasant.

In the end, he'd had no choice but to force his fourteen-stone frame along to the Plaza shopping centre on Oxford Street, where he'd signed up to the Virgin Active fitness club—a strangely appropriate name given his status, Calum had thought. Initially, he'd hoped he might even find a girlfriend at the gym, but he'd been shocked on his first visit to discover the place was full of whip-thin model types who only ever gave him a second glance when he'd forgotten to wipe his sweat off the machine he'd been using, or if they perhaps thought he was about to expire on the treadmill. And besides, by the look of the Olympic-hopeful men who exercised there—or rather, hogged the weights machines while they spent ten minutes finding a particular piece of music on their phones, or pranced around the room in their vest-tops showing off their perfectly defined pecs and occasionally examining their six-packs in the mirror—if any of the girls were on the lookout for a boyfriend, Calum would be last in the queue. If he was allowed in the queue at all.

He looked down from the television, where he'd been fascinated by some rap video that looked more like the out-takes from a porno film, checked the bike's display, and saw he was coming up to the end of his session. Two hundred calories burned—a new record, he noted proudly, wondering whether he should have that Big Mac after all. This was progress. He'd realised this morning he could see his toes when standing up (if not touch them), and his age and trouser-waist size were getting closer (though Calum had to concede that was possibly as much down to the fact that he'd just celebrated his birthday). Feeling pleased with himself, he was just about to get off and go for some light stretching when the girl from the desk appeared at his shoulder.

'Hi,' she said, breezily. 'I'm Debbie.'

Calum began to slow down, but Debbie shook her head. 'Don't stop on my account,' she said, so he reluctantly kept going.

'Calum,' he wheezed, surreptitiously reducing the resistance a couple of notches.

'I know,' she said, and Calum almost fell off his bike in surprise. Maybe he wasn't as invisible as he'd thought.

'You do?'

Debbie nodded. 'We get a thing coming up on the computer whenever someone swipes in at reception.'

'Ah.' Calum's face fell. 'Right.'

'And I noticed you hadn't had your personal training session yet.' Debbie smiled at him, and Calum began to panic. 'Is it compulsory?'

'No. But it's complimentary.'

Calum looked down at his spare tyre and feared if Debbie saw that, she might not be. 'What does it involve, exactly?'

'Oh, don't worry. We like to make sure everyone has one when they first join.' Debbie rested a reassuring hand on his arm. 'It's nothing too strenuous. I just ask you a few questions about your fitness goals, then design you a program to help you reach them.'

Calum stared at her. The only thing he wanted to reach was a few inches taller—and by tonight, if possible. 'And when were you thinking we should do this?'

'Right now, if you like?' said Debbie.

'Now? But I've just…'

'Don't worry. It won't take long.'

Before Calum could respond, she'd scampered back to her desk, returning with a clipboard and pen. 'So,' she said. 'What is it you're trying to achieve?'

Calum thought for a moment. 'The usual, I suppose.'

'Which is?'

He shrugged, and a bead of sweat dripped off his glasses and onto Debbie's clipboard. 'Lose a bit of weight. Tone up. Add some muscle.'

'Well, you've come to the right place,' said Debbie, then she leant over and looked at the bike's display. 'Right, you should be nicely warmed up now. Come on.'

'Warmed up? This was all I was planning on doing,' he protested, but Debbie didn't seem to hear him.

'Follow me,' she said, heading across to the free weights area, where the dumbbells gleamed ominously in their racks.

With a sigh, Calum climbed reluctantly off the bike, gave it a cursory wipe with his towel, and did as he was told.

◦≀◦

Mark Webster was sitting in his office, searching the internet for 'Ten Pin Bowling tips,' just in case he got the chance to pass a few on to Julie Marshall later. So far, he'd learned it was all about how you gripped the balls, or perfecting your wrist action, though Mark couldn't work out a way to communicate either of those to her without appearing rude. Although maybe he should be rude. She might like that. A bit of flirting. It would be a good way of testing the water.

He moved his chair out of the way to begin practising his swing when a knock on his door startled him, and he looked round to find Nathan grinning at him.

'I won't ask.'

'Oh, it's you.'

'Good to see you too!' said Nathan.

'Sorry. I was hoping it might be, you know, her.'

'Still nothing?'

He shook his head. 'No.'

'Maybe she's waiting till tonight to make her move.'

'Unless I've offended her.'

Nathan shook his head. 'Doubtful. After all, she'd hardly be coming this evening if she didn't want to spend any time in the same room as you.'

Mark sighed. 'I suppose not. Though I still don't know how I'm going to play it.'

'Come on, then,' said Nathan. 'You can buy me lunch and give me that pep talk you promised me, and in return, I'll help you work out a strategy for later.'

Mark looked at his watch. 'You really think that'll help?'

'Which one?' Nathan laughed. 'Maybe neither. But I'm starving. And it'll help that.'

'Fine.' Mark got up and peered out of the window at the ominously grey sky. 'Though you're sure you don't just want to wait for the sandwich man to come round?'

'What for?'

'I've seen better days.'

'Don't be so hard on yourself.'

'I meant the weath...' Mark caught sight of Nathan's expression. 'Yes, very funny.'

'Come on.' Nathan nudged him. 'Where's your sense of humour?'

'Taking the day off. Like I'm beginning to wish I had.'

Mark grabbed his coat and followed Nathan through reception. 'Just off to lunch,' he told Mia-Rose as he passed her desk, then he walked through the door Nathan was holding open for him. 'Where do you fancy?' he said, as they headed out of the office and along Bateman Street. 'Pret?'

'Not if you're paying,' said Nathan. 'Let's go somewhere else.'

'Spank-o-rama?'

'On Valentine's Day? I didn't know you cared.' Nathan grinned. In all the years they'd worked at Seek, neither of them had ever dared to pay the club a visit, even though it was just around the corner. 'Do they even serve food?'

Mark grimaced. 'Nothing you'd want to eat, probably.'

They made their way round the corner and down Frith Street, where Nathan spotted a table outside Bar Italia.

'How about here?'

'Out in the street?'

'Why not?'

'It's February, for one thing.' He glanced up at the sky again. 'And it looks like it might rain.'

'They've got heaters, you big girl's blouse. And a canopy.'

'Okay.' Mark buttoned his coat up to his neck and sat down. 'But if I get a cold, and it ruins my chances tonight…'

Nathan picked a couple of menus up. 'The only cold thing you'll be getting is Julie's shoulder if you're not careful,' he said, passing one to Mark.

'I feel like I've had that already.'

Nathan gave him a look, then turned his attention to his menu. 'You can't have pissed her off. Like I said, she's still going tonight. And she knows you'll be there. That's hardly the behaviour of an angry woman.'

'Perhaps. But me following her around like a dog on heat is hardly going to make the best impression.'

Nathan smiled. 'What do you want?'

Mark rolled his eyes. 'I don't know. Just a date would be nice. To go out as a normal couple. For the two of us to get to know each other away from work. Is that too much to ask?'

128

'I meant, to eat.' Nathan grinned up at the waiter, who'd appeared at the table a few seconds previously. 'He's talking about a woman at work. Not, you know...' He indicated Mark and himself. 'Us.'

'Hey,' said the waiter, in heavily accented English. 'This is Soho. We don't judge.'

Mark smiled as he scanned the menu. 'Just a panini, please. Ham and cheese. Chips on the side. And a cappuccino.' He looked up and caught Nathan's disapproving expression. 'What?'

'Your body is a temple.'

'Pardon?'

'Of doom!' said Nathan, then he shrugged. 'What the hell,' he said. He turned to the waiter. 'I'll have what he's having.'

The waiter smiled down at him. 'How romantic,' he said, and Nathan glared back at him.

'So,' said Mark, once the waiter had disappeared back inside the bar. 'What do you reckon?'

Nathan puffed air out of his cheeks. 'Well, again, take my advice with as much of a pinch of salt as you like, but have you thought of just asking her out for a coffee and telling her you like her?'

'Of course I have. Trouble is, what if she doesn't feel the same way?'

'Well, I'm sure she'll let you down gently. Julie's a good-looking woman. She must get approached by men all the time. So she'll be used to telling them where to go!'

'Thanks, Nathan. That's a real help.' Mark shook his head. 'Though if that is the case, why isn't she going out with anyone?'

'Are you sure she's not?'

'Pretty sure.'

'How?'

'There's something I haven't told you.'

'Which is?'

'The Christmas party. She and I ... Well, we shared a cab home.'

'You don't live anywhere near her!'

Mark grinned guiltily. 'What can I say?'

'You sly old dog!'

'And then, in the cab ...'

'Hang on,' said Nathan. 'Do I want to hear this when I'm about to eat my lunch?'

'No, we ...' Mark lowered his voice and leant across the table. 'Kissed.'

Nathan widened his eyes. 'How do you mean, "kissed"? A peck on the cheek, or full-on tonsil-tennis?'

'The, ahem, second one. She was a little drunk. And she kind of jumped on me.'

'Well good on you.'

Mark sat back upright as the waiter set their order down on the table. 'But don't you see?' he said, warming his hands gratefully on his coffee cup. 'That makes it worse. She knows I went out of my way to be with her, and then we kissed, and she still hasn't responded. Which would suggest she's not interested.'

'Again, I'm hardly an expert here, but I'd say her leaping on you that night would suggest exactly the opposite.'

'Well, at the time, I thought so too. But since then ... Nothing.'

Nathan took a bite of his panini, nodding appreciatively as he chewed. 'Why do you think that is?' he asked, through a mouthful of food.

Mark shrugged. 'Beats me. Maybe she was just drunk.'

'Yeah, but you'd still say something, wouldn't you?'

'Would you? It's a small office. She's the new girl. Maybe she was thinking of her reputation.' He regarded his lunch thoughtfully, as if choosing the best place to take the first bite from.

'Why didn't you confront her about it?'

'I did. In a roundabout way.'

'How roundabout?'

'The following morning. I asked her if she'd had a good time last night.'

Nathan almost dropped the chip he was holding. 'And what on earth was she supposed to say to that? "Yes, I particularly enjoyed our drunken snog in the back of the taxi"?'

'Well...'

He laughed. '"Did you have a good time last night?" You have to admit, it sounds a little sleazy.'

Mark threw his hands up in the air. 'What else was I supposed to say?'

'I don't know. Maybe you should have made a joke out of it. Apologised for kissing her or something.'

'But she kissed *me*.'

'And you don't think she might be a little bit embarrassed about that?'

'Well, I hadn't really thought...'

Nathan rolled his eyes. 'Come on, mate. She gets a little tipsy, or she's overcome by lust, or whatever, but she goes and does something arguably unladylike in drunkenly jumping you in the back of a cab... You're a bloke. Of course you're not going to turn down the chance of a free snog. So she has no idea whether you actually like her or not, she's perhaps a little ashamed about her behaviour, and instead of putting her at her ease, or telling her you like her, all you can say is "did you have a good time last night?" Plus, maybe if she was drunk, she doesn't remember how far you and she went.'

'Chiswick.'

Nathan downed half of his coffee in one gulp. 'That's not what I meant.'

'Sorry,' said Mark, sheepishly. 'I hadn't thought of it like that.'

'Well maybe that's how you should start thinking about it. Because all this stuff you're doing to remind her about that night... It might be having the opposite effect.'

Mark stared at him, then tore a corner off his panini and popped it into his mouth. 'So what should I do?' he said, once he'd finished chewing.

'Well, the way I see it, you've got two options.'

'Which are?'

'Be honest. Tell her you like her, and ask her out.'

'And risk a massive knock back, and make things awkward at work for the foreseeable future?'

'Or...' Nathan smiled. 'Put yourself in the same position as the Christmas party, and see if the same thing happens again.'

'I hardly think she'll want to play Pass the Balloon this evening.'

'Is that a metaphor?'

'Ha bloody ha!'

'I didn't mean you had to be so specific. Just buy her a couple of drinks—and I'd have a couple yourself, if I were you. Then later, when we're all leaving, you can just happen to offer to share a cab with her. Or jump on the tube together. Or even just walk her to the tube. Anything that gives you a little alcohol-fuelled you-and-Julie-on-the-way-home-together time. And then...'

'We'll see,' said Mark, uncertainly.

'Oh, and if you find yourself losing your nerve...'

'Yes?'

Nathan gulped down the rest of his coffee. 'Just remind yourself how horrible the last seven weeks have been.'

Mark nodded slowly. 'Good point.' He helped himself to another piece of his sandwich, then washed it down with a mouthful of cappuccino. 'So...'

'So?'

'How are you doing today?'

Nathan stared at his friend. It was a good question. 'Okay, I guess. I haven't really thought about it that much.'

'More than every five minutes?'

'It's not been that bad,' said Nathan, and the truth was, as long as he kept himself busy, it wasn't. 'It's only when I've got time on my hands, or something reminds me of Valentine's Day—like that anonymous card someone sent me—that I think about Ellie.'

'Ah yes. The card.'

'What about it?'

'What are you going to do about it?'

'Do? Well, seeing as I don't have the faintest who it's from, nothing.' He sighed. 'Besides, I'm not really that interested.'

'In whoever sent the card? Or in anyone?'

Nathan shrugged. 'Anyone, I guess. Not yet, anyway.'

'Nathan...'

'I know, I know. Maybe if someone really special came along...'

'Special? Or good-looking?'

'I don't know.'

Mark finished his coffee, then nodded to the next-door table, where a couple of attractive girls were chatting animatedly in between puffing on cigarettes. 'What about those two?'

'They're smoking.'

'You're telling me!'

'No, I mean, they're smokers. Ellie didn't smoke. And I could never go out with a smoker.'

'Well, what about her?' He pointed to a long-legged woman in a mini-skirt striding along the pavement towards them. As Nathan looked up, she caught his eye, and instinctively he looked away.

'Bit too tall.'

133

Mark made a long-suffering face. 'Nathan.'

'What?'

'There's something wrong with them all, isn't there?'

'No,' protested Nathan, though the truth was, there was something wrong with them all. And that thing was simply that they weren't Ellie.

Just then, Mark spotted Sophie hurrying towards the office along the opposite pavement, clutching a Selfridges bag as if it contained her life savings. 'Well, what about Sophie?'

Nathan followed his gaze. 'What about her?'

'She's attractive. Smart. And going tonight.'

'So?'

'So she's single.'

'Yeah, but...'

'But what?'

'Well, going out with someone at work, it's not really the done...' Nathan stopped talking, aware Mark was glowering at him.

'Thanks!'

'Not for you, obviously.'

'What's that supposed to mean?'

'Can we just change the subject?'

'Of course. Once you admit that you still think Ellie's the perfect woman, so no-one else can possibly compare.'

Nathan shifted uncomfortably in his chair. 'Of course I think she's the perfect woman. Why do you think I asked her to marry me?'

'But she obviously wasn't, was she?'

'Why not?'

'Because she didn't want to marry you. And because she was seeing someone else behind your back. That hardly makes her perfect, does it?'

'Well...'

'Admit it, Nathan. She's spoiled every other woman for you, hasn't she? Even someone like Sophie, who...'

Nathan bristled slightly. 'If you think Sophie's so perfect, why don't you go out with her?'

'Because I want to go out with Julie.'

'And she's perfect, is she?'

Mark shook his head. 'I'm not looking for someone who's perfect. Just who's perfect for me. And I think there's a difference.'

Nathan folded his arms. 'But I thought Ellie was perfect for me.'

'And you were wrong, weren't you?'

'Maybe,' admitted Nathan, begrudgingly.

'So don't you think maybe it's time to get over it?'

'Don't you think I want to?'

'No, actually, I don't.' Mark looked at his watch, then signalled to the waiter for two more coffees. 'And Anti-Valentine's proves my point.'

'What point?'

'That you are to Valentine's Day what Scrooge was to Christmas.'

Nathan looked at him blankly. 'I'm sorry, mate. My Dickens is a bit rusty.'

'I'm not surprised, after three years,' said Mark, and Nathan sniggered.

'So what do I do about it?'

'What Scrooge did,' said Mark. 'Confront the ghost of your Valentine's Past.'

Sophie Jones headed back along Bateman Street, clutching the Selfridges bag beneath her folded arms as if it were transparent and everyone could see its racy contents. She'd felt flattered by what had just happened—it had been a long time since anyone had seen her in her underwear, and even though the prospect of Nathan doing exactly that later was more than a little daunting, the incident hadn't done her confidence any harm at all.

She swiped herself into the building, smiling at Mia-Rose on her way past reception, then stuffed her purchase under her coat as she walked past the stairs that led down to the basement—the last thing she wanted was for Nathan to see what she'd bought before she was wearing it. She hurried upstairs and into her office, pushing the door shut behind her, and as she took the bag out from under her coat and put it on her desk, Julie cleared her throat.

'Have you just shoplifted that?'

'What? Oh, no. I ... I just didn't want to risk anyone seeing it.'

'Seeing what?'

'It's underwear.' Sophie felt herself start to turn the same colour as the bustier. 'For tonight.'

'For the bowling? I thought it was only our shoes we had to change.'

'It's for Nathan.'

'Are you sure it's his size?'

'No, I mean it's for me to wear, but, you know, for Nathan,' said Sophie, before realising Julie had been joking. She looked over her shoulder to double-check that the door was shut, then handed over the bag. 'I didn't think I'd be going out this evening when I got dressed this morning, and I'm hardly wearing my Sunday best. You know how it is?'

Julie nodded, although she didn't know how it was, given how the last piece of expensive underwear she'd bought had been a top-of-the-range sports bra. She'd read enough horror stories on the internet to know that training for the marathon carried various risks, though the one she'd been most concerned about was the prospect of her nipples ending up level with her knees.

'Nice,' she said, inspecting the bag's contents. 'And if tonight doesn't work out, you can always do a few shifts at that place round the corner.'

Sophie made a face. 'I knew it. Too tarty.'

'I'm kidding. I'm sure Nathan will...' She picked her words carefully. '...appreciate it.'

'He'd better.' Sophie felt a sudden surge of guilt as she remembered how much she'd just spent, and slumped down into her chair, still wearing her coat. 'Assuming it's his kind of thing.'

Julie smiled reassuringly. 'I'm sure it will be. Have you thought how you're going to ensure he actually gets to appreciate it?'

'Er...No.'

'Don't you think you ought to? Remember, marketing is all about creating a need in someone for something they don't know they want yet. And the best lingerie in the world isn't going to do you any good unless Nathan actually sees you in it.'

'I suppose not.'

Julie thought for a moment, then looked at her watch. Her own love life might be a disaster, but that didn't mean she couldn't try to play cupid for Sophie. 'Have you eaten yet?'

Sophie shook her head. Given how much she'd just spent in Selfridges, she'd been considering skipping lunch. And for a couple of months, at least.

'Okay. Come on, then. My treat.'

'Should we be leaving the office unattended?'

Julie laughed as she picked up her handbag. 'We're in marketing, Sophie,' she said, heading for the door. 'We're hardly the emergency services. What's going to happen—some customer suddenly has a "we've-run-out-of-brochures" emergency?'

Sophie shrugged. 'I suppose,' she said, following her boss downstairs and out of the building.

'What do you fancy?' asked Julie, once they were standing on the pavement. 'A sandwich?'

Sophie thought for a moment. 'I'd prefer something hot,' she said, wrapping her scarf around her neck.

'Will you stop thinking about Nathan for one moment?'

'Ha ha.'

'Soup? There's a new place on Old Compton Street.'

'Why not?' said Sophie.

They made their way through Soho until they found a freshly painted building with a neon sign above the doorway proclaiming 'Souped Up' in bright pink letters, and walked inside.

'What can I get you?' said the man behind the till, as they approached the counter.

Sophie scanned the menu on the wall behind him and quickly spotted her favourite. 'Carrot and coriander,' she said.

'You sure?' asked Julie. 'It's got garlic in it.'

'And?'

'Tonight? Nathan? Kissing?'

'Ah. Good point.' She looked at the menu again, checking each soup's list of ingredients. 'What have you got without garlic?' she asked.

'Winter vegetable,' said the man.

'Sounds good,' said Sophie.

Julie ordered the same for herself, ignoring Sophie's raised eyebrow while waving away her offer to pay—something Sophie was grateful for, having spent her last bit of cash on the coffees that morning. As the man poured their soups, they helped themselves to bread, then carried their lunch to a nearby table.

'So,' Julie said, though a mouthful of poppy-seeded bloomer, which Sophie didn't dare eat, not wanting to spend the afternoon picking the seeds out of her teeth. 'Any thoughts as to how you're going to get a bit of one-on-one time? Maybe even a bit of the aforementioned kissing?'

Sophie stirred her soup thoughtfully. 'I don't know. I was kind of hoping to rely on alcohol.'

Julie almost dropped her bread into her soup. She knew that worked—but given what had happened subsequently with her and Mark, she wouldn't necessarily recommend it as a strategy. 'You mean get him drunk? Or make sure everyone else is drunk, leaving the two of you on your own?'

'I haven't really thought that far ahead.'

'What are you trying to achieve, exactly?' Julie blew on a spoonful of soup. 'Just a drunken snog? Because that might not lead anywhere.'

'Of course not,' said Sophie, though in truth, if that was all she was going to get, it wouldn't have been a bad result.

'Have you and Nathan ever actually spent any time together? You know, just talking?'

'Well, no. At least, nothing more than office chit-chat,' said Sophie, not wanting to own up to their conversation during his card delivery earlier. 'But that's not how it works, is it? I mean, relationships nowadays kind of happen the other way round, don't they?'

'Do they?'

Sophie nodded. 'Yeah. You know, meet someone, get drunk, sleep together, then keep doing that until one of you gets fed up with the other one.'

'Whatever happened to getting to know each other? Spending some time finding out what you have in common before you, you know?'

Sophie let out a short laugh. 'Yeah, right.'

Julie swallowed her spoonful of soup, conscious she might be sounding like Sophie's mother. 'Well, what time does it start this evening?'

'Five-thirty, I think.'

'And assuming it was just you and Nathan on your own, how long do you think you'd need to work your womanly charms on him?'

'How long will it take me to get him drunk, you mean?' Sophie did a quick calculation in her head. If last year was anything to go by, everyone was pretty well away after three or four cocktails. And at one cocktail every fifteen minutes... 'I don't know. An hour?'

'Okay. So all you need to do is make sure you get that window of opportunity.'

Sophie watched in amazement as Julie started on her second bread roll, worried that if she followed suit, the lingerie she'd just bought wouldn't fit. 'And how do we do that?'

Julie smiled. 'We don't,' she said, dunking the bread into her bowl. 'You do.'

'Huh?'

'Think how a marketing campaign works.'

'What do you mean?'

'Say we were trying to run a seminar. What's the first thing we'd do?'

Sophie wondered whether her boss was testing her. 'Book the venue.'

'Which Nathan's already done. Next?'

Sophie scratched her head. 'Well, we'd send out a mailer. Try and get people interested.'

'Which you've already done.'

'Huh?'

'Your Valentine's card.'

'Oh. Right.'

'Exactly.' Julie smiled encouragingly. 'Then?'

'Well, then we'd...' Sophie frowned, unable to see any more parallels.

'Qualify the prospects. And we've done that by establishing Nathan's not gay.'

'Right. Of course.'

'And at the event itself?'

Sophie stared into her bowl of soup, as if hoping she might find the answer there. Aside from making sure there were enough chocolate biscuits to go with the coffee—and she wasn't sure what parallel Julie would draw with that particular observation—she couldn't think of anything else she'd have to do. 'Er...'

'We want them to buy something. Which means we need to create a need.'

'How?'

'By presenting our product as attractively as possible.' Julie fished a soggy piece of crust out of her bowl, popped it into her mouth, and swallowed it without chewing. 'Which you've just ensured, thanks to your recent Selfridges purchase.'

'But I can hardly walk around in my lingerie in front of every-one, can I? It's hardly likely to turn into a game of Strip Bowling.'

Julie laughed. 'Come on, Sophie. We work in the marketing department. If we can't run an effective campaign to get you to that point, then who can?' She smiled. 'What's the surest way to win the sale?'

'Um...'

'Eliminate the competition.'

'That's a bit drastic, isn't it?'

Julie shook her head. 'Not at all. Look at it this way—you want a date with Nathan, but you're too scared to ask him out, right?'

'Right.'

'And as far as we know, he's unlikely to be asking you out.'

Sophie made a face. 'I suppose not.'

'And how would you define a date, exactly?'

Sophie knew the answer to this one. 'Two people, out for the evening,' she said, confidently.

'And you're going out tonight, aren't you?'

'Well, yes, but like I said, with loads of other people. That might cramp my style a little.'

Julie smiled. 'My point exactly.'

'I'm sorry,' said Sophie. 'I'm not quite following you.'

'Get rid of the rest of them. Or delay them. That way, it'll just be you and Nathan. At least, for a while.'

Sophie's eyes widened in admiration. It was a brilliant plan. Though she could see one small flaw. 'So how do I do that, exactly, short of going round and telling everyone individually that it starts an hour later? And even if I managed that, how on earth do I stop it getting back to Nathan?'

Julie picked her bowl up and, forgoing the use of a spoon, drained the last of her soup in one go. 'Think laterally.'

'Huh?'

'Don't get everyone there late. Get Nathan there early.'

'And how do we—sorry, I—do that?'

Julie eyed the rest of Sophie's soup hungrily. 'Easy,' she said.

෴

142

Sophie felt more than a little guilty as the two of them walked back to the office—Julie was being so helpful in her quest to land Nathan, and without knowing that she was actually the object of his affections—though not guilty enough, she reflected, to actually tell her that. But what was it she'd been reminding herself ever since losing out on that promotion, and that handbag, and even the seat on the tube this morning? Nice girls finish last. And today, she couldn't afford to be a nice girl—though as they strolled back along Frith Street, she almost lost her nerve. There, sitting outside Bar Italia, was the object of her affection, drinking coffee with Mark Webster.

As they neared the bar, Sophie began to panic—the last thing she wanted was to give Nathan a chance to compare her with Julie, side by side, particularly since knowing her luck she was bound to have soup somewhere on her face. Mark had just stood up, so Sophie hung back a little, hoping they might be leaving and she'd be safe, but Nathan was showing no sign of going anywhere, and Mark had disappeared inside the café, leaving Nathan sitting there, alternately sipping his coffee and scanning the street. What if he saw her, spoke to her, even, and mentioned something about sending—or receiving—a card this morning? Sophie feared she'd turn into a jabbering mess, and Julie might put two and two together, and surely that would mean game over.

Sophie decided this was one meeting she could do with avoiding. Julie didn't seem to have seen them, so she tried to steer her across the road to where they'd be obscured by a double-parked British Telecom van, but judging by the sudden mischievous look that had appeared on Nathan's face, it was too late. Especially when his loud shout of 'Soph!' rang out. She reddened, and pretended to be fascinated by something in a nearby shop window, but just as she'd decided the best (if not only) strategy was to simply ignore him, she felt Julie grab her arm.

'Maybe you won't have to go to all that trouble after all.'

'Pardon?'

'Someone seems to be calling you.'

'But... No. I can't. I...'

'Come on.' With a smile, Julie tightened her grip and marched Sophie along the pavement. When they reached Nathan's table, he nodded towards the two empty chairs.

'Join us?'

'That would be lovely,' said Julie. 'Wouldn't it, Sophie?'

Without waiting for an answer, she guided Sophie down into the seat next to Nathan, and seemed to be wanting to make a break for it herself, but Nathan wasn't about to let that happen.

'Here,' he said, shifting his chair round. 'You come and sit here.'

Julie caught Sophie's pleading look. 'Well, okay,' she said, lowering herself into the chair.

'In between me and Mark,' continued Nathan.

'Mark?' Julie froze, her backside not quite touching the seat.

'Yeah. He's...' Nathan frowned towards the interior of the café. 'Well, he was here. Perhaps there's a queue for the toilets.' He peered towards the door, where Mark—having spotted the new arrivals—was lurking, a look of panic on his face. Nathan glared at him, then furiously waved him over. 'There he is.'

Realising he'd been spotted, Mark reluctantly made his way back to the table and took his seat, and the four of them sat there in silence.

'Well, this is nice,' said Nathan, eventually.

'Yes,' agreed Julie. 'We don't do this often enough. Do we, Sophie?'

Sophie glanced across at Mark. By the looks of him, and given the awkward way she was feeling, that statement wasn't strictly true. She shook her head reluctantly, and Nathan smiled.

'Everyone looking forward to tonight?'

'Oh yes,' said Julie. 'Aren't we, Sophie?'

'Yes,' said Sophie, quietly.

'Great,' said Nathan. 'I thought we'd split into two teams.'

'Don't tell me,' said Julie. 'Girls against boys.'

He nodded. 'Isn't that the way of the world?'

'That's a bit unfair, surely?' said Julie. 'On the boys, I mean.'

Nathan raised both eyebrows. 'That sounds like a challenge. Want to make it interesting?'

Julie let out a short laugh. 'The only way to achieve that would be to do something other than bowling.'

'Very funny,' said Nathan sarcastically, then he smiled. 'So, Julie...' he said. 'Did you do a lot of this at your last company?'

'A lot of what?'

'You know. Socialising out of work.'

'Not really. Why?'

'Some places do, some don't. I just wondered whether you enjoyed it. I mean, the Christmas party was...Fun, wasn't it?'

'Yes,' said Julie, flatly. 'It was.' She tried not to glance across at Mark, which was just as well. He couldn't have looked more awkward, though that was partly because he was trying to kick Nathan's shin underneath the table.

'Apart from when poor Mary ran out in tears when some drunk shouted out something about her facial hair,' said Sophie, desperate to contribute to the conversation and dazzle Nathan with her witty repartee—or at least, break up the private chat he and Julie seemed to be having.

'Yes, well, some people can't handle their drink,' said Nathan, and Mark had to force himself not to meet Julie's eyes.

'Or their balloons,' said Sophie, before she could stop herself, and Julie made a face. 'Without bursting them, I mean.'

'Mary's not that...' Julie stopped talking, remembering how she'd been fascinated by Mary's five-o'clock shadow earlier. 'I suppose it is rather an unfortunate nickname.'

'Isn't it?' said Sophie, sensing an opening. 'Quite a few people in the office have got one.'

'Such as?' said Julie.

'Dominic in pre-sales. 'Last minute dot Dom.''

'Pardon?'

'He's late with everything. Leaves all his work to the, you know...'

'Last minute?' said Julie.

'Exactly.' Sophie smiled. 'And there's Fiona.'

'Consultant Fiona?' said Nathan. 'The one from Newcastle?'

'Fee-earner.' Sophie grinned. 'And then there's Benedict, the intern.'

Mark made a face. 'The one with the, ahem, personal hygiene problem?'

Sophie nodded. 'Eggs Benedict.'

Nathan winced. 'That's unfortunate,' he said, before fixing Sophie with a look she couldn't quite return. 'So—what's mine?'

'What's your what?'

'You said quite a few people have got one. What's mine?'

'I don't think anyone's...' She blushed. '...given you one. That I know about, anyway.'

He laughed. 'Good cop-out, Soph.'

She met his gaze this time. 'I don't make them up.'

Nathan grinned back at her. 'And what would Julie's be?'

Sophie paled, a little annoyed that Nathan kept turning the conversation back to Julie, but at least she hadn't had to admit she'd heard her own nickname amongst the admin girls was 'Bridget' Jones due to her ongoing singleton status. Though that was something she was planning to do something about this evening. 'Well, again, I haven't really heard anyone say anything.'

'Thank goodness,' said Julie, and Nathan leaned over and nudged her on the arm.

'It's funny,' he said.

'What is?'

'How you can work with someone every day and still not know the first thing about them.'

'It is?'

Nathan nodded. 'Of course. I mean, take Mark, for example.'

As Mark shifted uncomfortably in his seat, everyone turned to face him. 'What about him?' said Sophie, eventually.

'You probably just think he's some boring accountant. But underneath that grey-suited exterior...'

'Lies a grey interior, who unlike you, actually has some work to do,' said Mark, glancing at his watch, then waving at the waiter and making the universal 'bill' sign.

'Well, that's what days like today are for,' said Nathan. 'To disprove that kind of thing. And so we can all get to know each other a little better.'

'You mean, nights like tonight?' said Julie.

'Either,' said Nathan, with a smile.

And as the waiter arrived with the bill, Mark Webster realised he'd never been more grateful to see anyone in his entire life. And little did he know it, but Sophie was thinking exactly the same thing.

6

Sophie Jones was stomping her way back to the office at an impressive pace—so impressive, in fact, that despite the amount of training she'd been doing, Julie was struggling to keep up.

'Are we late for a meeting I don't know about?' she said, as Sophie angrily swiped the door open. 'Or do you just need the toilet?'

Sophie glared at her, then bounded up the stairs without answering, Julie following a few breathless steps behind. Once they'd reached their office, Sophie rounded on her.

'What was that all about?'

'Don't you mean "you're welcome"?'

Sophie's jaw dropped open. 'I'm welcome? What for? You were all over him.'

'All over who?'

'Nathan!'

'Nathan?'

'Yes, Nathan!' said Sophie, marching over to her desk, picking up the Selfridges bag, and dropping it into the bin.

'What are you doing that for?'

'He's quite clearly not interested in me. Or rather, he's obviously more interested in you. And you seemed rather interested in him too. How could you sit there and flirt with him, when you knew I…' Sophie sat down angrily at her desk. 'I confided in you.

I told you I liked him.' She was struggling to stop the tears coming. 'I thought we were friends.'

As Sophie's lower lip started to tremble, Julie didn't know how to react. She'd never been a particularly girly girl, and physical demonstrations of affection put her a bit out of her comfort zone. To be honest, not counting that time in the taxi with Mark, it had been a while since she'd had any physical contact with anyone, even Philip.

'We are friends,' she said, settling for a brief pat on Sophie's shoulder. 'I was simply trying to find out if Nathan was single.'

'So it seemed.'

Julie bent down and retrieved Sophie's discarded purchase from the waste bin. 'For you,' she said, dusting the bag off and putting it back on her desk.

'You could have fooled me.'

'Honestly, Sophie. I'm not interested in Nathan.'

'Why not?'

Because I'm interested in Mark was Julie's first reaction. But to admit that would be…Julie almost laughed. She didn't have a clue what it would be. Then, ashamedly, she realised the word 'wrong' should have leapt to mind, given her marital state.

'Anyway,' continued Sophie. 'It doesn't matter anyway.'

Julie perched on the end of Sophie's desk. 'Why ever not?'

'Weren't you listening? Because he fancies you, not me!'

'Nathan?'

'Yes, Nathan!'

'Whatever makes you think that?'

'Let me see.' Sophie began counting off on her fingers. 'Because of the way he asked you to sit next to him. Because of the way he was talking to you—or should I say flirting with you.' She looked up, red-eyed. 'And because he sent you that card.'

'What?'

'The Valentine's card that was on your desk when you came in this morning. It was from Nathan.'

'How do you know?'

'Because I was here when he walked in and put it there,' said Sophie, in between sobs.

Julie reached into her desk drawer and removed a box of tissues. 'Why didn't you say anything?' she asked, handing Sophie one.

'Because...' Sophie blew her nose loudly. 'Because he asked me not to. And because I thought if you didn't know he was interested in you, then you couldn't possibly be interested in him.' She shook her head. 'But that doesn't really matter now, does it?'

Julie stared at her. Because if Nathan had sent the card, then that meant he'd probably sent the balloons and chocolates too. And that meant... Well, it meant that Mark wasn't as interested in her as she'd thought.

She almost felt like crying herself. The one ray of light she'd been holding on to in the midst of the nightmare situation she was in with her husband was... Well, it was looking like she'd imagined it all along, and that made her feel foolish. But it was more than foolish. She felt lonely. Lost. Hopeless. Helpless. A combination of emotions Julie wasn't used to, and certainly didn't like. But while she might not have known what to do about her own situation, Julie felt she owed it to Sophie to try and make things a little clearer for her

'Listen, Sophie, here's what we'll do. First things first, don't let Nathan see you like this.' She glanced at her watch, then made for the door. 'You go and wash your face, and I'll...'

'Where are you going?'

'To the toilet, actually. Too much soup. Then I've got a meeting with the ad agency. But after that, I promise I'll go and tell Nathan in no uncertain terms I'm not interested in him.'

'And how will that help me, exactly?'

'Well...' Julie thought for a moment. 'If you stick to the plan we've just discussed, it might even work in your favour. He'll be vulnerable this evening, and you never know—he may decide to drown his sorrows. If he is—or does—you might be able to swoop in and offer him a shoulder to cry on. And once he sees you in that...' She nodded towards the Selfridges bag. 'You'll have a field day. Or, at least, a Nathan Field day.'

Despite her tears, Sophie half-smiled at Julie's joke. Besides, she realised, that approach might just work, and she'd be more than happy to offer Nathan her shoulder—or any other part of her body—to cry on. And so what if she got him off the back of Julie's rejection, or even just because he was drunk? She'd still be getting him. It was better than nothing. And nothing was all she had at the moment.

❧

Mark Webster was standing outside the newsagent's on Frith Street, unable to work out why Julie had seemed so disinterested in him, and come to think of it, why she'd been showing so much interest in Nathan. Nathan, on the other hand, was doing his best to be encouraging, though he was mystified as to why Mark had cut the encounter short.

'What were you thinking? We could at least have walked back to the office with them.'

'Were you sitting at the same table I was?'

'Yeah. Went well, eh?'

Mark shook his head. 'I am so waiting to see how you can put a positive spin on what just happened.'

'Well, she was very chatty, at least.'

'To you.' Mark sighed. 'Nathan, face it, Sophie showed more romantic interest in me. And she hardly said a word.'

'I wouldn't say that.'

'I mean, it's like the kiss never happened.'

'You're sure it did?'

Mark made a face. 'Not so much anymore, no.'

Nathan smiled. 'I'm sure it's just a front. Like you said, she's not exactly an open book, is she? So she's hardly going to throw herself at you over coffee with the four of us.'

'She threw herself at you.'

'What?'

'You didn't notice?'

Nathan frowned. 'Well, no, to be honest.'

'And you seemed quite interested in her.'

'What?'

'If I didn't know you better, I'd think you were... Never mind.'

'Yeah, well, someone had to make conversation. Otherwise the four of us would have sat there like lemons.'

'Yes, but, did you have to make so much conversation?'

Nathan grinned. 'I was just trying to see what I could find out about her.'

'By steering the conversation round to talk about me? And what did you find out, exactly? That she didn't say a single thing to me, and instead, preferred to spend the whole time flirting with you about tonight.'

'She was hardly flirting...' Nathan caught sight of the look Mark was giving him and held his hands up. 'Okay, okay, it may have seemed like that on the surface. But it's a good double bluff, isn't it? Or...'

'Or?'

'Maybe, she was trying to make you jealous.'

'Make me jealous? Why on earth would she...'

Nathan stepped off the kerb to let a mad-haired old woman pushing a dog in a pram pass. 'Think about it. She might be thinking exactly the same as you. This kiss allegedly happens...'

'It did happen.'

'And afterwards, you're hoping the person you kissed will mention it, perhaps even ask you out, but...Nothing. No response. In fact, whenever you bump into him in the corridor, he seems to do the exact opposite. Avoids even mentioning it. Looks away awkwardly when you even try to pass the time of day. If it was me, I'd think they were maybe embarrassed. Ashamed, even. And certainly didn't want a repeat performance.'

'I still don't see where the "jealousy" part comes in.'

'So maybe she was trying to do the same as you are today with all your balloons and sweets. Provoke a reaction.' Nathan fished in his pocket and removed a handful of coins. 'Wait here.'

He disappeared into the newsagent's, so Mark leant against a nearby postbox and tried to analyse what he'd just heard. He supposed it was possible he'd put Julie off by his shyness, and his lack of acknowledgement of what had happened between them. After all, weren't women supposed to want men who were direct, confident, and not afraid to go for what they wanted? It had been she who'd made the first move in the taxi, and since then...Well, he could see how it might look as if he wasn't the slightest bit interested.

As he waited on the pavement, Mark realised that if Nathan was right, it was a wonder Julie was even speaking to him, the way he'd heartlessly kissed her—or rather, kissed her back—then not even mentioned it. After all, why should he have expected her to? That wasn't fair. Certainly wasn't the done thing. While Mark was no chauvinist, he liked to think of himself as a gentleman, or at least a modern man, and being a modern man, he should have followed things up. Taken the lead. Or at least 'grown a pair,' as his boss in the US was fond of saying.

He looked up as Nathan emerged from the newsagent's clutching a packet of Extra Strong Mints. 'So?' he said, offering Mark one.

'It's a bit extreme, isn't it?' Mark helped himself to a mint and popped it into his mouth. 'Trying to make me jealous. It's the kind of thing you'd do in the playground.'

'Like sending cards without your name on them?' Nathan began walking back to the office and Mark duly followed him. 'Or anonymously giving someone a packet of balloons. Or sending them chocolate "kisses."'

'Well, what would you do if you were me?'

Nathan puffed air out of his cheeks. 'Again, I'm hardly the best person to ask for advice, mate. Last time I tried to give someone something on Valentine's Day, they pretty much threw it back in my face.'

'You don't think...No.' Mark shook his head. 'That's not possible.'

'What?'

'Well, it could just be the case that if she was drunk, then she was so drunk she doesn't even remember who she was in the taxi with, and therefore, who she kissed. Maybe she thinks it was you. And so maybe that was her way of finding out.'

'Why would she think it was me?' Nathan shook his head as they turned the corner into Bateman Street. 'And if she did, surely she'd have said something by now?'

'I refer you to your earlier "embarrassed" observation.'

'Fair point.'

'Unless...' Mark stopped dead in his tracks. 'Are you sure she didn't see you deliver the card?'

Nathan nodded. 'Yup. Hundred and ten percent.'

Mark bit his tongue to stop his inner accountant from pointing out that that was a numerical impossibility. 'You're positive?'

Nathan nodded. 'And I told Sophie not to say anything either.'

'What?'

'Sophie. I told her not to say anything.'

'When?'

'This morning.'

'Why would Sophie have said anything?'

'Well, she was in the office.'

Nathan had started walking again, and Mark hurried to catch him up. 'What office?'

'Her office. You know, the one she shares with Julie?'

They'd reached Seek's building now, so Mark lowered his voice. 'Let me get this straight. When you delivered the card this morning—my card for Julie—you walked into the office she shares with Sophie and—in front of Sophie—put the card on Julie's desk?'

'Yeah.'

'Nathan.'

'But like I said, Julie didn't see me.'

'But Sophie did,' Mark almost shouted.

'So?'

'So Sophie might think the card was from you.'

'But I...' Nathan's jaw dropped open as he quickly replayed this morning's encounter with Sophie in his head. 'Ah.'

'And so what if she's told her?'

'She won't have,' said Nathan, looking a little less confident.

'No? Why ever not?'

'Like I told you, I asked her not to,' he said, weakly.

'And women always do what you ask them, do they?'

'Point taken,' said Nathan, grinning sheepishly.

'You didn't think adding "it's not from me" or "I'm delivering it for a friend" might have helped a little?' Mark shook his head, then pulled his key card from his pocket and swiped the door open.

'But Sophie…'

'Is a woman. So is Julie. Women talk. They don't have secrets. Ever.'

'Sorry, mate,' said Nathan, following him inside. 'I thought…'

'Yes, well, it's not what you thought that counts, is it? It's what she thinks. And what on earth am I going to do about that?'

As Mark unlocked his door, Nathan clapped him on the shoulder. 'I'll sort it. Just leave it with me,' he said, before making for the stairs that led down to his office. Though in truth, he didn't have the faintest idea how.

❦

Calum Irwin limped slowly along Oxford Street, wincing with every step. Why, oh why, had he taken up Debbie's offer of a free personal training session, and today of all days? There had been no way he was going to get ripped abs by this evening, and the muscles he suspected he'd torn in his lower back were hardly the same thing.

He cursed under his breath, then lifted his arm gingerly and looked at his watch. At least he still had four and a half hours until he was due to meet Emma, though given how the pain at the base of his spine wasn't getting any better, four and a half days wouldn't have been enough.

Ironically, it hadn't been the exercise that had done for him—instead, he'd been trying not to appear a wimp in front of Debbie by attempting to put a dumbbell back on the rack that some other member had forgotten to put away. And while he'd never been one to draw attention to himself in the gym, the loud yowling noise he'd made when he'd picked it up and felt his back go had certainly done that. As he'd lain on the mat, whimpering quietly, Debbie had run off to fetch the manager—an Amazon of a girl who'd looked as if she could have picked the dumbbell up in one hand and Calum in the other. She'd been a picture of concern, though it turned out she'd actually been concerned Calum was going to sue the club for his injury. When he'd put on a brave face and told her 'no harm done,' she'd looked relieved, and given him a couple of free passes for something called 'Zumba,' which had made Calum feel a little better until he'd discovered it was some sort of dance fitness class and not a tropical fruit drink from the juice bar.

He'd crawled out of the weights room, showered slowly, and—having found it impossible to reach any part of his body lower than his waist with his towel—dried his nether regions as best he could using the hand-dryer in the toilets. Getting his clothes back on had taken the greatest of efforts, though tying his shoelaces had been beyond him, and as he walked, he had to take care not to trip over them.

He caught sight of his shambling reflection in a shop window and wondered miserably whether he should text Emma to cancel, but decided to wait, hoping by some miracle his back might get better before tonight. Instead, he called into Boots to pick up some ibuprofen and a jar of something called Tiger Balm that Debbie had recommended (although he put that back on the shelf when he realised how bad it smelled).

Calum couldn't believe his bad luck. He couldn't even stand up straight, which made his claim of being over six foot tall look even more spurious. Still, perhaps the grimace he couldn't stop from appearing on his face every time he took a breath would be enough of a distraction, and Emma wouldn't notice. Or she might even regard a gym injury as some sort of badge of honour and be concerned enough about his health to offer to give him a massage... For the second time today, the words 'yeah' and 'right' formed a sentence in his head.

He sat down gingerly on a nearby chair, consoling himself with the fact that at least sitting didn't hurt too much, so as long as he and Emma stayed seated this evening he might just be okay. But as for anything else, Calum knew he might as well forget it. He found the packet of condoms in his jacket pocket and miserably checked the 'use by' date. While three years seemed a long time, if things continued like this, he'd be better off asking his mum if she'd kept the receipt.

With a sigh, he removed the tablets from his shopping bag and popped open the blister pack, then dry-swallowed a couple, wishing as they stuck in his throat that he'd paid the extra four pence and bought caplets, then hauled himself up onto his feet, walked slowly out of Boots, and headed back in the direction of the office. *Keep mobile*, Debbie had said to him as he'd left the gym, though the only degree of mobility he had right now involved shuffling with his left foot permanently in front of his right one, and he doubted that would help him much. He reached Seek's building and swiped his way inside, glad Mia-Rose was taking a late lunch—he could do without explaining himself—then surveyed the daunting flight of stairs in front of him. As he cautiously lifted his foot onto the first one, Nathan peered up at him from halfway down the basement stairs.

'What happened to you?'

'My back's gone.' Calum tried to get his other foot onto the same step, and the effort made him break out in a sweat.

'Oh no. How bad is it?'

'On a scale of one to ten? Eleven.'

Nathan made a sympathetic face. 'Have you taken anything?'

'About half an hour to get here from Oxford Street.'

'No, I meant tablets.'

Calum nodded. Even that hurt. 'Neurofen.'

'Can you touch your toes?'

'No,' said Calum. 'Though that's nothing unusual.'

'What are you going to do?'

Calum shrugged carefully. 'Hope it gets better, I suppose.'

Nathan thought for a moment. 'You should get a massage.'

'Round here?' Calum almost laughed, but didn't dare in case the convulsions sent his back into spasm again. 'I want to get less stiff. Not more.'

Nathan grinned. 'They're not all that kind of massage parlour. I meant one of those places in Chinatown. They've got to be worth a go.'

'You think?' Calum glanced carefully at the clock above the reception desk. He should have enough time before this afternoon's conference call. 'Okay.'

'Great. Just let me go and check nothing urgent has happened work-wise, and I'll take you.'

As Nathan ran down the stairs to his office, Calum swivelled round on the step, wincing with the effort. The way he was feeling, even a trip to Spank-o-rama would be worth a try.

As Julie Marshall pulled the door shut behind her, Sophie helped herself to another tissue and dabbed the mascara stains from her eyes, trying to fight off the feeling of loneliness that was washing over her. Why had she given up the safety, security, and—let's face it—adoration of Darren for this? And on top of everything, even he seemed to be deserting her now, given the non-arrival of his usual card this morning.

She typed her password into her laptop and checked her Hotmail account, hoping he'd perhaps sent her a Valentine's message by email instead, but despite hitting 'refresh' three times, there was nothing from him (or anyone)—in her inbox, or her 'junk' folder, or even in 'deleted items,' though how it would have got there without her actually deleting it, she didn't know. A thought occurred to her, so Sophie hurriedly logged in to Facebook. It was the twenty-first century after all—cards were so last year— so perhaps someone had messaged her this way instead. Even a Valentine's 'poke' would be something, but her face fell even further when she saw that, like her inbox, the notifications bar was bare.

On a whim, she typed Darren's name into the search box— maybe seeing what he was up to would cheer her up—but after she'd found his profile, instead of the reassurance she was hoping for, Sophie found herself unable to believe what she was reading. Why would Darren write something like that—and today of all days?

She stared at the screen, trying hard to stop the tears from coming again, and wished she hadn't bothered looking. She'd been able to handle it when Darren's relationship status had said 'in a relation- ship,' had even been pleased for him, but... Engaged? And who the hell was Sarah Miller?

Sophie clicked impatiently on the link but, frustratingly, Sarah Miller's profile was for friends only, so she toyed briefly with the idea of sending her a friend request, hoping she was one of those people for whom amassing friends on Facebook was a sign of social status, rather than simply social network status. Maybe she'd accept the request just to add Sophie to the—what was it?—four hundred and sixty seven friends she had already, then she could snoop all she liked. Check whether she and Darren were having fun. Look at their intimate photos. See snaps of them on holiday. And most importantly, check whether Sarah Miller was prettier—or thinner—than she was.

Her finger hovered over the 'send' button, then—as if her laptop was about to explode—she propelled herself away from her desk on her wheelie chair, wondering why on earth she was still so interested in what Darren was doing now. She'd never wanted him back (although now, she realised miserably, that was pretty academic), and she wanted him to be happy. Though not, it seemed, if it meant her being unhappy.

Sophie sighed loudly. At least this explained why she hadn't received a card this morning. She stood up and walked over to the door, cracked it open, and peeked out into the corridor. Julie was safely ensconced in the meeting room, but Sophie didn't want to risk her popping back in on the way to break Nathan's heart and catching her making an embarrassing personal call, so she picked up her mobile, grabbed her coat, and (after she'd checked to make sure it was smoker-free) made her way out onto the roof terrace. Quickly, before she could lose her nerve, she dialled the once-familiar number.

'Hello?' said a suspicious voice.

'Darren?'

'Who wants him?'

Sophie grimaced. Five years together, and he didn't even recognise her voice. 'It's me.'

There was a pause, and then, 'Sophie?'

'Hiya,' said Sophie, as cheerily as she could muster.

'Is everything OK?'

'Of course,' she lied. 'I just thought I'd call you up to wish you happy Valentine's Day. You know, seeing as it's...' She swallowed hard. 'Not appropriate for me to send you a card anymore.'

'Not appropriate because you left me, you mean?'

'Well,' Sophie took a deep breath. 'Yes. That too. But mainly because...' The words died in her throat, and she swallowed hard.

'Are you sure everything's OK?' said Darren.

She sniffed and wiped her nose on her sleeve. 'Why wouldn't it be?'

'It's just that you sound funny. Where are you?'

'I'm on the roof.'

'What roof?' said Darren, anxiously. She heard footsteps, and the sound of a window being opened. 'My roof?'

'No, silly. My roof. Well, my office roof.'

'You're not planning to jump, are you?'

'Jump? Of course not. Why would I...' Sophie stopped talking, and wondered if he could tell she'd seen his news. 'It's actually a roof terrace. For the smokers. I've not climbed out of the attic window or anything. Not that I smoke now. Filthy habit. It's the only place I can get any privacy here. You know, *busy busy hectic* otherwise...' She stopped herself, wondering why she was so nervous. 'Anyway, I just thought I'd call and congratulate you. On your good news.'

Darren paused again. 'My good news?'

'Yes you know...' Sophie forced herself to smile. She'd read if you did that while you were speaking on the phone, it made you sound all upbeat. Even if you were feeling the exact opposite. 'Getting engaged.'

'How did you know about that?' said Darren, flatly.

'How did I know?' Sophie was suddenly worried she'd come across as a stalker. 'I, um, saw it on your Facebook status update.'

'How did you see my status update? We're not "friends."'

Sophie felt her stomach lurch. 'Ha ha. That sounds weird, doesn't it? Because, of course, we are, but...No...Well, it's a funny story, really. You know how Facebook sometimes suggests you might like to "friend" people you may know? Well, I was on there earlier—I don't use it much, to be honest. Too busy at work. You know how it is...' She stopped talking again, conscious she was still babbling. 'Anyway, the funniest thing happened. I just happened to be looking at it in my lunch break. I don't know why. Like I said, I'm always really busy, but I just had a spare five minutes—well, two minutes, really—and strangely enough, it suggested you. What are the chances?' She could hear Darren breathing down the other end of the line, but he wasn't saying anything, and Sophie began to regret calling him. 'Like I said. Isn't that a funny...' It was freezing up on the terrace, and her nose had begun to run, so she sniffed loudly. '...story.'

'Hilarious,' said Darren, his tone suggesting otherwise.

'So I thought to myself, I wonder what old Darren's up to. Not that you're that old, of course, but you know what I mean. So anyway, I clicked on your profile, and then I saw that you'd just got—I mean, you were engaged. To...' Sophie didn't want to appear like she'd been studying his profile too closely. 'Samantha, was it?'

'Sarah,' said Darren.

'Sarah. That was it. Not Samantha. Do you even know a Samantha? And if you do, does Sarah know about her? Oops, what am I saying! None of my business anymore. Especially now.'

There was another pause, mainly because Sophie didn't have a clue what to say next, and Darren didn't seem to want to respond. Eventually, he broke the awkward silence.

'What's that noise?'

'Noise?'

'Like a machine gun. Where in London are you, exactly?'

Sophie realised her teeth were chattering, so she clamped her jaw shut and hopped about from foot to foot in an attempt to keep warm. 'Sorry. It's just a little cold up here. Another reason not to take up smoking. Not that I want to. Like I said, filthy habit.' She suddenly felt awkward, and worried she'd spoken out of turn. After all, she didn't know if Darren's fiancée smoked. 'Well, it's more of an addiction, really. You can't blame people who...'

'Sophie...'

'So,' she interrupted. 'Like I said, congratulations.'

'Thanks.'

'And so... When's the wedding?'

She heard Darren clear his throat. 'We haven't set a date yet.'

'Oh, that's a relief,' said Sophie. 'I mean, not for me. For you. And Samantha, obviously.'

'Sarah. And why is it a relief?'

'Because...' Sophie scanned the rooftops, hoping for inspiration, then spotted a woman with a baby through a window across the street. 'Because, obviously, it means she's not pregnant. So you're not marrying her under false pretences. Or having to rush into it.' She stopped talking again, and almost wanted to punch herself for her insensitivity. 'Not that I'm suggesting you would be. Though you're not rushing into it, are you? After...'

'You and me?' Darren laughed. 'That was two years ago, Sophie. I don't know what the actual time-scale for being on the rebound is, but I'm pretty sure it's not that long.'

'No. I suppose not. So...' Sophie was trying desperately to be chatty. 'What's she like? What does she do?'

'Does it really matter?'

'Well, no. Not to me, of course. You're the one marrying her. Till death do you part, and all that. I just...'

'She's twenty-eight. She works for the council. You'd like her.'

'Really,' said Sophie, already feeling the exact opposite. 'Is she...like me, at all?'

'What do you think?'

How would I know? thought Sophie. *The cow has set her profile to 'private.'* 'I don't know.'

'Actually, she is, a bit. Apart from one big difference.'

'Which is?'

'She wants to spend the rest of her life with me.'

Sophie felt her legs go weak, and she leant heavily against the railing, doing her best to ignore both its coldness and Darren's icy comment. 'Well, that's just...I mean, it's...'

'And what about you, Sophie?' said Darren. 'How's London working out for you? All those big dreams you had. The ones that were bigger than Eastbourne. Or at least, bigger than you and me.'

'It's...' Sophie searched for the right word. 'London's...' She could feel the tears start to build up again. 'I mean, I'm...'

'Sophie...'

'Really...'

'Sophie...'

'...so pleased for you,' she sobbed.

'Sophie!'

'What?'

'What's wrong?'

'Wrong? There's nothing wrong. I told you, I'm just a bit cold.'

'Well, why are you crying?'

'I'm not crying. I'm sniffing because I'm...'

'Cold. So you said.' Darren's tone softened slightly. 'Come on, Sophie. I know you.'

'I'm sorry. I . . . I am crying. But they're tears of happiness.'

'Really?'

'Really.'

'You sure you're OK?'

Sophie nodded—a pointless gesture over the phone, she knew. 'The news just . . . came as a bit of a shock, that's all.'

'I'm sorry. But I could hardly call you up and tell you, could I?'

'No. I suppose not.'

'Especially not today.'

Sophie gave another loud sniff, then hoped Darren hadn't heard it. 'I should have guessed when your card didn't arrive this morning.'

'Subtle of me, eh?'

'It got the message across.'

There was a pause, and then Darren sighed. 'Listen, Sophie, I'm at work, so if there's nothing else?'

'There is.'

'Well?'

'I just wanted to say . . .' Sophie thought of saying 'sorry,' but why should she be? By the sounds of things, she'd done him a favour. She fixed a smile on her face again, although the effort it took made her feel faint. 'Be happy, Darren.'

Sophie could almost hear him smile back. 'You too,' he said. And then he was gone.

She wiped her eyes on her sleeve, then slipped her mobile back into her pocket, and while she might not have felt a bundle of joy at this precise moment, Sophie realised she *was* happy for Darren. She'd always felt guilty for leaving him, though that was because she was worried she'd left him with nothing, and she had everything to look forward to—though look how that had turned out. And it wasn't that there was anything wrong with him: there just hadn't been enough right with *them*, and Sophie had begun to suspect she could do better. She hadn't meant better than Darren. Just better than Darren had been for her. And so, she'd known, could he.

She gulped down a few more lungfuls of the crisp London air, then leaned over the railing and peeked down. Darren needn't have worried about her jumping—the building was only two stories high, and chances were she'd have landed in one of Spank-o-rama's wheelie bins.

Though maybe that would have been appropriate, she thought, given how rubbish she was currently feeling.

※

The usual five-minute journey to Chinatown took Calum a depressingly slow quarter of an hour, which, combined with the way Nathan had been helping him along the pavement like an old man, wasn't particularly encouraging. As things stood, there was no way he was going to be able to meet Emma this evening, and to be honest, he couldn't even see how he was going to get home. Eventually, they reached Lisle Street and stopped in front of the first appropriate-looking establishment.

'What about this place?' said Nathan, pointing at the shop window, where a plastic model of a spine (at least, Calum hoped it was plastic, and hadn't been ripped bodily from some previous client) was arranged in a pleasingly upright way. The poster next to it was offering something called Shiatsu, and Calum frowned.

'Are you sure?'

'About what?'

'That this isn't a vet's.'

'A vet's?'

'There are bones in the window.' He pointed at the poster, wincing with the effort. 'And Shiatsu.'

'What about it?'

'Isn't that some kind of dog?'

Nathan laughed, and Calum would have joined in if it hadn't been so painful. 'What do you think? Does it look okay?'

With difficulty, Calum turned and peered up and down the street. From what he could tell, there were several identical shops offering similar services, and he didn't want to walk farther than was strictly necessary—or rather, he wasn't sure he could. 'I suppose so.'

'Great.'

Nathan pushed the door open and ushered him through, and a stern-looking Chinese girl behind the counter looked up from the magazine she was reading.

'Can I help you?'

'I hope so,' said Calum.

'It's his back,' said Nathan. 'Gym injury. And he needs to be fit for tonight.'

The girl looked Calum up and down. 'I won't ask,' she said. She pressed a buzzer, and an older Chinese lady who looked as if she weighed half as much as Calum emerged from a side door.

'This is Yu,' said the girl.

'Me? Great,' said Calum, pleased he wouldn't have to wait.

'No,' said the girl. 'She is Yu.'

As Calum forced a smile, Nathan nudged him. 'That's some pretty deep Chinese philosophy,' he whispered.

Calum ignored him. 'Sorry. Hello, er, Yu,' he said.

As Yu bowed in acknowledgement, Nathan looked at her, and then at Calum, comparing their relative sizes, then he turned to the girl behind the counter. 'Are you sure she'll...' He chose his next word carefully. '...manage?'

'She'll be fine,' said the girl, then she smiled at Calum. 'Have you ever had Shiatsu before?'

'No,' said Calum nervously. 'Will it hurt?'

The girl smiled. 'No more than your back does already.'

'Is that supposed to reassure me?'

'Do you want me to wait?' said Nathan, looking around for a chair.

Calum took one look at the woman, then grimaced as his back spasmed again. 'I think I'll be okay,' he wheezed. 'Thanks.'

'No worries,' said Nathan. 'And good luck.'

'Thank you.'

Nathan grinned. 'I was talking to Yu,' he said. 'Not, you know, you. Oh never mind...'

As Nathan left, Calum slowly followed Yu through the side door, and for a moment, wondered what kind of establishment he'd wandered into. Here he was, in a small room with a bed, and a not unattractive Chinese woman was helping him unbutton his shirt. He removed his glasses, and—relieved he had his best underwear on—started to undo his belt, but Yu held up a hand.

'Keep those on,' she said.

'You speak English?' said Calum, then he blushed. 'Sorry, I didn't mean "Yu—speak English!" as an order. I meant...'

'I know what you meant,' said Yu. 'Don't worry.'

Calum glanced around the room, and noticed a rope running along the ceiling. 'What's that for?' he asked, beginning to get a little concerned.

'I'm going to be walking all over you.'

'No change there,' joked Calum, as he sat cautiously down on the bed.

Yu smiled—as if she'd heard the remark a thousand times before—as she helped him onto his back. 'Okay. I need to flip you over onto your front,' she said. 'This might hurt a little.'

Calum almost laughed. Up close, she was even slighter than he'd first noticed. 'I don't think you'll be able to...Ow!'

'Sorry.'

For the next twenty minutes he lay face-down, staring at the carpet through the hole in the bed where his head was resting, as Yu worked on him, pushing, pulling, massaging, his eyes watering from the pain. After she'd loosened him up a little, Calum felt her step up onto the bed. Then she took hold of the rope and climbed gently onto his lower back.

'Are you sure this is safe?'

'Of course,' said Yu. 'I've got the rope to hold on to. And it's not that far for me to fall.'

'For me,' said Calum.

'Just my little joke,' said Yu. 'Like yours earlier. But funny.'

She let out a short, tinkling laugh, then began to walk up and down either side of Calum's spine, kneading and pinching with toes as strong as pliers, while ignoring the series of agonised yelps he couldn't stop himself from emitting. After a further twenty minutes, much to Calum's relief, she climbed off.

'You can get up now.'

'Are you sure?'

'Want me to help you?'

Calum shook his head. He didn't want a repeat of her earlier flipping—not with his back as sore as it was—so he rolled gingerly onto his side.

'That's amazing.'

Yu smiled. 'What can you feel?'

'Absolutely nothing.'

'You're paralysed?'

'No. I mean there's no pain. It's a little tender, but...' Not wanting to tempt fate, he eased himself off the bed and stood up, and when he caught sight of himself in the full-length mirror on the far wall, he even looked a little taller. 'It's a miracle.'

'It's Shiatsu.'

'Well, whatever you call it, it was...' Calum struggled for the right adjective. He didn't want to sound like he was referring to sex, but in the end, 'incredible' was all he could come up with. 'Thank you, er, Yu.'

Yu smiled, and bowed slightly. 'You're welcome,' she said.

Calum walked—normally, he was pleased to note—back out of the treatment room, paid the girl on the desk the best forty pounds he'd ever spent, then almost cartwheeled out of the door and back across Shaftesbury Avenue. He was feeling a little light-headed—maybe because of the treatment, but partly, Calum realised, because that had been the most amount of physical contact he'd had with someone of the opposite sex for, well, he couldn't remember how long, and he hadn't embarrassed himself that much, or said anything too inappropriate, or even started sweating uncontrollably.

And as he strolled jauntily back to the office, even though he didn't want to tempt fate, he allowed himself to believe it was a sign that perhaps, finally, his luck was changing.

7

Nathan Field averted his eyes as he stepped to one side of the pavement, then he silently let the couple walk past. It wasn't the fact they were holding hands that had unsettled him, or that the girl had reminded him a little of Ellie, but when he'd caught sight of the brown paper IKEA carrier bags they were clutching—today, of all days—it had pierced him through the heart.

As he always did when he spotted the familiar blue-and-yellow logo, he'd felt the insane urge to block the couple's path, rip the bags from their hands, and tell them the idea of peaceful co-habitation these screw-together symbols of perfect coupledom promoted was nothing but a myth. But instead (and again, as he always did), he'd simply stood back and let them go on their way, and then, unable to face going straight back to the office, he'd walked past Bateman Street and up into Soho Square, found a bench away from the buskers, and sat down heavily, resting his head in his hands, telling himself to breathe deeply until his heart stopped hammering, wondering when he'd stop feeling this way about what was just a Swedish furniture store.

Back when they were together, he and Ellie had gone to IKEA almost on a monthly basis. She forever seemed to be on the hunt for another rug, or a set of cocktail glasses, or strange items of furniture with innuendo-laden names, or even those scented candles she'd loved that to him just smelled like cheap air freshener. At the time, Nathan had humoured what he'd labelled her IKEAddiction, assuming she was nest-building. How wrong he'd been. She'd been stocking up for her escape.

He'd been back there once, just after they'd split up. Not through choice, or as part of some therapeutic plan, but he hadn't had much of an alternative, since Ellie had taken half the furniture and most of the kitchen equipment. She'd always used to tease him he kept the flat so tidy that you could eat your dinner off the floor, and when Nathan had discovered she'd taken the plates too, he'd almost had to. And while he was a fan of the minimalist look, what she'd left him with had been a little too sparse. So he'd braved the trip round the North Circular to Wembley on his Vespa, helped himself to a bright yellow bag and one of the paper tape-measures, tried to ignore the fact that he was the only man in the store who was on his own, and followed the arrows in search of crockery. And it had all been going fine until he'd turned a corner and seen them.

The couple—and he'd never laid eyes on them before—a few years younger than him and Ellie, had been sitting side-by-side on a sofa with a name Nathan couldn't pronounce in the mock-up of the forty-five-square-metre flat, gazing blissfully around the over-furnished room as if they'd just been transported to paradise. From that one snapshot, he could tell they were imagining the rest of their lives together, and how perfect it would be to live like this, as if a relationship was as easy to put together as a room-full of flat-pack furniture. Maybe it was, as long as you had all the pieces and followed the instructions to the letter, but as Nathan knew, there were no instructions, and if the most important piece was missing—love—then things were bound to fall apart.

He'd wanted to walk over and tell them how it really was. Shatter their dreams by letting them know in no uncertain terms that life wasn't as simple as that. But the looks of hope on their faces—and the delusion they were obviously suffering from—had rooted Nathan to the spot, and almost made him want to cry.

So he'd backed away from them, then dumped his yellow bag in the nearest receptacle and headed out the way he'd come in, a cardinal sin that had caused consternation on the faces of the wave of shoppers headed the other way—surely he knew you had to follow the arrows? But there and then, Nathan had decided to stop following arrows. After all, the one he'd followed that Cupid had fired into his heart had turned out to be pointing in the wrong direction entirely.

Since that day, he'd hated IKEA with a passion. In fact, he'd begun to dislike anything that promoted the idea of off-the-shelf happy-ever-after lives, like rom-com films, or even adverts on the TV featuring 'perfect' families with their two-point-four children and the inevitable dog, because Nathan knew that when the going got tough—as it invariably would—no matter how many Billy book cases you bought, how much stackable storage you owned, how many shelves you put up on a bank holiday Monday, or how many times you watched Matthew McConaughey eventually realise the girl he was competing with for that promotion was in fact the woman he loved, would make a difference. That kind of stuff was worthless and disposable. Much like their relationship had obviously been to Ellie.

But that, he knew, was what Ellie had always been about. PR was all about creating an illusion, and the idea that a few scatter cushions would make everything OK had certainly fooled him.

Though when she'd left, taking most of them with her, there hadn't been enough soft furnishings left to cushion his fall.

He looked up again, safe in the knowledge that the IKEA couple would be long gone, and sighed. Nathan didn't enjoy feeling bitter. He preferred feeling nothing. And that just wasn't possible today—or at least, not until he got a few drinks inside him later. He checked his watch, surprised to find he'd been gone for an hour, and came to the uncomfortable realisation that Mark had been right. He had to do something about how he felt. And soon.

Hauling himself stiffly up from the bench, he walked back towards the office and into reception, nodding at Mia-Rose as he passed. As he was about to head downstairs, he heard Mark call his name, so he backtracked to his office and stuck his head through the doorway.

'Yeah?'

'Where have you been?'

'I took Calum for a mass...to sort something out.'

'You've been gone ages!'

'Who're you? My boss?'

'Well, technically, yes. Though not actually technically, if you see what I mean. Anyway...' Mark waved him inside. 'Shut the door,' he said, and as Nathan did as he was told, Mark folded his arms.

'So?'

Nathan frowned. 'So what?'

'Leave it with me, you said. Well, in case you haven't noticed, time's running out.'

'Sorry, mate. Like I said, I got a little caught up with a problem Calum was having.'

'Yes, well, he's not the only one having problems. What am I going to do?'

Nathan thought for a moment. 'Just keep doing what you're doing, I guess.'

'And hope it all comes good later?'

'Why not?' He grinned. 'And anyway, I thought you were going to give me a pep talk?'

'Would you take any notice of what I said if I did?'

'I dunno.' Nathan sighed loudly. 'Probably not.'

Mark shook his head slowly. 'Is it really going to be like this every year? Us traipsing out to whatever Anti-Valentine's event you've organised, only for you to get progressively drunker and more morose as the evening wears on simply because you're scared to make another mistake like you did with Ellie?'

'It's not that easy, you know?' Nathan slumped into the nearest chair, then tapped his chest just over his heart. 'It's like I've got something in here that's left over from her dumping me which is obviously trying to avoid more pain, so it's stopping me from doing anything in case I get hurt.'

'Well...' Mark thought for a moment. 'Look at it from a technical point of view.'

'What do you mean by that?'

'You're the techie. So what would you do if you were having hardware issues?'

Nathan scratched his head. 'Start up in safe mode, so I could progressively check what works and what doesn't. But you can't really do that in relationships. And besides, there's nothing wrong with my hardware.'

Mark raised an eyebrow. 'I'll take your word for that. And if it's down to the software?'

'You make sure the old program's completely removed, then install a different one to see if it's any better,' said Nathan, though he suspected that was a problem in itself. While with a computer, it was easy to perform a factory reset to eradicate any old software, where people were concerned it wasn't quite so straightforward. No matter what he did, he'd always have an imprint of Ellie on his memory. 'But how on earth do I do that in this case?'

Mark shrugged. 'You could start by asking out the next woman you see.'

Nathan opened his mouth to protest, but a knock on the door interrupted them both, and they looked up to see Julie standing in the doorway.

'Nathan, have you got a minute?'

As Mark pretended to be fascinated by something on his computer screen, Nathan prised himself out of his seat. 'Well, maybe not the next one, eh?' he said to Mark, then followed Julie obediently out of the room.

❧

Calum was leaning back in his chair, gazing out of the window as he half-heartedly listened to his weekly conference call with the US. He was desperate for his usual mid-afternoon coffee, but didn't dare make himself one, worried he'd spill it down his miraculously still-crisp white shirt. Though given how good his back was feeling after his shiatsu treatment earlier, things seemed to be looking up. Most importantly, the date was definitely back on. Maybe he'd even suggest they go dancing afterwards. He'd impress Emma with his moves, and then, when the slow songs came on...

He became aware of the American voice on the other end of the line—Mike Peters, Seek's US Sales Director—mentioning his name, and Calum snapped out of his daydream. 'Sorry,' he said. 'The line went funny. Could you repeat that?'

'I was just asking you about your prospects, Calum.'

Calum thought for a moment, then he smiled. 'I'd say they're pretty good.'

'Excellent,' said Mike. 'Care to elaborate?'

'Well, I've got one very strong lead I've been working on for the past couple of weeks.'

'And when do you expect to close it?'

Calum smiled again, but a broader one this time. 'Tonight,' he said.

The call finished, and he stayed at his desk, wondering whether he could get away with not moving between now and six o'clock. Just a few short hours were all he had to get through, and what else could possibly go wrong? Nothing, if he didn't get up, or try to drink any potentially shirt-staining drinks, or attempt to contact (or respond to anything from) Emma. No, he'd finish writing the couple of proposals he'd promised to send out by close of play, then he'd have a little freshen-up and a shave before he left, make sure he got to Old Amsterdam in good time in order to get a good table, and . . . Well, the rest would be up to fate. Or rather, up to Emma.

He swivelled carefully round in his chair, first one way and then the other. His back seemed fine, and he was just considering risking a trip to the toilet when Sophie stuck her head around the door.

'How's it going?'

'Good, thanks.' Calum stood up slowly. 'Considering.'

'Getting nervous?'

He nodded. 'Yup. But in a good way, I think. How about you?'

She shrugged. 'Oh, you know. Julie's got me working on this campaign.'

'Tight deadline?'

Sophie nodded. 'Tonight.'

'Anything I can help you with?'

She shook her head, and then, as if reconsidering his offer, Sophie took a half-step into the room. 'Actually, Calum, there is something.'

'Name it.'

'I need to . . . play a joke on someone. Well, two people, actually.'

'April Fool's not for another six weeks.'

'No, it's for tonight. Nathan and Mark have been . . . Well, what they've been doing isn't important. But what I want you to do is. And requires the utmost discretion.'

'Does it involve any physical activity, or anything . . . messy?'

'Um, no.'

'Fine.' Calum grinned. 'Count me in.'

'Great. And remember, it's super top secret.'

'Sounds intriguing.'

'And we'll need a diversion. At around a quarter to four.'

Calum nodded. 'No problem,' he said. As far as diversions went, he knew just the thing.

৵৩

Julie Marshall strolled as casually as she could into Nathan's room, trying to keep a neutral expression on her face as he sat down behind his desk. She pushed the door shut behind her, then changed her mind and decided to leave it open a foot or so—she didn't want things turning nasty, and if Nathan had a temper anything like Philip's, she might need to make a quick escape.

She stopped herself, wondering when she'd become so cynical, knowing she shouldn't tar all men with the same brush. She'd just been unlucky with Philip—she had to keep telling herself that, at least—though she'd thought Mark Webster had been different, and look how that had turned out.

As Nathan smiled up at her, she flirted briefly with the possibility of briefly flirting with him—after all, he was very good-looking, and if he did have a thing for her, well, she knew she should be flattered. She'd never really studied him up close, and she could certainly see what Sophie... Sophie. Julie suddenly remembered why she was here.

'What can I do you for?'

'Well...' Julie wondered whether she should sit down, then decided to remain standing, reminding herself she might need to make a run for it. 'It's a little sensitive, actually.'

Nathan raised an eyebrow. 'Oh yes?'

'Yes. I...' Julie took a deep breath. 'Someone in this office has...' She cleared her throat. '...sent someone something.'

'An attachment?'

'No, not an attachment. And they've given them something too.'

'A virus?' Nathan looked puzzled. 'I've warned everyone about forwarding those chain emails. Or was it one of those Viagra advertisements? That stuff's not the real thing, you know. Not that I'd expect you to know that.' He laughed. 'Or be buying it, of course.'

'No. Nothing like that. It wasn't an email. And no-one's given anyone else a virus. I mean...' She felt herself colour slightly. 'Someone's actually sent someone a card.'

'An e-card?'

'No, an actual card. A Valentine's card.' Julie couldn't meet Nathan's eyes. 'Today.'

'Which, being Valentine's Day, would be appropriate.'

'Well, yes, of course. And yet, no.'

Nathan leant back in his chair and laced his fingers behind his head. Was Julie talking about the card he'd received this morning? 'I'm not quite following you.'

'Sorry.' Julie was beginning to wish she had sat down. 'What I'm trying to say is...' She thought for a moment, wondering exactly what it was she was trying to say, then remembered her earlier sur-real conversation with Mark and felt a sense of déjà vu. 'That's what I'm trying to say. Well, the opposite, actually. That it wasn't, like you said, appropriate.'

'The card? Or the person who sent it?' Nathan folded his arms. 'Or the person they sent it to?'

Julie scratched her head. 'Well, no, it was a lovely card. And I'm sure the person who sent it is lovely too. But like I said, it was...'

Nathan relaxed a little. So she wasn't talking about the card he'd found on his desk this morning. 'Inappropriate?'

'Exactly.' Julie nodded. 'And I don't know whether the sender felt that the, ahem, receiver had done anything to encourage them, but if they have, then it wasn't on purpose. So I just thought it was worth getting out in the open the fact that, while the person who received it was...' She tried to pick her words carefully, not wanting to sound ungrateful or hurt Nathan's feelings. '...flattered, there's just no way that the, shall we say, sentiment can be returned.'

'Right.' Nathan glanced briefly at his laptop screen, where an email had just pinged into his inbox from Mark, and he didn't have to open it to know what it probably said. 'And you're telling me this because...'

'Well, because I thought the person who sent the card might want to know that...' Julie paused again. Know what? She decided to end the sentence there. 'I mean, know that.'

Nathan had to stop himself from smiling. All this beating around the bush wasn't like Julie, though what it seemed to prove was that she couldn't have thought the card had come from him. No, unfortunately this was obviously her way of telling him she knew it was from Mark, and making sure the message got back to him that she wasn't interested without them having to have an embarrassing showdown at the bowling later. Though given how flustered she seemed, this was evidently embarrassing enough for her already.

He looked back up at her, and Julie couldn't tell whether he was offended or not. 'And you're sure, are you?'

'Sure about what?'

'That the sentiment's . . . unwelcome.'

Julie nodded, then shook her head. 'Not unwelcome, no. Just . . .'

'Inappropriate?'

'Exactly.'

'That's a shame,' said Nathan, already wondering how on earth he'd give Mark the bad news.

Isn't it? thought Julie, because it hadn't been Mark who'd sent the card. And while in truth she was flattered that Nathan, for want of a better word, fancied her, her disappointment at a lack of interest from Mark outweighed that by quite some way.

For a moment, she thought of telling Nathan that Sophie would be more than happy to step into her shoes, but now perhaps wasn't the time. That was a little like getting that card at Monopoly that said you'd won second prize in a beauty contest. And a consolation prize was never something to celebrate.

'So, am I understood?'

'Loud and clear.' Nathan saluted smartly, and to her surprise, Julie found herself a little miffed he didn't seem that upset. 'You are still coming tonight, though?'

'Tonight?' Julie thought quickly. She could still go—after all, even if there was an atmosphere, it would be preferable to the one at home. But the last thing she wanted was for Nathan to be spending the evening gazing adoringly at her as she bowled, while Sophie would no doubt be staring at her with the opposite sentiment. And even though she'd be missing an evening with Mark, and the possibility (though, admittedly, it seemed like quite a slim one now) of a repeat performance of what happened at Christmas, she knew that what she had to do would be best for all concerned. 'Sorry. No. I can't. Not because of this, you understand. It's just that . . . Something's come up. Work. You know how it is?'

Nathan smiled a tight-lipped smile. 'Well, that's a shame too,' he said.

And for the second time in as many minutes, Julie found herself agreeing with him.

~

Calum's phone pinged to tell him it was three forty-five, so he saved the proposal he'd been writing, took his glasses off and wiped the lenses with the end of his tie, then strolled downstairs and made his way towards the reception desk. He didn't know why Sophie wanted to play a trick on Mark and Nathan—he could only assume it was something to do with tonight—and seeing as he wasn't going to Anti-Valentine's, he'd decided the fewer questions he asked, the better. Mia-Rose was on a call, so he waited until she'd finished, then cleared his throat.

'If the phone rings again, don't answer it.'

Mia-Rose widened her eyes. 'Sounds exciting.'

'Not really. Just fire drill time. We need to test the system and make sure everyone pays attention.'

'Now?'

'Actually, in about five minutes. You remember how it goes?'

'You get them out, and I make sure they're all there.'

Calum blushed. 'Have you got the personnel list?'

'Sure.' Mia-Rose hit a couple of buttons on her computer, and then printed off a record of everyone whose key card swipes said they were in the building. 'Here.'

'Thanks.' He took the list, crossed his and Sophie's names off it, and handed it back to Mia-Rose. 'Right,' he said, leading her over to the alarm box in the corner. 'Usual drill, though today I'd like you to actually sound the alarm, if you don't mind?'

'Ooh,' said Mia-Rose. 'Are you sure I'm ready for the responsibility?'

Calum nodded, her irony lost on him. 'First thing you need to do is make sure the link to the fire station is disabled.'

'Why?'

'Because we don't want any firemen turning up.'

'Spoilsport.'

Calum sighed exaggeratedly, then reached up and turned the switch off. 'Then, you just press this one,' he said, pointing to the large red button next to it.

Mia-Rose peered at the panel. 'The one with "test" written underneath it?'

'That's the one,' said Calum, before realising she was teasing him.

'I think I get it.'

'Great.' He pulled his sleeve up to reveal his watch, then tapped the dial. 'And then, at four o'clock...'

'That's when the big hand's on twelve, and the little...'

'Yes, very funny. Just press the button, will you?'

Mia-Rose frowned exaggeratedly. 'Now?'

'No, at four...' Calum stopped talking, and wondered why he was always like this with women.

'You're so easy to get!' said Mia-Rose, with a smile. 'Don't worry. I'll make sure I push all the right buttons when the time comes.'

Calum blushed again. He could only hope he'd do the same for Emma later.

❦

For the fourth time since Julie had left his office, Nathan Field picked his phone up and began to dial Mark's number, then put it down again without making the call. Something about her attitude hadn't quite added up, as if... He didn't know what it was as if. His expertise, if you could call it that, was still a little rusty, and besides, what would he say, given how vague she'd been?

What was clear was that Julie had pretty much told him to warn Mark off, and Nathan suspected it was probably better to tell him that as soon as possible, rather than let Mark waste his time, or build his hopes up only to have them shattered when she didn't turn up this evening. And given that he'd already spent the best part of the afternoon avoiding the issue by dealing with a problem with Seek's server that could easily have waited, he decided he'd better get on with it.

He responded to the last couple of work emails that had come in while he'd been out with Calum, then popped to the toilet, helped himself to a drink from the water-cooler at the top of the stairs, then realised he'd run out of delaying tactics, so he walked as jauntily as he could into Mark's office and shut the door behind him. Before he could say anything, Mark pointed excitedly at the carrier bag on his desk.

'Look.' Mark removed a blue-cellophane-wrapped chocolate biscuit from the bag and handed it to him. 'It's a "Taxi."'

'I haven't seen one of these for years. Where did you get it from?'

'The retro sweet shop on Floral Street. You said to carry on with what I was doing, so I just nipped out on the off-chance.' He grinned, evidently very pleased with himself. 'I thought I'd go and bump into Julie in the kitchen, and see if she wanted to share it.'

'Huh?'

'Share a taxi. Can you see where I'm going with all this?'

'To an employment tribunal, if you're not careful.' Nathan peered closely at the bar and then, before Mark could stop him, he tore the wrapper open and took a bite.

'What are you doing?' Mark snatched the biscuit back and, for a moment, seemed to be considering trying to patch it up. 'That was the last one they had.' He patted his pocket to check for his wallet and made angrily for the door. 'I'll have to see if I can find one somewhere else now.'

'I wouldn't bother, if I were you.'

Mark stopped in his tracks, one hand on the door handle. 'Why not?'

'You won't need it.'

'What? Why not?'

'Because...' Nathan took a deep breath. 'That thing Julie wanted to see me about earlier...'

'Was?' Mark was sounding alarmed.

'Did you want the good news or the bad news?'

'I don't know.' Mark threw his hands up in the air. 'Is there good news?'

'Kind of.'

'I'll have that, then.'

'Great. Well, she definitely doesn't think I sent her that card.'

'How do you know?'

'She as good as said so.'

'As good as? Or actually?'

'As good as.'

'And does she think it was from me?'

Nathan nodded. 'Yup. Well, I'm pretty sure she does.'

'Pretty sure? But not...' Mark thought for a moment. 'One hundred and ten percent sure?'

'Stop splitting hairs. You told me you were worried she thought the card was from me. She doesn't. You should be happy.'

'Yes. You're right. Sorry.' Mark sat back down behind his desk. 'Hold on. You said there was bad news.'

'Oh yeah. That. Well, she's not coming this evening.'

'What?' Mark looked crestfallen. 'Why not?'

Nathan shrugged. 'Beats me. She just marched in and said so.'

'For god's sake, Nathan.' Mark stood up again, and began pacing anxiously around the office. 'What did she say, exactly?'

'Hey, don't shoot the messenger. She just came in and gave me some weird third-person speech about how that Valentine's card you'd sent her was inappropriate, and that she wasn't coming this evening.'

Mark stared at him. 'Inappropriate?'

'That's what she said.'

'What did she mean by that?'

Mark's pacing was getting more frantic, so Nathan got up, grabbed him by the shoulders, and steered him back into his chair. 'Er... The opposite of "appropriate," I think.'

'Thank you for explaining that so well.' Mark leant back and stared at the ceiling. 'Christ, I almost wish she did think the card was from you now.'

'Sorry, mate.'

'You're sure she doesn't.'

Nathan nodded. 'She referred to that night.' He picked up the remainder of the chocolate bar. 'In the taxi.'

Mark looked up sharply. 'I'm guessing it wasn't in a good way?'

'Well, no. She said she knew she'd done something to encourage you. But that it hadn't been...' Nathan cleared his throat. '...on purpose.'

Mark stared at him disbelievingly. 'Not on purpose?'

'That's what she said. Then she told me she'd have to cry off this evening.'

'Did you at least try and convince her she should still come?'

Nathan shrugged, then popped the last of the biscuit into his mouth and chewed it slowly, making Mark wait a frustratingly long time until he'd swallowed it. 'Didn't seem much point. Seeing how she'd said how the card was...'

'Inappropriate. I know.' Mark glared at him. 'She's definitely not going?'

'No. She said she had to stay here. Something to do with work.'

'Well, that's just brilliant, isn't it?' He slumped back into his chair. 'The object of my affections...'

'Objects to them?'

'Thanks, Nathan.' Mark shook his head slowly, then picked his phone up.

'Who're you calling?'

'Who do you think?'

'The Samaritans?'

'Julie. I've got to at least apologise to her.'

Nathan reached out and grabbed Mark's wrist. 'Hold on. Is that such a good idea?'

Mark placed the receiver back down, then put his head in his hands. 'What else can I possibly do?'

Nathan started to answer, but Mark couldn't hear him. The fire alarm had just gone off.

❧

Calum stood back as a flood of people in various states of agitation came streaming down the stairs. 'Don't panic,' he said, bracing himself for the usual grumpy comments, particularly as it looked like it had just started spitting outside. 'It's just a test.'

'Really?' Aisleen said sarcastically, almost tripping down the last step, before grabbing a huffing and puffing Mary for support.

'Good timing,' said Mary, nodding towards the mug of hot water and lemon she was carrying that Aisleen's grab had just made her spill.

He held his breath as Benedict strode past him, then waited until everyone else had made their way outside before marching smartly over to Mark's office and pushing the door open. Mark and Nathan were deep in conversation, so he cleared his throat loudly, and they looked wearily up from the desk.

'Didn't you hear the alarm?'

'Pardon?' shouted Nathan. 'I can't hear you for that annoying ringing sound.'

'I said . . . Yes, very funny.'

'I take it this is a drill?' said Mark.

Calum folded his arms. 'Not as far as you should be concerned. We have to do this at least four times a year. By law.'

'Yes, but in February?' Nathan looked at him pleadingly. 'Can't you at least reschedule these things for the summer months?'

'That's a good idea,' said Calum. 'Because fires never happen in the winter.'

'Well, in the future, can we at least not have them when it's raining? Because technically, fires and rain don't...'

'Outside, please. Now.'

'Okay, okay,' sighed Nathan.

Reluctantly, the two of them stood up, and as Mark reached for his briefcase, Calum cleared his throat again.

'Leave everything,' he said. 'You won't be there for long.'

As Mark did as he was told, Nathan walked out of the office and made for the stairs to the basement.

'Where are you going?'

'To get my phone. It's on my desk.' said Nathan.

'Leave it,' ordered Calum. 'No one wants to read "burned to death because he'd forgotten his iPhone" on someone's gravestone.'

'But it's the latest model.'

'Sorry.'

Calum held the front door open as Nathan reluctantly followed Mark outside into the street and then peered along the pavement, where the rest of the team were huddled impatiently under the awning of the shop next door. He smiled awkwardly as Mia-Rose gave him the thumbs-up, then turned to Nathan, who'd paused in the doorway.

'Problem?'

'Aren't you coming?'

Calum shook his head. 'Someone has to make sure everyone got out safely.'

Nathan rolled his eyes. 'Calum, the building's not really on fire.'

'Even so...'

He left Mia-Rose ticking off everyone's name on the register, locked the door to the street from the inside, then—pausing to switch the bell off on the panel—nipped into Mark's office and found his iPhone in his briefcase. As quickly as he could manage, Calum removed the protective leather case, stabbed at a couple of buttons on the screen and did as Sophie had requested, and then sprinted downstairs to the technical support room. He found Nathan's phone where he'd left it on his desk, pulled the black silicone case off, and fitted it onto Mark's phone, before slipping Nathan's phone into Mark's case. Then it would simply be a matter of putting them in their alternate locations, before...

'Whose phone is that?'

The voice made Calum freeze, though he relaxed when he spun round and saw it was Sophie.

'Mark's.'

'In Nathan's case?'

'Yup.'

'Great.' Sophie took the phone, touched the screen, and smiled. 'Thanks, Calum.' She placed it on the desk, then sat down in front of Nathan's laptop, and, thankful for her copy of 'Windows For Dummies' (which she'd spent the last half-hour consulting), Sophie right-clicked in the bottom right hand corner of the screen. A few key-presses later, she'd done what she needed to.

'Can I let them back in?' said Calum, peering up the stairs and out through the front door, where most of Seek's staff could be seen shivering on the pavement. 'They look like they're getting a little chilly.'

Quickly, Sophie scanned the office walls, relieved there wasn't a clock there, and allowed herself to believe her—or rather,

Julie's—plan might just work. 'Sure.' She pointed at Calum's hand. 'But hadn't you better put that where it belongs first?'

Calum stared at the phone he'd forgotten he was holding, then ran up the stairs to Mark's office, and slipped it into his briefcase. 'You ready?' he shouted.

'As I'll ever be,' replied Sophie.

As Calum unlocked the front door, Sophie got up from behind Nathan's desk, adjusted her watch, then headed out into the hallway, hiding round the corner until she heard Nathan come back in. Once he'd disappeared back into his office, she waited for a count of five, pulled her coat on, then stuck her head in through his open doorway.

'Right,' she said, cheerily. 'See you there, then.'

Nathan checked the time on his Omega, then smiled up at her. 'You skiving off early?'

Sophie made a play of looking at her own watch. 'I thought we had to be there at five-thirty.'

Nathan nodded. 'We do. But it's only...'

'Five to five,' said Sophie, innocently.

Nathan looked at his watch. 'No, it's five to four.'

'Five to five,' insisted Sophie. 'Look.'

She stuck her wrist out in front of him, hoping Nathan wouldn't laugh at her cheap Casio. 'Your watch must have stopped.'

Nathan frowned, then glanced at the corner of his computer screen, then—as Julie had predicted he would, checked his phone. 'But...' He tapped the dial of his Omega. 'Bollocks,' he said, leaping to his feet, then he blushed. 'Sorry, Soph.'

'That's OK.'

'I've got to run,' he said, reaching for his jacket. 'I promised everyone I'd get there early to sort out the shoes.'

'Sooner you than me.'

'You couldn't tell everyone else not to rush, could you?' said Nathan, grabbing his crash helmet, and as he ran past her and up the stairs, Sophie nodded.

'My pleasure,' she said, even though she wouldn't need to.

∾

Nathan steered his Vespa along Oxford Street, thankful that at least the rain had stopped but cursing the rest of his luck. The one day he needed to be on time, his trusty old Omega (the one present from Ellie he'd not either given to a charity shop or sold on eBay) had let him down. He almost found it ironic it would happen today, and while he didn't believe in fate, this... Well, Nathan had to admit it was a little spooky.

He knew these watches needed servicing, but in all the years he'd had it, it hadn't stopped once. He hadn't even ever needed to wind it, seeing as it was one of those automatic models: when Ellie had presented it to him, she'd told him it wound itself up every time he moved his wrist, and he'd observed that she'd better never leave him, otherwise he might over-wind it, and they'd both laughed until it hurt. Then she'd left him a few months later, and he hadn't found the joke the slightest bit funny.

The watch had been expensive, too. He'd admired it in the window of a shop on the Strand when he'd met her for dinner one evening, never expecting her to surprise him with it a couple of days later. Now he could see that perhaps she'd bought it out of guilt, but at the time, he just felt it showed how much she'd loved him. He'd been too wrapped up in their future to see it as just a present. And today, perhaps appropriately, it had stopped.

Still, at least he was making good time—for some reason the rush hour didn't seem to have started yet—so he accelerated round the roundabout at an unusually traffic-free Marble Arch (muttering 'yes' to himself as he managed to cut up two taxis in the process) and headed towards Lancaster Gate. He checked his mirror in case the taxis were chasing him, hell-bent on revenge, but they were heading down Park Lane, so he slowed down a little—the last thing he wanted was to be stopped by the police.

He rode on for a couple of minutes, then turned right up Queensway and made his way towards the Whiteleys shopping centre, relieved when he found a parking bay just outside the main doors. Pulling the Vespa onto its stand, he padlocked his helmet to the handlebars, made sure the bike's top-box was locked, and then checked his watch (then remembered it was an hour slow). With a shake of his head, he headed straight down to the basement and rushed breathlessly into the bowling alley.

'Hi,' said the girl behind reception. 'Can I help you?'

'I've got a booking.'

'For?'

'Field.'

'It's called a lane.'

'Pardon?'

'You bowl in a lane. Not a field.'

'No, my name is Field.' He nodded towards the computer. 'And I'm in a bit of a hurry.'

'Suit yourself.' The girl consulted her screen. 'At five-thirty, right? You can go on early if you like. No extra charge.'

Nathan nodded, deciding not to thank the girl sarcastically for the offer of the free ten minutes. 'Any of the others here yet?'

The girl peered exaggeratedly around the cavernous interior of the building. Apart from a Japanese family chattering excitedly by one of the lanes at the far end, the place was deserted. 'Unless that's them, then it doesn't look like it.'

'Right.' He fished in his pocket and handed her a piece of paper. 'They might be in a bit of a rush when they get here, so these are their shoe sizes, if you wouldn't mind…'

The girl made a face to suggest it might be the highlight of her evening. 'No problem.'

'Thanks,' said Nathan. 'Oh, is anyone booked after us? Just in case my lot are late, and we don't get started on time.'

The girl pursed her lips and looked at him. 'It's Valentine's Day,' she said. 'We're a bowling alley. I'm surprised we're even open.'

He slipped his shoes off and gave them to the girl, who took them at arm's length and then handed him a pair of red-and-white bowling shoes in return. Nathan did his best not to inhale as he put them on, then he made his way over to the bar, 'bought' himself his free drink, and took it to the lane to wait.

8

Sophie waited until she was sure Nathan had left the building, then ran back up to her office and collected the Selfridges bag from where she'd hidden it in her filing cabinet.

'Everything going to plan?' said Julie, looking up from her laptop. Her suit was speckled with rain from where she'd been waiting outside during the fire drill, and Sophie felt a little guilty.

'So far.'

'And are you ready?'

Sophie held the bag up and gave it a little shake. 'Almost.'

'Well, good luck.'

'Thanks,' said Sophie, making for the door. 'And don't take this the wrong way, but I hope I don't see you later.'

'Oh, don't worry. I've decided I'm not going anyway.'

'No?' Sophie paused in the doorway. 'Why ever not?'

Julie turned her attention back to her computer screen. 'I've got some work to finish. Besides, you're not going to be there, and the last thing I want is a drunken evening with that lot,' she said, flicking her eyes at the door.

Sophie made a face. 'I wish I had your confidence Nathan and I won't be there. After all, I've got a window of less than an hour.'

'Well, don't waste it talking to me, then.'

Sophie hovered in the doorway. 'You're sure you don't want to go?'

Julie shook her head. 'Like I said—work to do.'

'But Mark will be there.'

Julie looked up sharply. 'Pardon?'

'Mark Webster. He's going.'

'And what would that have to do with me?'

Sophie reddened. 'It's just...' Sophie pushed the door to. 'At the Christmas party. I mean, after the Christmas party...'

Julie tried to focus on her laptop. 'What about it?'

'I saw... Well, I thought I saw... I mean, it's none of my business, but you and Mark...'

'There is no "me and Mark," Sophie.'

'No, I'm not trying to imply anything. But...'

'But what?'

'Don't you think there could be?'

Julie swivelled round on her chair and folded her arms. 'No, Sophie, I don't. Especially since...' She caught herself, deciding now wasn't the time to come clean about her home situation, particularly given Sophie's time constraints. 'Well, especially since he didn't even send me a Valentine's card.'

'Ah,' said Sophie. 'Okay. Sorry.'

Julie forced a smile. 'Not to worry,' she said, as cheerfully as she could muster, and then tapped the face of her watch. 'Now go!'

'Yes boss.'

'And Sophie?'

'Yes?'

'I hope you get what you want.'

'Thanks. You too.'

As Julie bit off a hollow laugh, Sophie made her way to the toilet and locked herself inside the furthest cubicle. Mindful not to drop the bustier on the floor, she removed it from the bag, trying to avoid looking at the price tag as she tugged it off the label. Still, she told herself, it was an investment, just like the lottery ticket she bought herself every Saturday. Though if it was a choice between the roll-over jackpot or a roll-over with Nathan, she knew which she'd prefer.

She carefully hung the bustier on the hook on the back of the door, stripped down to her underwear, then took that off and dropped it into the Selfridges bag, feeling suddenly nervous at the prospect of being naked in front of another human being. She hadn't felt like this for a long time—she and Darren had been together for so long he'd even taken to using the toilet in front of her (not one of Sophie's favourite Kodak moments from their relationship) and when you got to that stage of familiarity, simply being naked in front of your partner kind of lost any embarrassment. But the fact that in just a few hours, she might be standing in front of someone new, undressed—and him like that in front of her...

Sophie's heart started to beat faster at the thought, and she supposed she should be grateful for the dress (or rather, undress) rehearsal she'd had in Selfridges earlier, and she was pretty sure that that, at least, had gone well. She shivered in anticipation, then found herself shivering from the cold, so she pulled the bustier on quickly, making sure she knew where all the hooks were so she could get it off without ripping it if she needed to undress in a hurry later. And while the thought was rather appealing, Sophie doubted she'd really sleep with Nathan tonight. She'd never been that kind of girl—apart from the odd drunken snog, she'd never had anything approaching a one-night stand.

Though maybe she was changing—after all, here she was, preparing to parade in front of Nathan dressed like this, with the sole purpose of trying to get him into bed. But this was what London girls did, Sophie reminded herself. They were modern. Liberated. Independent. Made their own rules. Could even behave like men, if that was what they felt like. And if that included going to bed with Nathan on their first 'date,' well, that was just what she'd do.

Sophie almost smiled, wondering whether she could remember what to do. Two years was a long time, after all. Then again, she'd waited this long, so what were a few more days? Maybe she'd just use her new look to entice Nathan. Drive him into a state of high excitement, and then she'd have him just where she wanted him... She shivered for a different reason this time and smoothed the bustier down with her hands, loving the way the lace felt. There was no doubt about it, this new underwear she'd bought was empowering. That kind of behaviour was never something she'd have thought about dressed in her granny knickers, but what was the phrase—if you feel good on the inside, then you'll look good on the outside? Surely the same applied to looking good on the inside too?

She checked her watch, then quickly pulled the rest of her clothes back on and exited the cubicle. Making sure the bathroom was empty, she adopted a 'bowling' stance in front of the mirror, unbuttoning her blouse so it gaped just enough to give a flash of the bustier when she bent over. Pleased with the result, Sophie strode out of the toilets, her head held high, nodding confidently at the girls in the admin team, and as she walked along the corridor, she stuffed the bag containing her old bra and pants into the nearest bin. No longer was she an M&S underwear kind of girl. Never again would she wear control pants, or big knickers, or anything that wasn't at least made out of lace. Maybe she wouldn't have to. Especially if, from tonight onwards, all her underwear would be a present from Nathan.

She strutted out of the office and along Bateman Street, and pushed her way through the smokers standing outside the pub on the corner, mindful of the heads that turned as she did so. Forget smiling when you were on the phone—this was the way to feel confident, and—dare she say—sexy. Throwing caution to the wind, and ignoring the lack of money in her bank account, Sophie withdrew her last twenty pounds from the cashpoint on the corner, then impetuously flagged down a passing taxi.

'Where to, my love?' asked the driver, and Sophie smiled.

'Yes,' she said, nonchalantly. 'That's exactly where I'm going.'

❧

Nathan was sitting in SuperBowl, frowning at his phone. That was the problem with these basement venues—no reception, especially, it seemed, where an iPhone was concerned—and for some reason, he couldn't even work out how to unlock the screen. Whether that was down to the lack of network, or some new feature on the latest model that he'd accidentally activated he wasn't sure, but the last thing he wanted to do was try and reset it when he was nowhere near his backup. Still, that was Apple for you, he thought. Style over substance. He knew a few people like that too. Perhaps he'd almost married one of them.

The other thing Nathan couldn't understand was where everybody was, seeing as no-one from the office had turned up yet. According to the clock on his phone (the one feature that seemed to be working), they should have been here changing their shoes and making the usual jokes about their balls ten minutes ago, but as yet, there was no sign of anyone. What was worse was he had no way of getting in touch with any of them—he didn't have time to go back to the office to call from there, and even heading upstairs to ring wasn't an option given his phone's mysteriously locked status—and the fact that he'd have to change his shoes. No, he'd just have to stick it out and hope they turned up soon.

Nathan supposed he should be pleased for them. Chances were their non-attendance meant they'd managed to get a date after all (though he was surprised they all had), but on the other hand, it made him look like a particularly sad Billy No-Mates, and that wasn't what he wanted from this evening at all. Plus, he enjoyed bowling—even though Ellie had hated it. She'd hated karaoke too, and ice-skating, and amusement parks, and in fact now he thought about it, most things that people had fun at, Ellie had seemed to dislike. All in all, Nathan wondered just what it was they used to do together—apart from visit IKEA, that is. Maybe he'd just imagined they'd had stuff in common. Maybe, just maybe, he was better off without her. Though not, he was sure, without anyone.

He wished he hadn't rushed over here. Now he was stuck with his Vespa, and he didn't want to leave it outside the shopping centre overnight in case it got vandalised, which meant he couldn't drink too much... All in all, not the best start to the evening. He picked up his beer and wondered whether he should just finish it and go. He could still ride home after just the one, and it was probably better to go now than risk having to fight his way through all the romancing couples on the streets. But just as he was about to do exactly that, he felt a tap on his shoulder.

'Soph!' Nathan put his glass down and stood up. 'I could kiss you!'

Sophie blushed. 'Feel free' had been her first response, though she hadn't dared voice it. 'Where is everyone?' she asked, as genuinely as she could.

Nathan shrugged. 'Beats me.'

Sophie made a play of looking at her watch. In truth, she'd been hiding behind the Coke machine in the corner for the last ten minutes, waiting for an appropriate time to come over, and while she'd almost lost her nerve, it was only when she'd suspected Nathan was about to leave that she'd plucked up the courage to make the ten-yard walk.

'Should we wait, do you think?'

Nathan shook his head. 'I'm not sure there's much point. You sure you still want to bother?'

Sophie gazed at her feet. 'After I've gone and changed into these fetching shoes? You bet!'

Nathan beamed at her, and her heart almost skipped a beat. 'Well, looks like it's just you and me, then.'

'Great. That is, if you don't mind...'

'Don't mind what?'

Sophie grinned at him, then walked over and picked up the nearest bowling ball. 'Losing.'

❧

Julie finished the report she'd been working on for the past hour, then she removed her spare running gear from her bottom drawer, locked her office door from the inside, and began to get changed. She hadn't been planning to run again this evening, but today just felt like a two-session day, and she always kept some spare running gear at the office, though partly because she never knew when the tube drivers might go on strike, and if that happened, running was as good a way of getting home as any.

She was still a little annoyed about missing this evening's bowling—and boy, did she need a drink after such an up-and-down day. She'd been so flattered when she'd thought she'd been the target of Mark's romantic campaign, especially when she'd seen how much thought had gone into it (she couldn't remember when she'd been so clever, so targeted on a marketing campaign, for example) and then, when the card and the balloons and the chocolates had turned out to have come from Nathan...Well, she supposed she was still flattered, but that had been somewhat outweighed by her disappointment both that they hadn't come from Mark and by her annoyance that he must have been bragging about what had happened the night of the Christmas party. How else would Nathan have known what to send her? She'd even eaten all the chocolate "kisses"—another reason she was going for a second run—though she'd been amused by Sophie's reluctance to share them as she'd 'not wanted to look fat' in her lingerie this evening. Julie smiled as she remembered their conversation—Sophie had a great figure, and even if she hadn't, underwear like that was probably worth at least a couple of dress sizes.

She finished lacing up her Nikes, then pulled her fleece running gloves on and began her stretching routine. She still found it strange Nathan could have been sweet on her and yet she'd had no idea about it, but then again, she'd had no idea about Philip having an affair and she'd thought Mark had fancied her, so maybe she was just rubbish at this whole 'men' thing. And to have married someone like Philip in the first place—well, maybe that just proved it.

Then again, people changed, didn't they? He certainly wasn't the man she married, and Julie had to face the fact she probably wasn't the same person either. Who'd have thought she'd have kissed one of her colleagues, then have had to let another one down gently, all in the space of a couple of months? More importantly, she never imagined she'd be training for the marathon, and here she was, off out running when she should have been out enjoying herself.

She lifted one foot up onto her desk and pulled herself into a painful hamstring stretch, wondering what the future held for her. Should she try and patch things up with Philip and pretend the whole affair never happened? More importantly, did she want to?

Certainly, he'd begged her to forgive him, though she was finding that hard. She'd never been very good at forgiving and forgetting, and what he'd done would take a lot of that. Plus she still didn't know why Philip had done it. He'd blamed her, but had it really been her fault? Julie had to concede that maybe she'd been too focused on her career. But so had he, and now he was focused on a different one, though despite his best efforts, his writing was hardly a 'career.'

And while Philip had managed to shrug off the countless rejections he'd had from the literary world, Julie was the one who felt rejected, as if she hadn't been enough for him. It was partly the reason she'd started running—to get into shape, perhaps make herself fanciable again. And maybe it was working—after all, Mark had fancied her enough to kiss her (or rather, kiss her back), and Nathan had fancied her enough to send her a Valentine's card. And while neither of those two things had come to anything, Julie told herself she should at least take heart from them both. And maybe she just had to treat her situation with Philip like the marathon training she was doing—at times, it was painful, but she was doing it so she could survive in the long run.

With a sigh, she made her way out of the building, pulled her bobble hat down over her ears, clicked 'play' on her iPod, and set off at a fast jog down towards the river.

∽

Calum waited until the office was nearly empty, then picked up his toiletries bag and headed into the toilets. He'd initially been worried about not having time to go back home to get changed between work and tonight's date, though in actual fact, he'd realised wearing his work suit was probably a good idea, given he wouldn't have known what was appropriate dress for a date anyway. 'Smart-casual' (whatever that was) was what the Frequently Asked Questions page on LondonDate had recommended, and though Calum had gone out clothes shopping at the weekend clutching a couple of torn-out pages from his latest copy of GQ for inspiration, he'd returned home empty-handed, having quickly come to the conclusion that skinny jeans were only good if you had skinny genes, and to wear anything else from the pages of the magazine would be to walk the dangerous line between either trying too hard and not trying at all. Besides, if he wore a suit, Calum reasoned, the easiest way to pull off the smart-casual look might simply be to take off his tie.

A double-check of the time told him he had just under an hour, so he unzipped the toiletries bag and spread the contents—electric shaver, moisturiser, toothbrush, toothpaste, dental floss, mouthwash, aftershave, deodorant—out on the shelf behind the sink, then examined his face in the mirror. Under the harsh bathroom light, his fast-growing but patchy facial hair wasn't a good look, hence the reason he'd waited until just before meeting Emma to shave, though for a moment, he considered going like he was. Perhaps Emma would like the 'designer stubble' look, though trouble was, with his bright red uneven growth, it looked like the designer was a five-year-old.

He switched the shaver on and carefully began shaving, under his left side-burn first, then across his cheek, down to the sporadic growth on his neck, and finally up over the left side of his chin and under his nose, then he stood back and rubbed that half of his face—as smooth as the proverbial baby's backside, to quote his mum earlier. If there was going to be kissing tonight—and he at least planned to go for a peck on the cheek at 'hello'—then that would surely do, especially once he'd moisturised. He'd never had a grooming routine until he'd started reading GQ, thinking that 'grooming' was something that only pet owners or paedophiles did, but nowadays the contents of his bathroom cabinet probably put David Beckham's to shame. It was only a pity he couldn't say the same thing about his abs.

He tilted his face to the light and checked his reflection, making sure he hadn't missed any bits, then readied himself to do the same to the other side of his face. But suddenly, the buzzing from his shaver began to get lower, and before he could start on his unshaven right side, the sound died completely. Calum froze, then flicked the shaver's switch off and back on again, but with no success. Trying to ignore the sudden feeling of panic rising in his chest, he hunted around inside his toiletries bag, tipping it upside down and shaking it over the sink, even turning the bag inside out in an attempt to find the power cord. The cord, he suddenly remembered, that was still attached to the shaver socket in his bathroom at home.

Calum examined his reflection in the mirror, wondering what on earth to do. He didn't have time to get home and back, and rushing out to the shops to buy a razor and some shaving foam just wasn't an option, given how his skin tended to develop a rash whenever he wet-shaved. He had some tweezers, so he toyed with the idea of simply plucking out the hairs on the right side of his face, but the one he tried made his eyes water so much with the pain that he soon gave up on that idea.

He told himself to breathe deeply as he considered his options. Short of emptying the shaver and trying to glue the recently removed hair back on again, he supposed he could sit for the whole evening with his hand covering the unshaven side of his face. Or, he could make sure he got one of the corner tables at Old Amsterdam, meaning he could sit sideways on to Emma for the whole night, but that would be tricky to maintain—particularly if she wanted to do one of those continental-style double kisses when they met. Alternatively, he could just pretend he was taking part in one of those 'grow half a beard' things for charity, which would have the added benefit of making him look like a particularly generous, virtuous type, and maybe if he chose the right charity—orphaned children, perhaps, or injured dogs, given Emma's love of them, perhaps even ones that had been hurt by sparks from log fires—he'd gain extra brownie points. Trouble was, whichever of those options he chose wouldn't stop him looking ridiculous.

Then, in the midst of his desperation, Calum had a brainwave. Tottenham Court Road was five minutes away, and the home of about twenty electrical shops—one would surely stock the right kind of power cord. If he hurried, he could be there, back, and shaved within fifteen minutes, still leaving him the best part of three-quarters of an hour before his date.

He stuffed his electric shaver into his trouser pocket, gathered the rest of his toiletries up and shoved them back into their bag, then ran to his office and grabbed his coat from the hook on the inside of the door, sprinted down the stairs, and out of the building.

❧

Mark closed the blinds on his office window, just missing out on what would have been the delicious sight of Julie Marshall running past on the pavement outside. Aware he was in danger of wearing the carpet out, he began pacing round his office, still unable to understand what had happened today—or rather, work out how his carefully laid plans had gone so wrong. He cursed the fact he hadn't been more up front with her, or even sealed the deal when the opportunity had presented itself to him, but then again, he wasn't a salesman, but an accountant. Ironic, then, that this was something he just couldn't figure out.

At the back of his mind, he wasn't convinced Julie had been warning him off. Something about what Nathan had said had made him suspect she might still think Nathan had sent her the card; otherwise surely she'd have mentioned him by name and told Nathan to let him know in no uncertain terms his advances weren't welcome, and yet she hadn't. In fact, she'd sounded more like she'd been warning Nathan off. And given how it had been Julie who'd kissed him... Well, that made her behaviour today all the more puzzling.

The more he thought about it, the more Mark was convinced something just didn't quite ring true. Julie hadn't refused to join them outside Bar Italia, and surely that would have been the obvious thing to do—or a good time to mention something. With both him and Nathan there (and Sophie as a witness) she could have said what she needed to say without any of this subterfuge, but instead she'd waited to catch Nathan on his own—which meant Julie must have thought Nathan had sent her the card. Plus she knew he and Nathan were friends, and because of that, she must have known her warning Nathan off would get back to him—which meant it could be possible she might—in a roundabout way—have been trying to tell him she was still interested. And if that was the case, well, he needed to confront her about the kiss now. See whether he had imagined it, and if not, find out whether it had meant anything at all.

He retrieved his jacket from the back of his chair and slipped it on, straightened his tie, then walked out of his office, carefully locking the door behind him. The building was pretty deserted already—no-one liked to hang around on these winter nights, though he'd often noticed Julie's light still burning long after Sophie and the others had gone home. He'd always been too scared to go and talk to her, though, preferring to pretend to be working late himself, his door open, listening out for her on the stairs, though usually settling for a hasty ''Night' as she hurried past with her head down. This evening, though, half of them would probably be out for a drink before heading over to Nathan's Anti-Valentine's night, and the rest, if they knew what was good for them, were probably off home for a Valentine's rendezvous with their other halves. Which meant he and Julie were unlikely to be disturbed.

He heard a thundering noise, followed by a breathless 'excuse me,' and stepped back quickly to avoid what looked like a half-shaved, charging-at-full-speed Calum, then nervously made his way up the stairs. All he had to do was talk to her like a man. Be honest. Tell her how he felt. Maybe not even that—perhaps he should start by asking her if he'd insulted her by his actions. Most importantly, he needed to ask her out.

But when he got to Julie's office, the lights were off, and the door was locked firmly shut. And Mark couldn't help feeling that was strangely appropriate.

❦

Sophie didn't know whether Nathan was just being kind, but so far she was ahead by around thirty points. She'd started off by pretending she didn't know how to play, and had nearly fainted when Nathan had held her briefly to demonstrate the correct way to swing her bowling arm, and then, when her game had 'miraculously' started to improve, she'd even had a strike, much to Nathan's delight (and Sophie's, when he'd hugged her in celebration). She'd almost wanted to text Darren there and then to thank him for the hours he'd made her spend on the Nintendo version.

Conscious of the time, she'd been playing as fast as she could, and in truth, she found actual bowling (as opposed to the on-screen type) hard going, but Sophie had wanted to make a good impression, so she'd tried not to wince at the effort of constantly lifting the heavy ball up to her shoulder, and done her best to ignore the weakening grip in her bowling hand. In return for the lesson, she'd bought Nathan a drink, in the hope he'd return the compliment elsewhere once they'd finished the game, and then she could go for a different kind of strike—a 'while the iron was hot' one—and certainly, the more she spent time with him, the more she thought Nathan was hot.

Every now and again, he'd glance at the door, though Sophie imagined this was probably to see whether anyone else from the office had turned up rather than because he was looking for an escape route. But she was also aware that after a couple more frames, the others would surely start to arrive, which meant her window of opportunity was closing fast. And it was possibly because that fact was making her nervous, or maybe that she was sweating from the effort of repeatedly lifting the heavy balls, or even that her hand was tired, or her fingers were wet from the condensation on her cocktail glass, but the one thing she hadn't planned on doing this evening was dropping her bowling ball from shoulder height in front of the whole bowling alley. And certainly not onto her foot.

For a moment, Sophie didn't know what to do. Her foot had exploded in the most intense agony, and even the fact that Nathan had lifted her up off her feet and was carrying her back to her seat couldn't take her mind off how painful it was. As he knelt down beside her and gently undid her laces, she was almost beside herself.

'Where does it hurt?'

'My foot,' she whimpered, fighting back the tears, and then, despite her pain, Sophie cursed her stupidity. 'I mean, the middle of my foot. Just behind the toes.'

Gently, Nathan eased her shoe off, and although Sophie was embarrassed at the old pair of socks she was wearing, that was nothing compared to how Nathan's gentle probing up and down her foot was making her flush.

'Can you feel this?'

'Oh yes,' said Sophie, responding to Nathan's gentle pressure.

'What about your toes?'

'What about them?' asked Sophie, worried Nathan was commenting on her cracked nail varnish, or the stupid bunion she was in danger of developing from those one-size-too-small shoes she'd convinced herself to buy from the Russell and Bromley sale.

'Wiggle them for me?'

Sophie did as instructed. 'Ow.'

'Well, they all work, at least.'

'How come you know so much about first aid?'

Nathan shrugged. 'Too many nights spent watching Casualty, I guess.' He gently squeezed her heel. 'How about here?'

'That's fine,' said Sophie, wishing she'd had a pedicure, or at least taken up that special offer that had come through her letterbox last week from some place in Harrow where you stuck your feet in a tank and fish nibbled the dead skin off them. At the time, the idea had revolted her (plus she'd actually considered writing to the place to tell them they should pay her, seeing as she was providing food for their fish), but right now, she'd have swum in shark-infested waters if Nathan had asked her to. At least she'd shaved her legs this morning, and maybe the bustier would distract Nathan from any other imperfections—though she'd look really sexy limping about in it later, she realised.

Just then, the girl from the desk appeared. 'Did you want me to call an ambulance?' she said, peering anxiously over Nathan's shoulder.

'No, I'll live,' said Sophie, allowing Nathan to help her to her feet. But when she tried to put a little weight on her foot, she squealed.

'Are you sure?' said Nathan. 'I'll come with you, if you like?'

Sophie thought for a moment. Through her pain, she pictured Nathan, dutifully holding her hand at her bedside, then perhaps taking her home afterwards. She'd invite him in for a coffee, and then maybe he'd carry her up to her bedroom, help her get undressed, and then... Well, the rest was up to fate. And her expensive lingerie.

'Maybe that would be best,' she said, weakly.

9

Sophie Jones couldn't believe her luck. Here she was, snuggled tightly up against Nathan, her arms wrapped around his warm body, her face pressed into his broadly muscled back. If only her foot wasn't killing her, she'd have perhaps enjoyed being on the back of his Vespa more.

So far, he'd turned out to be a bit of a knight in shining armour, insisting it'd be quicker if they went on the bike rather than waiting for an ambulance, then carrying her outside, even letting her wear his helmet when the spare he kept in the bike's top-box didn't fit her properly, and now they were roaring towards A&E at top speed. With the throb of the Vespa's engine half-deadened by the icy wind that was buffeting her, Sophie imagined it felt just like Leo and Kate must have felt standing on the front of Titanic, and she had a wild impulse to hold her arms out horizontally and pretend she was flying, but that would have meant letting go of Nathan, which she had absolutely no intention of doing until the last possible moment. Plus, given how they were weaving swiftly in and out of the traffic, she feared she might fall off the bike.

She became aware that Nathan was shouting something at her, so she removed her ear from where it was pressed against his shoulder blade.

'Pardon?'

'I said, is your foot hurting a lot?'

'Quite a bit,' she yelled back. 'Why?'

'You're just holding on to me very tightly, that's all.'

'Sorry.' Sophie reluctantly relaxed her grip a little. 'Is it far?'

'The hospital?' Nathan shook his head. 'Just another half a mile. A couple of minutes at most.'

Sophie sighed disappointedly. The journey would come to an end soon. Though on reflection, that was probably just as well, given how much her foot was hurting.

They sped round the next corner, the bike leaning at some dangerous angle, and Sophie tightened her grip again and shut her eyes, only opening them again when Nathan pulled the bike into a space near the hospital's entrance. He lifted it—and Sophie, she was impressed to notice—up onto its stand, then held out his hand.

'Here.'

Sophie took it gratefully, then tried to climb off the bike as elegantly as possible, though she only succeeded in banging her sore foot painfully against the exhaust pipe. As Nathan lifted her down the last few inches, she enjoyed the sensation of being in his strong arms again.

'Can you walk?'

Sophie thought quickly. Saying 'no' might mean he'd have to carry her manfully in through the doors, and though *An Officer and a Gentleman* was another of her other favourite films, she wasn't sure she could take the excitement.

'I think so,' she said, reluctantly.

'You sure?'

She placed her foot gingerly on the floor, and wondered who she was trying to kid. 'Maybe not.'

'Okay. Hold on.'

She shut her eyes as Nathan picked her up again, preparing herself for the long carry, but instead, Nathan just sat her back on the bike, and when she opened her eyes again, he was striding away towards the hospital entrance. Sophie leant against the handlebars, wondering what was going on, and was just about to try and hop after him when he reappeared, pushing a wheelchair.

'Jump in, and fasten your seatbelt!'

Sophie forced a smile, then climbed off the bike again, wincing as she accidentally put too much weight on her injured foot, and as she'd hoped, Nathan picked her up again, though this time, it was only to deposit her in the chair.

'Ready?'

Sophie nodded, hoping no-one she knew could see her as Nathan wheeled her up the ramp, through the automatic doors, and up to the front desk.

'Hi,' he said, as the stern-looking receptionist looked up from her computer screen.

'Can I help you?'

'Suspected broken foot.'

'You don't look like you've got a broken foot.'

'Not me.' Nathan pointed down to where Sophie was obscured from view, and as the receptionist stood up and peered over the counter, Sophie made what she felt were appropriate whimpering noises while pointing to the end of her leg.

'What's her name?'

'Jones,' said Nathan, and Sophie smiled to herself. This morning, she'd been worried he didn't even know her Christian name, and yet he quite obviously... She stopped herself. Nathan probably knew the full names of everyone in the office. He wouldn't be able to set them up with an email address if he didn't.

'OK,' said the receptionist, handing Nathan a clipboard and pen. 'Get her to fill this in.'

'It's my foot I've hurt,' Sophie called from her wheelchair. 'I haven't gone deaf.'

As the receptionist rolled her eyes, Nathan grinned, then wheeled Sophie over towards a spare chair in the waiting room and waited until she'd filled the form out. He dropped it back at reception, then sat down next to her.

'Bad news,' he said. 'There's about half an hour's wait.'

'Oh no,' said Sophie, trying to ignore the throbbing from her foot. Though as she sat there, close enough to smell his aftershave, she didn't think that was bad news at all.

❦

Calum was hurrying back through Soho Square, feeling a little less stressed. He'd managed to find the right power cord in the Maplin shop at the other end of Tottenham Court Road, and seeing as he couldn't remember whether the office bathroom had a shaver point, he'd decided to take the belt and braces approach by buying a plug adaptor as well. It had cost him nearly ten pounds, but that didn't matter—at least now he was sorted. More importantly, he still had half an hour. Plenty of time to finish shaving, complete the rest of his ablutions, and get to the restaurant by six o'clock.

He turned the corner into Bateman Street, ignored the sniggers at his half-shaved appearance from the assembled smokers outside the pub on the corner, and strode towards his office, knowing he'd have the last laugh. They were stood there, on Valentine's Day, drinking with their mates, whereas he—well, he was off on a date. And despite the fact he'd repeated that phrase enough times to himself to make the words lose their meaning, he still loved the way it sounded.

He reached inside his coat and into his jacket pocket to where he always kept his key card, then stopped dead in his tracks. He didn't have his jacket on—it was still over the back of his office chair. In his rush to get out and buy the shaver cord, he'd thrown his coat on and sprinted out of the building in such a hurry that he'd nearly knocked Mark Webster flying, not once stopping to think how he was going to get back in.

A feeling of dread washed over him as he peered through the glass panel in the office door—there weren't any lights on that he could see, as far as he knew the cleaners weren't due to arrive for at least another hour, and without his key card, Calum was stuck. He glanced anxiously at his watch, not knowing what to do, then checked his pockets again, even though he knew it was a futile exercise. On the plus side, he had his phone with him, so if it came down to it, he could call Emma and tell her he'd be late, but he didn't want to risk doing that until he actually *was* late. And while he could still go as he was—he had his wallet, after all—without shaving properly, or brushing his teeth, or bringing the red rose he'd been carefully guarding all day, he worried the impression he'd make would be worse than not going at all.

He got his phone out and dialled the Seek switchboard number, just in case by some miracle Mia-Rose was still there, then remembered she hadn't been at her desk when he'd left. From where he was standing, he could see the light flashing on the phone on the reception desk, and hoped someone would hear it and come down to let him in, but after a couple of minutes, Calum ended the call. *Where was everybody?* he wondered, then almost immediately answered his own question. They'd be at Nathan's Anti-Valentine's event by now.

He scrolled through his phone's menu and found the email Nathan had sent him. SuperBowl was in Bayswater, so all he had to do was get there, get someone's key card, and... Calum froze again. At this time of day, Bayswater was a good half an hour away by taxi, and he didn't dare try the rush-hour tube. He had to face facts—there simply wasn't time to get there and back if he wanted to be on time for Emma... Unless someone could come here, maybe send a key card in a taxi... Perhaps he should call Nathan, and... He cursed under his breath. Thanks to him, Nathan had Mark's phone, and Calum didn't have his number. Besides, from what he could remember about SuperBowl, it was way down in Whiteleys' basement, and a phone-reception-free zone.

Calum leant heavily against the door and gave it a couple of hopeful tugs, but it didn't budge. He took a step back into the street and looked up to see if there was a window open, then quickly dismissed that idea as ridiculous. He wasn't that good at climbing—ironic, he knew, for someone who'd said he was into adventure sports—plus he didn't want to ruin his trousers, and quite frankly, turning up late because he'd been arrested for burglary wasn't something he thought he could explain away to Emma later.

He sighed loudly and took stock of his situation—here he was, half-dressed, half-shaven, and half an hour away from the most important date of his life on the most important date of the year—and wondered whether this was payback. He knew he shouldn't have lied on his LondonDate profile, nor should he have helped Sophie out by doing something as sneaky as switching Mark's and Nathan's phones. And he'd been pushing his luck by going to the gym, and waiting until now to shave, and then daring to feel confident on his conference call.

He looked up at the star-lit sky, thankful that at least it wasn't raining, and wondered whether things could get any worse.

And as he gave the door one last desperate tug and felt his back twinge again, they did.

⁓

Julie Marshall was running along the South Bank, checking her progress on the GPS watch she'd treated herself to on her birthday, confident that while her nine-minute-mile pace would hardly qualify her for the Olympics, it should at least it keep her ahead of anyone running the marathon in fancy dress. She'd done a 10K fun run—or rather 'fun' run, given how she'd slogged round—the previous November in Chiswick, where she'd been out-sprinted on the final straight by a man in a gorilla suit, and had resolved there and then not to let it happen again. Especially when the man had crossed the finish line, removed his gorilla mask, and revealed himself to be pushing sixty.

She kept her head down as she ran, trying not to make eye contact with any of the male joggers coming in the opposite direction. Julie knew she attracted attention when she was out running—as a woman, it was almost impossible not to, due to the combination of Newton's laws of motion and having breasts. She was grateful for the heavy-duty sports bra she'd invested in, though at the same time, the thought depressed her. How she'd have loved to be Sophie, spending her money on fancy lingerie at Selfridges, rather than on something with a Nike logo that she'd seen receive a five-star review for 'support' in *Runner's World* magazine. She almost laughed at the irony—Sophie was hoping her underwear would end up on the floor, whereas Julie had bought hers so her boobs wouldn't.

Tonight, of course, fewer than the normal number of people were out pounding the pavement past the Tate Modern. Most of the usual crowd would be foregoing today's training session to get ready for their big nights out, or perhaps they'd be saving their energy for a different type of physical activity this evening. For Julie, the choice had come down to this or bowling. And sadly, this had won.

It occurred to her she could still go to the Anti-Valentine's night—even with any awkwardness among her, Nathan, and Mark, it would beat sitting on her own in a restaurant. But if Nathan did have feelings for her (and assuming Sophie hadn't managed to work her magic on him in the hour they'd had together), it wouldn't be fair on Sophie, and if Mark didn't have feelings for her, then it wouldn't be fair on him. She wondered whether Nathan had told Mark she wasn't going, and if so, how he'd reacted, though just as quickly she realised he probably didn't care, given how he'd seemed quite happy to sit back and let Nathan have a 'crack' at her today.

She side-stepped through the tourists making their way into the gallery and cut right across the Millennium Bridge (or the wobbly bridge, as most Londoners knew it), enjoying the view as she ran across the river, the sight of St. Paul's Cathedral illuminated brightly against the black, cloudless sky taking her breath away more than the cold February night air did. Dodging round a couple holding hands in front of her, she ran down the other side of the bridge, then sprinted easily up the steps towards the cathedral, resisting the impulse to do a Rocky-like celebration at the top, before running back down and beginning the final stretch towards her office. Julie knew she was in good shape, and she should be— these were the best years of her life, after all. It was just a shame they didn't feel like them. But that wasn't her fault, surely? After all, Philip was the one who'd changed. He was the one who'd cheated on her. Though given how that was the case, why was she the one who felt guilty?

Turning away from the river, she jogged up past Embankment station, crossed the Strand, and ran through Trafalgar Square, scattering the pigeons as she went, then weaved through the theatre-goers on St. Martins Lane. Julie loved running through central London, perhaps because it reminded her there was so much vibrant life here—unlike the leafy mummy-land Chiswick seemed to have become. She sprinted up Frith Street and turned triumphantly into Bateman Street, where she clicked off her stopwatch, checked her distance and average speed, then almost tripped over Calum, who was sitting on the pavement outside the office, his head in his hands.

She pulled her earphones from her ears and switched off her iPod. 'Calum?'

'Julie!' Calum hauled himself gingerly to his feet. 'Thank god!' he said, fighting a wild impulse to hug her.

'What's the matter?'

'I've got a date. In fifteen minutes.'

'Are you meeting her here on the kerb?'

'No, I...' Calum was hopping from one foot to the other, as if he needed the toilet. 'I locked myself out. And I need to get back in and finish shaving, and brush my teeth, and get the rose I've bought her, and...'

Julie noticed his half-stubbled chin, and put a reassuring hand on his arm. 'Say no more.' She un-velcroed the wallet round her arm and removed her key card from where it was nestled behind her iPod. 'Where is this date, exactly?'

'Old Amsterdam.' Calum followed her towards the door. 'On Charlotte Street.'

'Okay. That's only two minutes away, so you've got plenty of time. Come on.' She unlocked the door and pushed it open, holding it wide as Calum hurried inside. 'What can I do to help?'

Calum wheeled round. 'I don't know!' he said, staring wide-eyed at her, so she took him by the shoulders.

'Relax,' she said. 'Breathe.'

Calum did as instructed. 'Sorry,' he said, after a few moments. 'I'm fine now.'

'Right. You go and finish shaving. What else do you need?'

'Everything's in my briefcase,' said Calum. 'In my office. And my jacket's on the back of the door.'

'No problem.' Julie smiled. 'I'll collect it all together, then wait for you here. Now take your time. And don't cut yourself shaving.'

'With an electric shaver?' Calum made a face. That would be just his luck.

As he disappeared into the toilets, Julie made her way up to his office and collected Calum's bits and pieces, then returned to reception, stretching lightly as she waited for him. When he finally appeared, perspiring more than she had been after her run, Julie looked him up and down

'Right.' She helped him into his jacket, then held out his brief-case. 'Have you got everything?'

Calum took the briefcase and peered inside. 'Red rose...' He patted his jacket pocket. 'Con...' He stopped talking, hoping Julie hadn't noticed the condoms, and cleared his throat. '...tact lens solution. I think so.'

'Great.'

'How do I look?'

'Same answer.' Julie smiled reassuringly. 'Now, you've still got five minutes. What's her name?'

'Emma.'

'Well, Emma's a woman, remember, so she'll probably be late. So all you need to do is keep calm, walk there slowly, and find your-self a nice table. And Calum?'

'Yes?'

Julie gave his arm a squeeze. 'Good luck,' she said, for the second time that evening.

She held the front door open, then watched Calum hurry along the street, a smile on her face, though it quickly faded. So far, she'd helped Sophie get a date with Nathan, and Calum get to his date with Emma, and what did she have to look forward to? Dinner for one, followed by a miserable night at home.

She glanced at Mark's door on the off-chance he might still be in his office, but it looked firmly shut, so instead, and with nowhere to go and no rush to be there, Julie carried her change of clothes into the toilets and showered slowly. She knew her situation was her own fault. When it had come down to it, she simply hadn't been able to go all the way with Mark after the Christmas party, and then, when she should have followed it up, something had stopped her. And while she'd have liked to blame Philip, in reality, Julie realised it was her problem and no-one else's.

She looked at her watch. Six-fifteen was certainly a respectable time to go for a drink, but that would mean drinking alone, and on a night when the pubs and bars around her office would either be full of couples drunk on their love for each other, or drunk on happy-hour beer because they were single. Besides, Julie decided, she'd better head for a restaurant instead, otherwise she'd be drinking on an empty stomach, which might make her do something rash, and being drunk and emotional on Valentine's Day probably wasn't the best combination if you were planning to spend the evening ignoring your cheating husband.

Though the concept of a happy hour was something that appealed. Julie hadn't had many happy hours since she'd found out about Philip's affair, and when she thought about it, there hadn't actually been that many before it either. The people who'd told her that her wedding would be the happiest day of her life had been right—if only because every day married to Philip since then had become progressively more miserable. Though the interesting thing had been how a part of her had been relieved when she'd found out about the affair. She'd suspected things hadn't been great between the two of them for a while. And his sleeping with someone else? Well, that had pretty much confirmed it.

She felt an insane urge to take the lead, call Mark, and perhaps suggest they go for a drink, but then realised miserably she didn't have his number. Besides, he was probably out having a great time at the bowling.

Her stomach rumbled, so Julie finished dressing and, with a last longing gaze at Mark's door, headed out in search of something to eat.

❧

Mark Webster was walking along Oxford Street, his hands stuffed into his pockets against the cold. He'd contemplated flagging down a cab and going to join the rest of them at Anti-Valentine's, but the way he was feeling this evening, being around people was the last thing he wanted.

He turned into Tottenham Court Road and made his way towards the entrance to the Underground, battling his way through the crowds of commuters while waving away the numerous free newspapers being pressed on him. As he reached the station, he nearly tripped over a fat, dishevelled-looking man sitting on the floor just inside the entrance.

'Watch where you're going,' said the man.

'Watch where you're sitting!' replied Mark, crossly, then immediately felt guilty. 'Sorry,' he said.

The man looked up at him. 'That's okay. Tough day?'

Mark nodded. 'You could say that.'

'Well, whatever happened to you, it can't have been as bad as sitting outside an Underground station in February hoping some kind stranger will spare the price of a cup of tea.' The man picked up an old Starbucks paper cup containing a few copper coins and jingled it. 'I said, hoping some kind...'

'Okay, okay.' Mark nodded, and fished in his pocket for a fifty-pence piece. 'Here,' he said, dropping it into the cup.

The man peered into the cup, then frowned up at him. 'You obviously haven't bought a cup of tea for a while.'

'What? Oh, sorry.' Mark found a pound coin, and dropped that in too, and the man smiled.

'Thanks. And don't worry. It'll get better.'

'If only.' Mark sighed as he walked on, and the man rolled his eyes, then he pulled himself up by the handrail.

'Don't tell me. Woman trouble?'

Mark paused at the top of the stairs. 'How did you know that?'

'I'm a medium.'

'Really?'

The man held his hands up. 'I know, I know. You're probably thinking I'm more of an extra-large. But seriously, I'm a psychic. And before you say anything, no, not like Robin, or Tonto.'

'Huh?'

'Sidekick. Just my little joke.' The man grinned. 'I used to have my own show.'

Mark peered at him. 'Have you been on TV?'

'Only the "CC" variety.' He mimed a 'bum-tish' drum roll. 'But seriously, you're having a problem with the lay-deez, right?'

'Well...' Mark looked around, feeling a little awkward, but the constant flow of commuters certainly weren't paying any attention as they passed. 'Seriously, how could you tell?'

The man tapped the side of his nose with his index finger. 'Like I said—psychic. Well, that, plus the fact that it's Valentine's Day, and you're walking towards the tube on your own wearing an expression like your dog's just died.'

'Okay,' said Mark. 'Well, thanks for the lovely chat, but I've really got to go.' He started down the stairs, but the man put a hand on his arm.

'What's your name?'

Mark frowned. 'Shouldn't you know that already?'

'Do you want my help or not?'

'Well, actually...' Mark stared at him, then sighed resignedly. After the day he'd had, he realised he was prepared to try anything.

The man nodded down towards a hand-written cardboard sign next to where he'd been sitting, where 'Fortunes told—£2' had been scribbled in black marker pen. 'Traditionally, you're expected to pay beforehand.'

'What—cross your palm with silver?'

'Something like that.'

'You'll be telling me you've got a crystal ball next.'

'No, it's just the cut of these trousers.'

'Yes, that's very funny.' Mark shook his head slowly as he found another fifty pence in his pocket. 'Here.'

'What's this?'

'Fifty pence.'

'It's two pounds for a fortune-telling.'

'I've already given you one pound fifty.'

'That was a donation.'

'And this is daylight robbery.'

'No it isn't,' protested the man. 'For one thing, it's dark.'

Mark rolled his eyes. 'Okay. Give me my money back. This is obviously...'

'It's a woman, right?'

'I already told you that,' Mark said, making for the stairs again.

'And you're not married, and you don't have a girlfriend.'

Mark stopped in his tracks. 'How did you know that?'

The man shrugged. 'No wedding ring. And you're obviously on your way home, but without a bunch of flowers or a box of chocolates.'

'Listen,' said Mark. 'As...fascinating as this is, I really have to...'

'Tell me one thing before you go. Do you believe in fate?'

Mark thought for a moment. 'What do you mean?'

'Do you believe that things are predestined? That you've got no control over what's going to happen to you? That your life is going to go in one direction, and there's absolutely nothing you can do about that? Fate.'

'Well, that's an argument I can't really win, isn't it? I mean, whatever I say, whatever happens happens, doesn't it? So I've got no way of proving...'

'That wasn't what I asked,' said the man. 'I said, do you believe in it?'

'What's the difference?'

'Because if you do, then like you say, there's nothing you can do about what happens. But if you don't... Well, you can change it, can't you? Or at least have some control over what happens.'

'Huh?'

'I'm guessing there's someone you like. I'm also guessing she hasn't responded in the way you'd like?'

'Well, not that it's any of your business, but no, she hasn't.'

'What did you do?'

Mark stood there for a moment and considered the absurdity of his situation. Here he was, on Valentine's Day, standing at the top of the steps leading down to Tottenham Court Underground station in the middle of rush hour, contemplating explaining his dilemma with Julie to a stranger to whom he'd just given two pounds to tell him his fortune. And almost immediately, he decided *what the hell*.

'Well, we kissed after our office Christmas party, but the next day, she pretended she'd been drunk and didn't remember it, and so I've sent her stuff all day to remind her what happened that night, and it turns out she probably thinks they were from someone else. So all that effort, all that planning, all that...'

'Expense?'

'Well, now you come to mention it, yes. It all appears to have been for nothing.'

The man nodded slowly. 'And you're thinking it just isn't meant to be, right?'

'It's starting to look that way.'

'So you do believe in fate?'

'No, actually,' said Mark. 'I don't.'

'Well, why are you acting as if you are?'

'I'm not.'

'Yes you are. You've just said it isn't meant to be. If it wasn't meant to be, why are you so bothered? There was nothing you could have done about it, it was never going to happen...'

'Because I...Look. This is ridiculous.'

'Do you think you could have a future together?'

Mark let out a short laugh. 'Shouldn't I be asking you that?'

'Hey—I do the jokes.'

The man made a mock-offended face, and Mark half-smiled. 'So what should I do? Or can you put in a good word for me with the spirit world?'

The man shook his head. 'I said I was psychic, not a miracle worker. But I can tell you what will happen if you leave it to fate and don't do anything.'

'What?'

'Nothing.'

Mark stared at him for a moment, then felt himself bristle. 'You'll excuse me if I don't take the advice of someone who's... Well, who's touting for business on a street corner. Do something proper. Rather than this... rubbish you've been spouting, try selling the *Big Issue*.'

'Sounds like you're the one with the big issues, pal.'

'Yes, well...' Mark puffed air out of his cheeks exasperatedly. 'Much as I'd love to spend the rest of Valentine's Day standing here, I have to go.'

'Where?'

'Home.'

The man shrugged. 'Suit yourself. But don't you think you'd be better off going and telling this woman what you've just told me?'

'And why exactly are you so qualified to give me advice? Married, are you?'

'Three times,' said the man.

'And that's something to be proud of, is it?'

The man nodded. 'Better to have loved and lost, etcetera, etcetera,' he said, enunciating the last two words like a circus announcer. 'And correct me if I'm wrong, but it's three times more than you.'

Mark's jaw dropped open, then he shook his head, let out a long, loud sigh, and walked down the steps to the station.

಄

Calum was sitting in Old Amsterdam, alternating between staring at his phone and staring at the door. He'd been anxious to get here early so he could choose a decent table, then even more anxious because his shaving problems had put paid to that, though given how Old Amsterdam didn't seem to be a popular choice for Valentine's Day dining, even though he'd cut things a little bit fine, he'd still pretty much had the choice of any one he liked.

In the end, he'd chosen a table that gave him a good view of the door, yet couldn't be seen from outside through the window. This way, he'd reasoned, Emma would have to actually come into the restaurant to see him (he didn't want to be rejected on looks alone from outside) and he was planning to wave her over as soon as she entered, through the drawback of that strategy was that he didn't know who he'd be waving over. Still, he thought, if any single women walked in, caught sight of him, then turned round and walked straight out again, he'd have a pretty good idea who they might be.

He peered at his phone again to check for messages, and dropped it on the table in shock when it chose that exact moment to ring. 'Hello?' he said, as coolly as he could muster.

'Calum? It's your mother.'

'Mum!' He glanced around furtively, hoping no-one had heard him. It would be just his luck for Emma to walk in and catch him on the phone to the mother he hadn't told her he still lived with. 'Is everything OK?'

'Fine, fine. How's it going?'

'She's not here yet.'

'Oh, Calum.'

'She's not supposed to be. It's only just six o'clock.'

'Well, I'm glad I've caught you. Listen, I need to tell you something.'

'Right now? I don't have a lot of time.'

'And nor might I, Calum.'

'Don't talk like that!'

'I'm not saying anything that isn't true. So I just wanted to say... When you're with her... Don't you be thinking of me.'

'Mum, that's just weird.'

'Not like that. I mean it's time for you to be making your own life now. To be thinking about yourself. I'll be fine on my own if it comes to it. So don't you feel you have to be responsible for me anymore.'

'But...'

'I mean it, Calum. I love you, and I'm proud of you, but the sooner you get on with your life, get settled down...'

'What?'

'The sooner I get some grandkids!' Calum knew his mother had meant it as a joke, but her voice was trembling as if she was on the verge of tears, and Calum swallowed hard.

'Mum, please!'

'You're a good boy, Calum. You deserve to be happy. And if this girl can't see that...' There was a sniff, followed by a moment's silence, and then his mother's voice reappeared on the line. 'Now get off the phone, and good luck!'

'Bye mum. Thanks. And...' He glanced nervously at the next-nearest table, and lowered his voice. 'I love you too,' he said, but she'd already gone.

Calum smiled to himself, peering self-consciously at the other diners—a couple of families, a group of three girls—relieved no-one seemed to have heard him. Just across from him sat one solitary man, and he found himself praying there wouldn't be two solitary men by the end of the evening. He noticed he'd dropped his serviette and, without thinking, reached down and retrieved it from the floor. At least his back seemed to have calmed down a little since he'd tweaked it again by tugging on the office door—though he didn't want to risk moving too much, and he'd just taken his final two Neurofen, so he hoped they'd at least last him the evening.

He slipped his phone away, picked up the over-sized menu, and peeked at the girls over the top of it, beginning to worry that Emma was one of them. Perhaps she'd brought her friends along for solidarity (or even as a smoke-screen) in case she didn't like the look of him, but he told himself that was unlikely—the three of them had just ordered their dinner, and surely they'd simply have had a drink and left if that had been the case. And besides, Calum reminded himself, as Sophie had pointed out, she'd already seen him—or his photo, at least. The only thing he really had to be worried about was the fact that he wasn't as tall as he'd led her to believe (and was maybe a bit, ahem, wider than his head-shot suggested). Maybe if he didn't stand up for the whole evening he could get away with both those things, but then again, Calum had always been taught you had to stand up when a woman arrived at your table.

The door to the restaurant swung open again, and Calum slipped his glasses on briefly to see who'd come in, but it was just a couple of teenagers sneaking in to use the toilet. He wondered whether he should remove his jacket, as he was feeling pretty warm, but he'd been sweating, and visible damp patches under each arm weren't the most attractive of sights.

'You ready to order?'

The waitress's voice made him jump. 'No. Not yet. I'm...'

'Waiting for someone. So you said.'

The waitress, a middle-aged woman dressed in what Calum guessed was supposed to be a version of Dutch national dress, looked like she was starting to doubt him, which was funny, because Calum was starting to doubt himself too. As she walked away from his table, her clogs squeaking on the bright orange carpet, he checked his phone again, compared the time on the display to what his watch said, and then checked that with the clock on the restaurant wall. Give or take a minute, it was five past six.

He wondered whether he should phone the speaking clock just to make sure, but then worried Emma might choose that precise moment to call to say she was running late, and he might miss her, and... Maybe she'd already called, when he was on the phone to his mum. Perhaps he'd missed her voicemail... Anxiously, he checked his phone's screen again, and even though there was no notification icon, he dialled his voicemail anyway, then stopped mid-call, worried Emma would actually be ringing him now.

Calum almost laughed as he wondered how it had come to this, though at the same time, he knew exactly how it had come to this. He forced himself to take a few deep breaths and sipped nervously at the sparkling water he'd ordered when he arrived, careful not to drink too much and make himself need the toilet any more than his nervousness was making him already. He'd wanted a beer, but didn't want to gulp it down and make the wrong impression, or have beer breath when he kissed Emma hello. A Coke had been his next choice, but even then, he didn't want to risk the caffeine making him hyper—he was bad enough as it was—so he'd gone for water, but even so, he was regretting not ordering still, as the bubbles were making him want to burp.

Was nothing safe? To be honest, a part of him wanted to get up and leave before Emma arrived. He'd put too much pressure on this evening already, and the omens had hardly been promising. The way he was feeling, he was probably going to stammer and sweat his way through dinner anyway, and if that was the case, Emma was bound to make her excuses and leave before they'd even got on to dessert.

He kept trying to remind himself he was a salesman, and a good one, too. And if he could sell software via cold-calling, then surely he could sell hardware in the flesh—especially when he knew the product so well. And anyway, what was the old sales maxim—'sell the sizzle, and not the steak'? Calum could do that, if only he could work out what his sizzle actually was, and deflect Emma from how much steak he was actually carrying round his waist. Besides this was hardly a cold call. He and Emma had exchanged two hundred and seven emails (Calum had counted) and live-chatted late into the night on more than one occasion. So they got on. Shared several interests, including watching *The Wire* and *Modern Family*, and they'd even been to the same Keane concert a couple of years ago—not that either of them had known it at the time. In fact, he told himself, they were practically soul mates.

He checked his watch again—ten past six—and decided he'd give her another twenty minutes to be fashionably/female-ly late before he left, then realised he was kidding himself. He'd wait all night if necessary. He glanced down at the red rose in his briefcase, which was looking a bit worse for wear. Maybe he should be holding it between his teeth when she arrived—or maybe not. It had thorns, after all, and bleeding lips probably weren't the best look, or any good if he was planning to at least kiss Emma goodnight later.

Calum wondered how Nathan's evening was going. The last two Anti-Valentine's nights had been excellent fun, if a little alcoholic.

Last year, they'd ended up in some flash hotel on Berners Street where cocktails had set them back twelve quid a go, and he'd ended up having three, then falling asleep on the night bus home. He'd been lucky to escape without a hangover, though—the long cold walk back from the depot to his flat had sobered him up pretty quickly.

A strange rumbling sound made him look up, until he realised it was his stomach. Missing lunch had been a silly idea, partly because the last thing he wanted was to 'entertain' Emma with sounds from his midriff, but also because it hadn't (as he'd hoped) made him look that extra bit thinner, and now he was even more worried that the first drink he had would go straight to his head. He thought about not drinking at all, but it was important to be himself, and Calum liked a drink—though he made a mental note not to repeat that phrase to Emma. The people at work who 'liked a drink' sometimes disappeared to the pub at midday and didn't come back to work until late afternoon, if at all. And Calum didn't want to be associated with any of them.

He looked at his watch again, then glanced up at the doorway, just in time to see a girl walk in, and he caught his breath. She was pretty, her short dark hair partly hidden under a grey, knitted hat, her curvy figure accentuated by the belted coat she was wearing, and even without his glasses on, Calum thought she looked familiar. He noticed she was smiling, and Calum found himself smiling too, especially when he realised she was smiling at him, though when she came a little closer, he saw it was only Mia-Rose, and his face fell.

She walked over to where he was sitting, and Calum shifted uncomfortably in his seat.

'Hi, Calum!'

'Er, hi.'

Mia-Rose shrugged her coat off, and nodded at the table. 'May I?'

Taken a bit by surprise, Calum nodded, and as Mia-Rose squeezed herself into the booth, he began to panic. If Emma was to arrive now, and see him with another woman...He jumped up quickly, and then, not knowing what to do, just stood next to his chair.

Mia-Rose looked up at him, an amused expression on her face. 'Normally the man's supposed to stand up as the woman arrives. Not when she sits down.'

'Sorry.' Calum shook his head in disgust at his lack of manners as he slipped back into the booth, then he positioned the menu so it partly obscured the two of them and hunkered down behind it.

Mia-Rose peered at him. 'Are you hiding?'

'No.' Calum flattened the menu on the table. 'It's just that...I'm kind of waiting for someone.'

'Me too,' said Mia-Rose. 'I'll wait with you, shall I?'

'Um...'

'What's the matter?'

'It's just that it might be a little awkward. You know, if she sees you. With me.'

'It's a she?' Mia-Rose raised both eyebrows. 'And who is this mystery girl?'

Calum swallowed. 'Just someone I've met.'

'Does she have a name?'

'Emma.'

Mia-Rose peered around the restaurant. 'What does she look like?'

'Why?'

'Just curious.'

He cleared his throat. 'I don't know,' he said, awkwardly

'You don't know?'

Calum decided he had no choice but to explain. 'I met her on the internet. We haven't actually met yet.'

'And tonight's the night? How romantic.'

'You think?' he said, though 'how foolish' was beginning to seem more like an appropriate description.

'Definitely! Not to mention exciting.' Mia-Rose glanced furtively at the other diners. 'She might be here already.'

Calum started to panic. Maybe she *was* one of the three girls who were sitting at the table by the window, currently tucking into their main courses. Maybe Emma had brought along a couple of friends so she could pretend not to be here if she decided he wasn't what she wanted, or so she had some backup, or because she wanted a second (or even a third) opinion, or simply so if she did decide to join him, she wouldn't have to leave her friend sitting on her own. And now she'd seen him with Mia-Rose... Well, Calum couldn't imagine what she'd be thinking.

'Listen, Mia-Rose, I don't mean to be rude, but...'

'You'd like me to sit at another table?' Mia-Rose nodded slowly. 'Wow. This Emma must be really special.'

'She is,' insisted Calum.

'And what makes a girl you've never met so special?'

Calum pretended to stare into the distance as he considered his answer, though in reality, he was sneaking another look at the clock on the wall. It was twenty past, and he was beginning to fear that Emma had been and gone already and he hadn't noticed. Why had he stood up when Mia-Rose had sat down? Emma might have come in at that very moment, spotted him, realised he wasn't as tall as he'd claimed, and gone home in disgust.

'We just...click.'

Mia-Rose laughed. 'That's funny.'

'Why is that funny?'

She reached over the table and punched him lightly on the arm. 'You met online. And you "click." Get it?'

Calum forced a smile. Normally he would have found that funny, but where was she? While under different circumstances he'd be relishing a one-on-one with someone as pretty as Mia-Rose, he was more worried this was completely blowing his chances with Emma. Besides, when Mia-Rose's date arrived, he'd be left on his own to be stood up in full view of someone from the office.

'So,' she continued. 'How do you "click," exactly? What do you know about her?'

Calum exhaled loudly, wishing again he'd ordered a proper drink. 'Not much. I mean, she lives in London, and she likes dogs, and long walks, and roaring log fires... But it's not those things. It's more that that we just...'

'Get on?'

'Right.' Calum looked at his watch again. 'Or at least, I thought we did.'

'And why did you arrange to meet her here?'

Calum shrugged. 'She insisted we "go Dutch" tonight. So I thought...'

Mia-Rose tilted her head back and burst out laughing. 'That's very funny.'

'You don't think it's a bit... lame?'

'Not at all. It's hilarious. Women love a man with a good sense of humour.'

Calum smiled, encouraged slightly by Mia-Rose's comment. Though as he caught sight of his reflection in the mirror on the far wall and saw himself sharing a laugh with a pretty girl, he realised that if Emma walked in now, a sense of humour would be the one thing she'd need to have.

10

'Don't feel you have to stay,' said Sophie, guiltily, as she cautiously rested her foot on the pillow Nathan had procured from one of the passing nurses. 'I mean, it's Valentine's Day, and all that.'

Nathan cast a wary eye round the waiting room, which, despite the relatively early hour, had already started to fill up with the usual assortment of drunks and druggies that hospitals seemed to attract most evenings. 'Not a problem,' he said, leafing through one of the old, tattered copies of *Hello* on the table in front of him, before spotting a battered vending machine in the corner of the room. 'Coffee?'

Sophie shrugged. 'Sure. Cappuccino, please. But let me get these.'

'No, I insist,' said Nathan. 'I owe you a drink. And besides, you might spill them.'

He fished in his pocket for some change and headed over to the machine, leaving Sophie miserably reflecting how this wasn't exactly the kind of drink she'd hoped Nathan would be buying her this evening—and certainly not in this setting—though when he reappeared a minute later with two paper cups full of steaming brown liquid, he seemed reluctant even to hand her one of them.

'One's a cappuccino, one's a latte,' he said, regarding them suspiciously. 'Though I can't really tell which is which.'

'Thanks,' said Sophie, taking the nearest cup.

'You're welcome. Sugar?'

Sophie's heart leapt momentarily as she assumed Nathan had invented a pet name for her; then she saw the small white packet he was offering her.

'Er, no, thanks.'

'Sweet enough already, eh?'

'Something like that.' She smiled at him, and they sipped their coffees in silence for a few moments, until Sophie suddenly noticed the huge clock on the waiting room wall just behind where Nathan was sitting. 'Are you sure you don't want to get back?' she said, fearing he was bound to spot it and see what the actual time was. And how on earth would she explain that?

'What would be the point?' Nathan looked at his watch and shook his head. 'I still can't believe the others didn't turn up.'

'Well, maybe they...' Sophie stopped talking, worried she'd only be getting herself into trouble. 'Me either. People, eh?'

Nathan rolled his eyes, then sat back in his chair. 'So, tell me all about yourself, Soph.'

'Me?' She tried to ignore the throbbing in her foot, though at the same time, felt it probably served her right. 'Well, there's not really that much to tell.'

'No?'

Sophie shrugged. 'No, I'm just... Ordinary, I suppose.'

'Sophie, you're anything but that.'

She looked at him with a start. 'What do you mean?'

'Well, you're smart. You're funny. You work for an exciting company in the centre of one of the most vibrant, multicultural cities in the world. And on top of all that, you're pretty...' He took a sip of coffee, and Sophie found herself hoping that was the end of the sentence. '... good at ten-pin bowling.' He leaned over and nudged her again. 'I wouldn't say there was anything ordinary about you.'

'I don't know…'

Nathan glanced absent-mindedly around the waiting room, his eyes settling upon a flickering fluorescent light in the ceiling. 'It's funny, isn't it?'

'What?'

'Like I was saying earlier outside Bar Italia. How you can work with someone for so long and not know what they're like? Or what they like?'

Or who they like, thought Sophie. She took a deep breath. 'How about yourself?'

'Me?'

'Yes. You didn't quite answer me earlier.'

'Earlier?'

'In the office. When I asked you what exactly you had against Valentine's Day.'

Nathan stared at her for a second, and while his first instinct was to clam up, he was struck by the realisation that (apart from his mum) he'd never told another woman what had happened—and perhaps a woman's perspective might actually help. He opened his mouth, wondering where on earth to start, and then it all came pouring out. About Ellie, and her turning his proposal down, and why she'd turned his proposal down, and how that had made him feel, and why he hated IKEA, and what had happened in the coffee shop this morning, and how he'd felt when he'd seen the couple this afternoon. When he'd finished, he felt strangely dejected, and so did Sophie, though she perked up a little when he told her he'd finally realised it was time for him to change.

'Why? Or rather, why now?'

Nathan shrugged. 'Because I got this card today.'

Sophie's heart leapt. 'And?'

'And I didn't know how to feel.'

'About the card? Or about the person who sent it?'

'Either. Both.' Nathan was slumped in his chair, as if the admissions had drained him. 'I don't know.'

'How did it make you feel?'

Nathan looked like he was struggling to put it into words. 'I don't know. Flattered. Scared. Somewhere between the two.'

'Why scared?'

'Because love hurts, Soph. And I don't want to be hurt like that again.'

He was staring straight at her, and Sophie had to fight hard not to look away. 'Nathan, lots of things in life hurt. Dropping a bowling ball on your foot, for example. But they stop hurting eventually. And it doesn't mean you can never go bowling again. Just don't do it with, you know, sweaty hands.'

'That's very deep, Soph. Though I'm not quite sure I understand it.'

Sophie smiled. Nor was she. 'So, what are you going to do?'

'I don't know.' He shrugged. 'Unfortunately, people aren't like computers. You can't just turn them off and on again and expect them to forget the past. They have memories.'

'Well, technically, so do computers.'

'You after my job or something?'

Sophie laughed. 'Hardly. Though I do know the best way to get rid of a bad memory. And I'm talking computers—and people.'

'Tell me.'

'Replace it with a good one.'

Nathan stared at her for a second, then broke into a smile. 'That's pretty good advice. Even though it might be easier said than done.'

Sophie swallowed hard. She could say exactly how to do it—and whom to do it with—although one thing was puzzling her, or rather, there was one thing she needed to know. 'So, tell me something.'

'Sure.'

'Why did you send Julie that card?'

'Eh?'

'If you don't believe in Valentine's Day.'

'What card?'

'This morning. The one you put on her desk.'

Nathan frowned at her. 'That was from Mark. I was delivering it for him.'

'From Mark?'

Nathan nodded. 'That's right. Don't tell him I told you, but he's had a thing for her for ages.' He grinned. 'You didn't say anything, did you?'

Sophie felt herself start to colour again. 'Er...'

'Soph...' Nathan leant back in his chair and gazed around the room in disbelief, and then he caught sight of the clock on the wall. 'Funny.'

'What is?' asked Sophie, nervously.

He checked his watch, and then his phone. 'What time is it?'

Sophie stared at him, and before she could help herself, she burst into tears.

'Nathan, I'm so, so sorry.'

'For what?'

'For this,' she sobbed. 'Ruining your evening.'

'You didn't do that. The others did that by not turning up.' He reached over and put a comforting arm round her, but Sophie was feeling too guilty to enjoy it.

'Yes, well...' Sophie wiped her eyes on her sleeve. 'I'm sorry about that too.'

'Huh?' Nathan looked down at her. 'What do you mean?'

'I...I changed the clock on your computer. And the one on Mark's phone. And then I got Calum to swap your phone with Mark's. And then I changed the time on my watch, and told you you were late for Anti-Valentine's.'

'What?' Nathan slipped his phone out of his pocket and peered at it. 'Why would you do that?'

'Because...' Sophie sniffed, and launched into an explanation of her own, telling Nathan all about Darren, and moving to London, and how she'd embarrassed herself in front of him that day with her 'Outlook' comment, and about missing out on everything else since then, and how this morning she'd determined that today would be the day when everything changed. 'And I thought if we spent some time together,' she said finally, 'just the two of us, and got to know each other, you might like me. And maybe even ask me out. Seeing as my card didn't work.'

'You sent me that card?'

Sophie nodded. 'Yes,' she said, quietly.

Nathan stared at her for what seemed like the longest time, then opened his mouth as if to say something, but just at that moment, Sophie heard her name being called from reception. And while it occurred to her to ignore it, her foot was incredibly painful.

'That's you,' said Nathan matter-of-factly, then waved towards the desk.

'Nathan...'

But before she could say anything else, a well-built male nurse came over and began to wheel her away, and while something like this would normally be the highlight of her evening, Sophie hardly noticed. Instead, after a final, lingering look over her shoulder at a still-stunned Nathan, she did her best to pull herself together, fished her phone out of her jacket pocket, and quickly composed a text.

〜

Mark Webster allowed the crowd to carry him off the tube at Bank, then followed the signs towards the Northern Line platform and stepped miserably onto the next available train. He'd had such great plans for tonight, but they'd all come to nothing, and as far as he was concerned, it served him right. The way things were going, it'd be him organising the Anti-Valentine's event next year.

He rode the couple of stops in a daze, then got off at London Bridge and walked slowly along Tooley Street, past the London Dungeon and the World War II exhibition, before heading under the viaduct and down Bermondsey Street. He loved where he lived—the variety of restaurants, the attractions on his doorstep—but at the same time, Mark knew these things were only really fun if you had someone to enjoy them with.

He reached his flat and made his way inside, just in time to hear his home phone ringing in the hallway. Hoping it might be Julie, he lunged at it, only succeeding in knocking the handset off the hall table. Though when he eventually retrieved it from where it had fallen behind the radiator, instead of Julie's dulcet tones, he heard Nathan's voice.

'Hello, mate. Haven't interrupted anything, have I?'

'No,' said Mark, disappointedly. 'More's the pity.'

'Good,' said Nathan. 'Listen, I've got to keep this brief, because I'm just at the hospital...'

'The hospital? Are you all right?'

'Yeah, I'm fine. It's Sophie, actually.'

'Sophie? Is she OK?'

'Yes, she... Actually, mate, that's not important, and I'm on a payphone, and I think I'm just about to run out of money, so shut up and listen, will you?'

'Sorry. Yes, of course. What to?'

'It's Julie.'

'What about her?'

'She...' The line went dead, and he stared at the receiver in disbelief. 'What?' he shouted. 'Nathan. Nathan.'

He punched Nathan's number into his phone, then almost jumped out of his skin when his own mobile started ringing, though when he answered it, all he could hear was a strange echo. He ended the call, then stood there, waiting for Nathan to call back, until he realised he'd be unlikely to if he had, in fact, run out of money, so hurriedly he dialled 1-4-7-1 to return the call, and to his relief, after half a ring, Nathan answered.

'Finally!'

'What do you mean, 'finally'?'

'I've had to fight off two drunks and an old lady with a walking stick. She had the stick, I mean. I didn't use one to fight her off.'

'Get on with it, Nathan, please.'

'Oh yeah. Sorry.' Nathan laughed. 'Well, to cut a long story short, you were right. Sophie did tell Julie the card she saw me putting on her desk this morning was from me. Which, if you think about it, probably explains everything else today, including why she didn't come to Anti-Valentines. Probably thought she wouldn't be able to resist me...'

'Nathan!'

'Anyway, I just thought you ought to know that it wasn't you she was rejecting. It was me.'

'But that means…'

'Yeah.'

'And she doesn't…'

'Nope.'

Mark shook his head as it all fell into place. No wonder Julie had hardly said two words to him all afternoon. She must have thought he wasn't interested in her at all, and that he'd told Nathan all about what had happened the night of the Christmas party, and been happy to let Nathan try and remind her of it. And what must she think of him if that was the case?

'Why did you leave it until now to tell me?'

'Because I've only just found out. And you've got my iPhone, and I've got yours.'

'What? How did that happen?'

'I'll explain tomorrow. Anyway, what it all means is the coast's now clear for you to make your move.'

'But I'm at home.'

'So?'

Mark looked at his watch. 'And it's six-fifteen.'

'Which means you've still got five-and-three-quarter hours of Valentine's Day left to…' There was the sound of a commotion, and then Nathan appeared back on the line. 'Listen, mate, it's getting a bit ugly here, so I'd better get off the phone. And you'd better get on yours. Or rather, mine.'

'OK. Great. Thanks. Will do. Right away.'

'Go on then!'

'Sorry. Of course.'

Mark put the phone down, then picked his mobile up and prepared to call Julie, then cursed under his breath, remembering that her number was on his mobile, not Nathan's. He hit redial on his land-line, planning to call Nathan back to ask him for Julie's number, but unsurprisingly the payphone at the hospital was engaged.

He slammed the phone down in frustration and began pacing around his front room, wondering what to do. He had his laptop, and supposed he could send Julie an email, but she might not see it until the morning, and besides, what would he write? And short of jumping on the train to go and see her... Mark almost laughed. That wasn't him at all—and nor, now he thought about it, was some panicked phone conversation. No, far better to just wait until the morning, try to catch Julie at the coffee machine, and have a laugh with her about what a huge misunderstanding today had been.

He walked into his kitchen and opened the refrigerator, looking for something to drink, then realised he'd finished off his last bottle of wine the previous evening while trying to think of something witty to write in Julie's card, so he picked up his keys from where he'd dropped them in his earlier scramble for the phone and headed out to the Sainsbury's Local in Bermondsey Square. The bar opposite was full of couples sitting holding hands, and he tried to ignore them as he made his way into the store.

Picking up a basket from the pile near the entrance, he walked up and down the aisles, considering his evening dining options. He hadn't expected to be here, surveying the 'Taste the Difference' pizza selection—given the choice, he'd rather have been gazing at Julie across a table in a romantic Soho restaurant, but things just hadn't worked out that way. And as for that rubbish that so-called 'psychic' had been spouting at Tottenham Court Road, about believing in fate... That was a short step away from the likes of 'today is the first day of the rest of your life,' and all that other American-speak that people at those motivational seminars the company arranged from time to time were always quoting. Well, if that was the case, then tomorrow could be too. And at least tonight he could have something tasty, if not, well, *tasty*…

As his hand hovered over the last pepperoni pizza, a short, heavy-set banker type wearing a suit and a New York Yankees baseball cap reached past him and snatched it from his grasp. Mark opened his mouth to protest, but the man just grinned.

'Sorry, buddy,' he said. 'You snooze, you lose.'

For a second, Mark stared at him. Then he placed his basket carefully on the floor, made his way measuredly out of the supermarket so as not to attract the attention of the security guard, and sprinted back towards the station.

༄

Julie Marshall was sitting in There's No Place Like Rome near Embankment tube station, working her way through a large plate of spaghetti carbonara, although in truth, she was really just eating the spaghetti—the chef had taken the 'carbon' part of the dish's name too literally, and the burnt chunks of bacon were beyond her.

She'd spotted the restaurant—a fast-food Italian with plastic tables, fixed-in-place chairs, and the kind of over-bright décor usually aimed at tourists—on her run earlier, and had selected it on the assumption that no-one in their right mind would take someone here for a romantic Valentine's dinner. So far she'd been proven right—aside from a couple of groups of tourists and an old man in the corner reading a book, she was the only diner.

Not that it felt like it—trying to attract the attention of the surly, bored-looking Eastern European waiter to complain about her food had proven impossible, so in the end, Julie had just pushed the bacon bits to one side of her plate and concentrated on working her way through the rest of it, along with what was already her second large glass of red wine. It was depressing, she knew, but better than the prospect of another night at home with Philip, which—tonight, of all nights—might just have made her want to kill herself. Or kill him, which she realised was perhaps a more appropriate response to what he'd done.

She looked at her watch and wondered how Sophie was getting on with Nathan, whether an hour had been long enough for her to have charmed him, and whether he'd been able to transfer his affections *just like that.* He hadn't seemed that disappointed when Julie had told him he was wasting his time, but he was a man, and there was always someone else on their radar—even if they were married, it seemed. As for Mark, well, Julie had to face up to the fact that she'd blown it. He must have felt completely snubbed—and she couldn't blame him for what had happened today. Maybe he'd simply confided in Nathan and told him what had happened, that she hadn't seemed interested, and so Nathan had decided to have a 'go.' Wasn't that how men worked? No loyalty. Just after one thing. At least, the ones she knew seemed to be.

As she contemplated a third glass of wine, the waiter appeared at the table next to her, where a group of strikingly blond men were chatting animatedly in a language she didn't recognise. He looked down at their half-eaten meals and cleared his throat, and they stopped talking.

'You finish?' he said, his thick accent making it sound more like an accusation than a question.

The tallest one grinned. 'No, we're from Sweden,' he said, in perfect English, and the rest of the group burst out laughing. Julie couldn't stop herself from joining in. Sadly, she realised, it was the first good laugh she'd had for a while.

As the waiter sullenly cleared their plates, her iPhone beeped— Philip, probably, wondering where she was, checking up on her, even though what she was up to was none of his business. But instead, when she glanced down at the screen, the number displayed was Sophie's.

Julie found herself hoping it was good news, but she feared the worst. Sophie would hardly be texting her already unless she was a really quick worker—although that lingerie had been pretty stunning. She opened the message, and almost did a double take as she read it.

'Nathan didn't send you that Valentine's card,' it said. 'It was Mark.'

∽

Calum sneaked another guilty look at his watch, though it was unlikely Mia-Rose would notice seeing as she was sitting in the adjoining booth with her back to him. This way, he'd reasoned, they could still talk, but when (or if) Emma appeared, she wouldn't see him sitting with another woman and be put off. He'd felt really awkward asking her to move, but Mia-Rose had understood, though as the minutes ticked by Calum had begun to feel worse about his request, certain as he was by now that Emma wasn't going to turn up at all, and worried Mia-Rose would think he'd made her up just to avoid her sitting at his table.

Suddenly, he heard what sounded like a glass breaking behind him and reminded himself not to look round, worried his back couldn't take the twisting. 'Are you okay?' he called over his shoulder.

'I'm fine,' said Mia-Rose. 'That's just my phone telling me I've got a text message.'

'It's not from Emma, is it, by any chance?' asked Calum, glumly, and Mia-Rose laughed.

'My mother, would you believe? Asking what time I'll be back.'
She laughed again. 'Honestly!'

'You still live at home?'

'There's nothing wrong with living at home, Calum,' scolded
Mia-Rose.

'No, I wasn't inferring...I mean, I do too. Well, with my Mum.
She's not so well.'

'I'm sorry to hear that.'

'Thanks. It's not terminal. Unless you get her talking about
it, that is, and then you'd think her days were numbered. She
just needs a bit of looking after from time to time. And it was
just easier.'

'Well, I think it's sweet,' said Mia-Rose.

Calum brightened a little; perhaps Emma would feel the same
way—if he ever got the chance to tell her, that was. Though he had
to consider perhaps she'd been and gone already. Maybe she hadn't
liked the look of him—even though he had been careful to sit
up straight so she couldn't tell he wasn't quite as tall as he'd said.
Perhaps, as he'd initially feared, she'd already seen him talking to
Mia-Rose, and had dismissed him as just like all the rest. With a
final glance towards the door, then at his watch, then his phone,
then the clock on the wall, he let out a long sigh.

'What's the matter?' asked Mia-Rose.

'She's not coming.'

'How do you know?'

Calum swivelled round in his chair, wincing with the effort,
then pulled up his cuff to expose his watch. 'Because it's six-thirty,'
he said, tapping the dial with his index finger. 'And we'd arranged to
meet half an hour ago.'

'And you're positive she's not here already?'

'Unlikely.'

'I might as well come back and join you, then.' Mia-Rose got up from her booth and sat back down in front of him, and despite his depression, Calum was grateful not to be sitting there alone. 'What are you going to do?'

Calum shrugged. 'I don't have a clue. I really thought...'

'What?'

'That she was someone special.'

'Maybe she's just shy. Maybe she feels awkward about how the two of you are meeting. Maybe she's sitting at one of these tables hoping you'll recognise her, and waiting for you to make the first move.'

Calum looked dejectedly round the restaurant. It was quite busy now, and apart from the two of them there were a few couples, and a number of groups of girls, though none of them seemed to be looking in his direction. No change there, he thought.

'But how can I find out? I can hardly go up to every girl in the place and ask if she's called Emma, can I? Even if I did, she could still lie, and say "no."'

Mia-Rose thought for a moment. 'Have you got her mobile number?'

'Well, yes.'

'Then I'll tell you how you can find out. Send her a text. Then if any of the girls in here looks at their phone... Bingo!'

'No, I couldn't. That'd be...'

'Making the first move?' She nodded towards his mobile, which was sitting on the table in front of him. 'How about it?'

Calum stared at his phone, then peered at the other diners, and realised it wasn't such a bad idea. 'Okay. But what should I write?'

'Easy.' Mia-Rose picked his mobile up. 'What's her number?'

'It's on speed dial. 142.'

'142?'

'Today's date.'

'Nice touch.' She tapped on Calum's phone for a second or two, then handed it back to him. 'Here.'

'What?'

'You should be the one to actually send it, don't you think?'

Calum took his phone, and stared at the message. Mia-Rose had written, which said simply 'Surprise!'

'Surprise?'

She smiled. 'Because it will be.'

He held his breath and pressed 'send,' and almost immediately, the sound of breaking glass came from Mia-Rose's handbag. He watched, wordlessly, as she fished inside, removed her mobile, and smiled at the screen.

'But…'

Calum stopped mid-sentence. He'd spotted the initials stuck on the back of Mia-Rose's phone case. Two silver letters. M-R.

Emma.

With an embarrassed smile, Mia-Rose reached across the table and gently closed his freshly shaven, carefully moisturised, gaping-open jaw.

∽

Julie read the message a third time, just to be sure of what it said, then quickly dialled Sophie's number.

'Are you sure?'

'Positive. He just told me.'

'And it wasn't just some…' Julie searched for the right phrase. '…pillow talk?'

Sophie decided not to admit the only pillow she'd seen was the one she'd been resting her injured foot on. 'Chance would be a fine thing. No, I poured my heart out to him and told him how I felt, and what I'd done, and he... Well, let's just say he set me straight regarding today.'

'I'm sorry, Sophie. But you're sure the card came from Mark?'

'Yes.'

'And the balloons, and the chocolates?'

'Well, I'm guessing they weren't from Nathan either, so there's a pretty good chance. Apparently Mark's had a thing for you for ages.'

'Oh. Right.'

As Julie processed that particular piece of information, she heard what sounded like an ambulance siren, and then Sophie came back on the line. 'Listen, Julie, I've got to go.'

'Where are you? You sound... Strange.'

'I'm at the hospital.'

'The hospital?'

'It's a long story. Anyway. I just thought you ought to know. About Mark. And I'm sorry.'

'For what?'

'For giving you the wrong information. I hope I haven't spoiled your day.'

'Not at all,' said Julie, though she wanted to add quite the opposite.

She ended the call and sat staring at her half-empty plate. So Mark did like her, and yet earlier she'd gone in and warned Nathan off... She felt foolish, then even more so as she realised to her horror that Nathan could have thought she'd been giving him a message for Mark.

She glanced at her watch. Six-thirty. Maybe she could go and catch him at the bowling, but if Nathan was going to be there, that might be a little awkward. Or would it? Perhaps they could all have a good laugh about it, and then she'd suggest she and Mark go on for a drink, and then...

Her train of thought was interrupted by the arrival of the next-door table's dessert order, and Julie looked at the plates hungrily as the waiter tried to remember who'd ordered what.

'Who's the tart?' he said, and Julie felt herself blush. She'd be, if she did anything more with Mark, and the last thing she wanted was to end up feeling just as guilty as she had after the Christmas party. There was something—or rather, someone—she needed to sort out first, and while she and Philip had never had the final 'divorce' conversation, and Valentine's Day perhaps wasn't the most sensitive time to do that, she knew she didn't have any choice. Not unless she wanted to risk completely pissing Mark off—and that, she somehow knew, would be a huge mistake. She just had to hope the lawyer in Philip wouldn't take her to the cleaners, though Julie reminded herself that was unlikely. He hadn't taken her anywhere in ages.

She gathered her things together, then turned round and tried to attract the waiter's attention from where he'd gone back to the far corner of the restaurant to read his copy of *the Evening Standard*. She tried noisily clearing her throat, but to no avail. Eventually, she took a deep breath and shouted 'Hey!', and the waiter looked up reluctantly.

'Hello?' she said, then waved. 'Over here!'

He put his paper down on a nearby table and ambled over towards her. 'You want something?'

Julie nodded. 'The bill, please. Quickly.'

The waiter gave her a look that inferred she'd just asked for his first-born, and sloped off towards the counter, while Julie fumbled in her handbag for her purse. When, after five minutes, the waiter was still jabbing at the till's buttons while cursing in a language Julie didn't recognise, she found a twenty-pound note in her purse and dropped it onto the table, then made her way quickly out of the restaurant.

She pushed her way through the early evening crowds and towards the Underground, wondering what on earth she was going to say, and how she could possibly start a conversation like the one she was planning on having. Maybe Philip would be drunk, but even if he wasn't, she was sure they'd have a row—it was all they seemed to do nowadays. And if she had to move out... Well, that's what she'd have to do. As to where she'd go—well, Julie would cross that bridge when she came to it.

As usual, the station was jammed—the evening rush-hour was in full swing, and Julie knew she stood little chance of getting on the first train. Just her luck—according to the announcer, it was a Chiswick train, too. She sighed as the crowd inched forward, gauging the number of people on the platform ahead of her against the amount of space on the train, and simultaneously readying herself for the ten-minute wait before the next Chiswick-bound one turned up.

She managed to get about a foot away from the doors before they began to close, and glared at the train as it left, envious of those passengers on their way home, but at the same time grateful for the extra few minutes it would give her to think. Relax, she told herself. That was the most important thing. To approach this in a calm, composed manner. Not to get overexcited. To keep her cool.

Though when she spotted Mark Webster in one of the carriages, a determined expression on his face, Julie almost had a heart attack.

11

'It's just in here,' said the nurse, wheeling Sophie through the ward and into a small, blue-curtained cubicle. 'The doctor will be along shortly to take a look, and then we'll get you X-rayed.'

She nodded, and the nurse disappeared, so Sophie sat her in her wheelchair to wait. A flimsy green hospital gown was hanging over the chair on the corner, and Sophie wondered if she was supposed to put it on. Gingerly, she stood up, then poked her head out through the curtains—the two other patients she could see were both wearing them, so she began to undress. Balancing awkwardly on her good foot, she removed her skirt and her blouse, placing them carefully over the back of the chair. She felt ridiculous, standing there in the bustier-and-knickers combination that had looked so nice in Selfridges, but seemed more than a little out of place in the cold starkness of the A&E department, and almost wanted to cry again. This certainly wasn't how she'd seen her evening going.

She regarded the gown suspiciously. It looked like it wouldn't quite fasten round her, and she was just debating whether it would be best to have the gap at the front or at the back when she heard the swish of the curtains being parted. She wheeled round, just as the best-looking Indian doctor she'd ever seen stuck his head through the gap.

Sophie stood there, mortified, as the doctor looked her up and down, then to her surprise, he swept the curtain completely open, revealing a group of his colleagues behind him.

'Very funny,' he said.

As his colleagues looked on in surprise, the doctor walked towards her. 'And what's your name?'

'Sophie,' said Sophie. trying desperately to cover herself with the gown.

'Sophie, eh?' The doctor turned and gave his colleagues a knowing look. 'And where exactly does it hurt, Sophie?'

'It's my...'

The doctor held a hand up. 'No, don't tell me. It's your chest.'

'My chest?' Sophie shook her head. 'No, it's my foot.'

'Your foot.' The doctor grinned. 'And you just had to strip all the way down to this because you had a sore foot, did you?'

'I just thought...' protested Sophie.

'I'll bet you did.' The doctor turned to face his colleagues, most of whom were looking anywhere but at Sophie—something she was extremely grateful for. 'So, which one of you was it?'

As they stared blankly back at him, a tall, spotty man Sophie thought was probably younger than she was cleared his throat. 'Which one was what?'

'You know! The one who arranged the stripper?'

'What stripper?' said the man.

'This stripper,' said the doctor, turning back towards Sophie. 'The one with the bad...' He looked down at Sophie's foot, noticing for the first time the bruising that had begun to develop on the top of it, and then his face went pale. 'Oh my god. I'm so sorry.'

As his colleagues tried hard not to laugh, the doctor took a quick step backwards and yanked the curtain shut. Sophie gratefully took the opportunity to slip the gown on, and was sitting on the bed by the time she eventually heard the doctor say 'knock knock.'

'Yes?'

'Are you decent?' he said, from the other side of the curtain.

Sophie looked down at herself. That, she knew, as she thought about how she'd tricked Nathan earlier, was a matter of opinion. 'Just about.'

The doctor opened the curtain a few inches and slipped in through the gap. 'I'm so terribly sorry,' he said sheepishly, closing the curtain carefully behind him. 'It's just, well, today's my birthday.' He jabbed a thumb over his shoulder. 'And I'd heard they were planning to play a trick on me. So when I saw you standing there in your... Well, dressed like that, I just assumed...'

He couldn't look at her, and while Sophie knew she had every right to feel insulted, in truth, after the evening she'd had, she found it a little funny. And she was a little flattered, too— while she'd hoped the money she'd spent in Selfridges might get her more than simply being mistaken for a stripper, she supposed his reaction meant she couldn't have looked too bad.

'That's OK,' she said. 'It can't be any fun to be working on your birthday. Or to have a birthday on Valentine's Day.'

'How do you mean?'

'Well, having to send cards to other people when it's your special day.'

'Oh, I didn't send any...' The doctor stopped talking. 'I'm sorry,' he said, still a little embarrassed. 'It was your foot, wasn't it?'

'Yes,' said Sophie, with a smile. 'My foot.'

He knelt down in front of her, and Sophie couldn't stop herself from letting out a short laugh.

'What's so funny?'

'I'm sorry. It's just...This. It would be most girls' idea of a result.'

'What would?'

'A good-looking doctor, down on one knee in front of them on Valentine's Day.'

As the doctor reddened even more, then turned his attention to examining her injury, Sophie almost pinched herself. It was the stuff that dreams were made of. Or at least, it would have been, if her foot hadn't still been throbbing.

'We better get you to X-Ray,' said the doctor, whose name, Sophie saw from his badge, was Doctor Jonesh. She caught her breath. Now there was a sign—it was nearly the same as hers. She repeated it a couple of times under her breath and liked the sound it made. More importantly, once they were married, she could still (nearly) be Sophie Jones. She wouldn't even have to get new business cards. Just add an 'h' onto her existing ones.

'Is there anyone here with you?'

Doctor Jonesh's voice snapped her out of her daydream, and she suddenly felt guilty. Ten minutes ago, she'd still hoped she and Nathan might have something, yet now, she was already contemplating being a doctor's wife. 'Yes. They're waiting in the, you know...'

'Waiting room?'

'Right.'

'Okay. Well, you'd better warn them they might be there for a while.'

Sophie swallowed hard and sat heavily back down in the wheelchair. 'Sure,' she said, though she knew she couldn't count on Nathan still being there when she came out. Not after how she'd behaved.

Doctor Jonesh called for the nurse, who wheeled Sophie through to the radiology department. As they passed through reception, as she'd feared, Nathan was nowhere to be seen, and Sophie realised she shouldn't be surprised. He'd probably be on his way back to Anti-Valentine's, and she couldn't blame him. Suddenly, she heard someone running up behind her.

'Sorry, Soph. Just had to make a phone call. And nice outfit!'

'Thanks a lot,' said Sophie, sarcastically. She'd blown a hundred and thirty pounds, and this was what Nathan ended up noticing her in.

He nodded down at her foot as he kept pace with her wheelchair. 'What's the diagnosis?'

Sophie gave what she hoped was a brave smile. 'Just off to X-Ray now.'

'Want me to hang around? I can give you a lift home afterwards if you like?'

Sophie thought about this for a second. As appealing as holding on to Nathan for the forty-minute journey back to Harrow was, she already felt guilty enough, and wasn't sure she wanted to put him out any more. And besides, if her foot was broken, then riding on the back of a Vespa might not be the safest way to travel.

'No, thanks. You've been brilliant. I'll get a minicab.'

'I don't mind. Honestly.'

'Nathan, please just go. I feel bad enough already'

'Sure?'

'Sure.' Sophie forced herself to smile. 'And Nathan?'

'Yes?'

'I'm sorry.'

'Forget about it.'

'Do you forgive me?'

'Nothing to forgive, Soph.' He smiled, then reached down and gave her hand a squeeze. 'I'll see you tomorrow.'

Sophie nodded disappointedly. 'See you tomorrow,' she said. Then as Nathan turned to leave, she told the nurse to wait.

'Nathan,' she called, and he walked back over to where she was sitting.

'Yeah?'

'I just…' Sophie hauled herself out of the wheelchair, stood up on tiptoe—on one foot, at least—and kissed him on the cheek.

'What was that for?'

'For looking after me,' she said, gazing up at him. 'For being such a gentleman.'

He smiled, then leaned down and kissed her on the forehead, and Sophie had to fight the urge to throw her arms around his neck and kiss him properly, though she knew nothing more would happen between them. Which she had to accept was probably what she deserved.

She sat heavily back down in the wheelchair, and as the nurse wheeled her away, Sophie wasn't sure what was hurting more—her foot, or the pain in her chest.

�○

Calum's first reaction had been to get up and leave—not because he didn't like Mia-Rose, but because, well, he felt…In truth, he didn't know what he felt. 'Surprised' was the first word that had sprung to mind, followed quickly by the word 'cheated,' but then again, Mia-Rose hadn't really cheated him, she just hadn't revealed herself to him until now. And if they were going to talk about cheating, she only needed to ask him about his height or adventure sports, so in the end, he'd stayed, staring mutely at her across the table.

'But... Why?' was all he could eventually manage.

'Well...' Mia-Rose paused—the waitress had appeared at their table, so she ordered herself a glass of white wine. 'Did you want something?'

Calum nodded. 'Beer,' he blurted out.

As the waitress left, Mia-Rose leaned across the table. 'Because you're funny, and kind, and polite, and nice looking, and I liked you, and suspected you liked me too. But no matter how many times I tried to bump into you in Pret, or flirt with you during a fire drill, you didn't seem to want to ask me out. I thought maybe you had a girlfriend, though you'd never mentioned one. And then by chance, I was having a quick skim through my potential matches on LondonDate when your photo caught my eye—one of the advantages of you being, you know...' Her eyes flicked up at his hair. 'What d'you call it? Strawberry blond? Anyway, I couldn't believe my luck, so I sent you that message.' She smiled. 'I thought it would be a good way for us to get to know each other properly, and if it turned out we didn't get on online... Well, seeing as you didn't know it was me, there'd have been no harm done. No awkward meetings by the photocopier. And I wouldn't have to hide behind my desk every time you walked past reception.'

'But...' Calum stared at her, conscious all he was saying at the moment were words of one syllable. He could see Mia-Rose's approach had made sense, and yet... It still didn't seem quite right.

The waitress reappeared and set a glass of wine the size of a goldfish bowl down on the table in front of Mia-Rose, followed by a bottle of Dutch beer, the name of which Calum couldn't pronounce. As he frowned at the label, the waitress frowned at him.

'Glass?'

Confused, Calum picked up the bottle and tapped it with a fingernail. 'Er, yes, I think it is.'

'No—did you want a glass? said the waitress, and when Calum shook his head, Mia-Rose laughed.

'See? You're funny!'

He stared back at her. So far, he couldn't say the same about this evening.

'Are you ready to order?' asked the waitress.

Calum shook his head again. 'No,' he said, abruptly, and as the waitress scuttled off, Mia-Rose's face fell.

'What's the matter?'

'It's just...The pretence.'

'It was only my name that was different, Calum, and even then, not that different. And you know what it's like on those sites. You've got to protect yourself a little bit. But the rest...The person you got to know—that was the real me. And haven't we all pretended to be someone else at least once in our lives?'

Calum couldn't meet her eyes. After all, she had him there. 'I'm sorry. This just wasn't how I pictured this evening going. It all feels a little...'

'What?'

'Strange.'

'Strange? That doesn't sound good.'

Mia-Rose took a large mouthful of wine, then stuffed her mobile back into her bag, and Calum began to panic.

'What are you doing?'

'I think I'd better go.'

'What? Why?'

'Why do you think?'

Mia-Rose looked as if she was about to cry, and Calum suddenly felt awful. She stood up, and he did the same, knowing he had to think on his feet—in both senses.

'Please,' he said, reaching over and putting a hand on her arm. 'Stay.'

'You're just saying that because you feel sorry for me,' said Mia-Rose, her eyes glistening with tears.

'Not at all.' Calum reached into his jacket pocket for his handkerchief. 'Here,' he said, but he'd forgotten the condoms were in there, and as he pulled out the handkerchief, the box fell out too, and tumbled into Mia-Rose's wine glass. He stood there, mortified, but instead of stomping out of the restaurant as he'd feared, Mia-Rose suddenly burst out laughing.

'Oh Calum, you old romantic.'

'Huh?'

'I've heard of men presenting girls with engagement rings in a glass of champagne on Valentine's Day, but this . . .'

'I'm so sorry. They . . .' Calum stopped talking. Telling Mia-Rose he only had the condoms because his Mum had presented him with them this morning would probably make things worse. He retrieved the box from the glass, dried it on his napkin, and slipped it back into his pocket. 'At least let me buy you another drink.'

Mia-Rose hesitated. 'Are you sure?'

Calum nodded. 'I'd hardly expect you to drink the rest of that one. And I'm sorry. I was just a little . . .'

She smiled tentatively. 'Surprised?'

'And flattered. I never thought someone as lovely as you would . . .' Calum decided to leave it there. If ever there was a reason to stop putting himself down, it was standing right in front of him. 'Would you like to start again?'

To his relief, Mia-Rose sat back down. 'Yes, please.'

He waved at the waitress and indicated another glass of wine, then moved out of the booth, before reversing his steps and sitting back down himself. 'Hi,' he said, holding his hand out so Mia-Rose could shake it. 'I'm Calum.'

'Mia-Rose,' said Mia-Rose, giving his fingers a polite squeeze. 'M-R to my friends.'

And although it might simply have been down to static from the carpet, Calum could swear he felt something resembling a spark.

'It's lovely to see you,' he said.

ᘐ

Mark Webster was sitting nervously on a District Line tube to Chiswick, trying to psych himself up, or at least work out a strategy, and so far, the only one he could think of was to simply tell Julie how he felt. Somewhere inside him a voice kept saying *Don't go there* (either with Julie, or to Chiswick), but Mark had run out of ideas—and patience. And quite honestly, he needed to know what Julie was playing at. If she was playing at anything.

He got off at Gunnersbury and made his way out of the station, aiming for Fairfax Road, taking in his surroundings as he walked. Chiswick was certainly different to where he lived—the funky mix of modern flats and warehouse conversions were what had attracted Mark to Bermondsey in the first place, and in contrast, Chiswick's wide, tree-lined streets seemed more genteel, more established, more traditional; the only Warehouse here was the shop he'd just walked past on the high street. He'd memorised Julie's address a while ago when he'd debated (and chickened out of) sending some flowers to her home, and as he followed the route he knew so well (thanks to numerous Google Street View journeys from the safety of his office), he found his way blocked by mothers with oversized buggies, or loading children in and out of massive four-wheel-drive vehicles parked haphazardly up on the pavement.

As Mark did his best to dodge round them, receiving a couple of painful bangs on the ankle for his trouble, he was also struck by the absence of single people. Everywhere he looked, there seemed to be young couples, or mothers with children. Unlike central London or where he lived, Chiswick had more of a feel of a place for families, and he wondered why Julie lived somewhere like this, and realised just how little he knew about her, and the thought almost made him want to turn around and go home. Though perhaps it was good running territory. Perhaps she was from here. Perhaps he was being stupid, putting himself on the line for what effectively had been just one kiss. Or was he? Mark had kissed (he totted it up in his head as he walked) fourteen women in his life in more than a peck-on-the-cheek kind of way, and none of them had ever made him feel like that kiss with Julie had. And while he wasn't naïve enough to think that something like that was the basis for a relationship, it certainly wasn't a bad place to start.

He reached Fairfax Road and strode along the pavement until he found number twenty-three, a tall, red-brick building he recognised from Street View (though the ivy growing down one side had flourished since Google's camera car had visited), so he walked up the steps and stood staring at the front door. He was feeling nervous, but at the same time, Mark knew he had nothing to lose— apart from his credibility, and his job, perhaps. He took a deep breath, located the buzzer for the ground-floor flat, and pressed the button, still not knowing what he was going to say to her, but in the absence of anything else, the truth seemed like the best idea, and if today wasn't a good day for telling someone how you felt about them, then Mark didn't know when was.

When there was no answer, he waited for a moment, then pressed the buzzer again, then considered stepping into the garden to peer through her window, but he worried he'd attract the attention of the neighbours—or possibly the police. Plus that might seem desperate. And even though that was how he felt, he certainly didn't want Julie to know that.

Mark wondered where she could be. She'd left the office before him—he'd been sure about that—but why hadn't she come straight home? Unless she'd changed her mind about Anti-Valentine's (although surely Nathan would have said), or even had a date—though that was one possibility he couldn't allow himself to entertain.

He pressed the buzzer one last time, waited a few more seconds, then turned and headed dejectedly back down the steps. As he reached the pavement, he heard the sound of a bolt being drawn, so he bounded back up to the door and fixed a smile on his face. Perhaps Julie had been in the shower. Maybe she'd appear, wrapped only in a towel, her hair wet, and as she reached out to greet him, the towel would fall...

'Yes?'

Mark's smile faded almost immediately as a grumpy-looking man in a dressing gown answered the door.

'I, er...' He stood back, and looked at the number on the door. It would be just his luck to have been ringing the wrong bell. 'This is number twenty-three?'

'Yes,' said the man, gruffly.

'Garden flat?'

'Yes.'

'Fairfax Road?'

The man tutted. and pulled the belt of his dressing-gown tighter. 'What do you want?'

'I...' Mark glanced at his watch. 'I'm sorry. Did I wake you?'

'Is this some kind of doorstep survey on sleeping habits?'

'Sorry. No. I'm...Is Julie in?'

'Julie?' The man looked him up and down suspiciously. 'Who wants her?'

I do, thought Mark. 'It's Mark. From her office?' He'd phrased it like a question, but the man showed no sign of recognition.

'Well in that case, you should know she's still there.'

He moved to shut the door, but Mark held up a hand. 'I'm sorry. And you are?'

The man looked at him contemptuously. 'Her husband,' he said, before slamming the door shut.

Mark stood there for a moment, staring at the brass letterbox as it clattered shut. Julie was married. But she'd never said she had a husband, and as far as he could remember, she didn't wear a wedding ring.

He felt a little light-headed, and reached a hand out to steady himself against the wall. Even though he hated to admit it, now it all made sense. She'd drunkenly kissed him, and then of course she hadn't wanted to mention it. As the pieces all fell into place, he felt angry, used, and that he'd wasted the last seven weeks. Why couldn't she have told him? Well, maybe he could understand that too. In fact, the only thing that still puzzled him was what Julie was doing married to someone like that.

With a shake of his head, he walked back down the steps and headed miserably towards the tube station.

❧

Nathan Field smiled to himself as he rode his Vespa out of the hospital car park. He'd been flattered by Sophie's attention, not angered by what she'd done, and the fact that someone would go to such lengths to get close to him...Well, he had to see that as a real confidence boost—and it was the first time he'd had his confidence boosted by a woman in a long while.

He checked his watch, remembered it was an hour fast, and wondered what to do with the rest of his evening. The office crowd might still be at the bowling, but they'd probably all be angrily wondering where he was, so turning up now, particularly when they were several drinks ahead of him, probably wasn't the best idea. No, he decided, he'd stop off back at the office, check his emails, then simply head back home with a takeaway.

As he steered his bike back towards the West End, the one-way system took him left and down towards the Strand, and Nathan suddenly realised he was riding down the street where Ellie worked. He'd been here several times after they'd split up, skulking behind the postbox on the other side of the road so as not to be spotted, usually when he was feeling depressed, or lonely, or a combination of the two (i.e. the last two Valentine's Days), watching her as she'd headed out to lunch, wondering whether she'd be meeting what's-his-name at the tapas bar around the corner, just like the two of them used to do all those years ago.

He shook his head as he remembered his trip here last year, how he'd gazed up at her window and felt a little sick when he'd spotted the once-familiar mane of blonde hair. As seemed to be the norm for her job, Ellie had been talking animatedly on the phone, the handset jammed between her shoulder and her ear as she typed something on her keyboard. Always multitasking, was Ellie, never happy unless she was doing two things at once. That was something he'd found out to his cost.

He'd watched her for a while, remembering her voice, half-smiling in recognition as she tilted her head back and laughed, then flicked her hair out of her eyes with her hand. He'd loved that about her, those little mannerisms—along with a lot of other things too. Though as he thought about them today, he began to realise they were just that: things. And things (as he'd found out when he'd eventually gone into Habitat a few days after the IKEA incident and bought a job lot of crockery) could be replaced.

He slowed the bike down as he neared her building. While the thought of bumping into her always used to make him nervous, today he was pretty confident he could relax. It was gone seven, and no-one in a relationship would still be at work at this time on Valentine's Day. Not if they knew what was good for them.

As he approached the zebra crossing outside her office, he noticed a group about to cross, so squeezed hard on his brakes, bringing the Vespa to a sudden halt just before the black-and-white lines, causing the man at the front of the group to jump sharply backwards. Nathan made an apologetic face, nodded that they should cross, and found himself looking straight at Ellie. As she stared back at him, his heart started thumping, and he fought the urge to twist hard on the throttle and screech away, but he knew it was already too late. She'd obviously seen him, and while she looked almost as shocked as he suspected he did, to Nathan's surprise, her expression quickly morphed into a smile. She waited until the rest of the group had made it across the road, then walked over to his side.

'Hello, stranger!'

'Hello yourself.' Nathan willed the hammering in his chest to stop. 'You're looking...'

'You look...'

They laughed at having spoken simultaneously, and then Ellie put a hand on his arm. 'It's nice to see you. How are you?'

'Good, thanks. You?'

'I'm...' A honking sound from behind him made Nathan jump, and he realised he was still sitting in the middle of the road, blocking the car behind him. 'Hold on,' he said, pulling the bike over to the pavement.

'This isn't your normal route.'

He switched the bike's engine off and removed his helmet. 'No, I've just been to the hospital.'

Her smile wavered. 'The hospital? Is everything OK?' she asked, and Nathan was touched by the concern in her voice.

'Yes, fine. A friend just had a minor accident. I was just dropping...'—he stopped short of saying 'her'—'...them off.'

'Oh,' said Ellie. 'Right.' She regarded him for a moment, as if weighing something up, then her smile reappeared. 'Got time for a coffee?'

He made a show of looking at his watch. The thought of spending any time with Ellie today of all days was making him a little uncomfortable, but Nathan also suspected it might be—what was the word that Mark kept using?—cathartic.

'Well, I was heading back to the office, but I suppose I've got a few minutes.'

'Great.'

He lifted his bike up onto its stand, then followed Ellie into the Costa on the corner, trying not to think about how good she looked, doing his best to ignore how the smart black business suit she'd seemingly been sewn into accentuated her figure as they walked up to the counter.

'Double espresso for me,' she said to the barista. 'Nathan?'

'Latte,' said Nathan. 'Decaf.'

Ellie raised one eyebrow. 'Decaf?'

'What's wrong with that?'

She handed a few pound coins to the man behind the till, simultaneously waving Nathan's offer to pay away. 'I didn't know you drank decaf.'

Nathan shrugged. He hadn't, back when they were together, regarding it in the same light as non-alcoholic beer, or diet Coke, or kissing without tongues—in his opinion, all of those things were worse for having had their key ingredient removed. But now he could see that at times, all you needed was the taste, without any of the after-effects.

'So,' she said, as they waited for their coffees. 'How are things?'

Nathan considered the question. It was a pretty innocuous one, he supposed, even though he couldn't think how on earth to respond. 'Fine,' was what he eventually settled for. 'You?'

'Good. Work's really busy. We've just landed this huge new account, and the client wants us to make a big splash by...' She smiled. 'Well, I'm sure you don't want to hear about the intricacies of PR.'

Nathan shrugged. 'I don't mind. As long as you'll let me bore you afterwards with how I upgraded our office system to Windows 7 last weekend.'

'Point taken.' Ellie rolled her eyes. 'You and computers. I still haven't forgiven you about that Facebook thing. That was one page I didn't "like."'

As the barista placed their drinks on the counter, Nathan stared at her incredulously. Ellie looked like she was trying not to smile, so he couldn't tell whether she was being serious, but then he supposed he shouldn't be surprised. He'd never been able to tell if she was being serious in the many arguments they'd had over the stupidest things when they'd lived together, and he certainly hadn't been able to tell she wasn't serious about him. But surely she couldn't think what he'd done in changing her status update was worse than her infidelity?

'Well, I haven't forgiven you for cheating on me with what's-his-name,' he said, picking up their coffees and carrying them over to a nearby table. 'So we're even.'

'People I knew saw that status update. My boss. Clients.'

'Was it wrong?'

'Of course it was.'

'I meant the facts. Not what I did.'

'Come on, Nathan. That's in the past.'

'It might be for you...'

'It should be for you, too.'

'Well, that's easy for you to say. You've got...' Nathan frowned as they sat down. What was his name?

Ellie couldn't meet his eyes. 'I don't, actually.'

'What do you mean?'

She turned to stare out of the window. 'We split up.'

'When?'

'A couple of months ago,' she said, ripping open a sachet of sweetener and pouring the contents into her cup.

'Oh.' Nathan tried to keep his voice level as he passed her a stirrer. 'I'm sorry.'

'Yeah. He...' Ellie looked directly at him. 'He'd met someone else.'

'Ellie, that's...' Nathan struggled to find a different word to 'fantastic.' 'Terrible. Are you OK?'

She nodded. 'I suppose you think it's funny.'

'Not funny, exactly. Just, well...' To tell the truth, Nathan wasn't sure what he felt about it. On the one hand, this was revenge—and unlike changing Ellie's Facebook status, not one that he had to feel bad about getting. But on the other hand, he knew how much this kind of thing hurt, and he wouldn't wish that kind of hurt on anybody. 'Ironic, I suppose.'

Ellie stirred her coffee slowly. 'Is that why you're here, today of all days? To dredge this all up again?'

Nathan shook his head. 'Not at all. I was just passing by accident. I assumed you'd be long gone by now. And in fact, you were the one who mentioned it.'

'Sorry.' She nudged him. 'As you should be for telling the world I was having an affair.'

'Don't tell me you want me to apologise?'

Her eyes flicked up at his, and she half-smiled. 'I suppose not.'

He picked up his coffee and sipped it thoughtfully. 'You know the funny thing? It wasn't the cheating and the lying that really bugged me.'

Ellie looked surprised. 'It wasn't?'

'Well, maybe a little. It was more... How did I get it so wrong?'

'How do you mean?'

'I wanted to marry you, and I thought you might feel the same way. How did I misread the signs?'

Ellie smiled, and took his hand, and Nathan had to stop himself from flinching. 'If you remember, there weren't any signs. That's how I got away with it.'

'Yes, but...'

'Nathan, there wasn't anything to get wrong. Maybe it was just bad timing. We were young. People change. And I knew I still had some changing to do.'

'But why were you seeing... him? When you knew I loved you. Wanted to be with you. For the rest of my life.'

'I suppose because I was scared.'

'Scared?'

Ellie nodded vigorously. 'You don't think it's scary? The rest of anyone's life...It's a long time. I wasn't sure you weren't right for me, but equally, I wasn't sure you were. And how was I going to be sure—say "yes" to you, then hope for the best?' She sighed. 'And then Chas came along...'

Chas, thought Nathan. *Thank you.*

'...and I was flattered by the attention. And equally, in some perverse kind of way, I thought it might make me more sure about how I felt about you. About us.'

'And it did, didn't it?'

'Yes, actually. You were offering me forever. Chas was a bit of fun. And back then, I wanted fun.'

'We were having fun. We could have had more fun. Being married might have been fun.'

Ellie leant forward in her chair. 'But it might not have been. And that's what I was worried about. Particularly if it was going to be for the rest of my life.'

Nathan picked his coffee up, then put it straight back down again. 'So you went off with him because you were worried about us?'

She shook her head. 'No, Nathan. Because I was worried about me.'

'But to just go with him, to leave so abruptly, and cut me off like you did...'

'What would you have preferred—that I kept on seeing Chas behind your back? The only thing I knew was I couldn't possibly find the right person if I was still hanging on to the wrong one...'

'Ouch.'

'I didn't mean it like that.'

'Basically, you're saying the problem was me, right?'

Ellie looked at him imploringly, as if needing him to understand. 'It was both of us, Nathan. People are complex. Different.

So what are the chances of meeting someone who feels the same way about you, while feeling the same way you do about everything else, at the exact same time you do?'

'Loads of people do. Or at least, they think they do.'

'And more than half of them get divorced. What was I going to do—marry you, knowing that eventually we'd make each other miserable and become just another statistic, and maybe have wasted the best years of our lives on something that was always likely to end in tears?' She sighed. 'I was twenty-seven. I didn't want to get married.'

'To me.'

'To anyone. Until recently, that was. But he didn't want to marry me. So I suppose I got my just deserts.'

Ellie stared into her cup, and Nathan was surprised to find himself feeling sorry for her. Eventually, he smiled. 'If it's any consolation, you do get over it. In time.'

'Really? How long does it take, exactly?'

Nathan decided not to answer, though he found himself thinking that three years should just about cover it.

'It's funny,' continued Ellie. 'I knew you'd understand.'

'Yes, well, that's only because you did the same thing to me, remember?'

'Yes, Nathan,' she said. 'I remember.'

They regarded each other for a moment, and then Nathan picked his cup up and held it out towards her. 'Happy Valentine's Day, Ellie.'

Ellie returned the gesture, and they clinked cups across the table. 'Happy Valentine's Day,' she said, then seemed to be considering something for a moment. 'Listen, did you ... No. Forget it.'

'What?'

'I was just thinking. I'm not doing anything this evening—obviously—and if you weren't ...'

Nathan looked at her levelly. For the last three years, he'd wondered what he'd say if Ellie ever wanted him back. And while this was hardly the same thing, he was shocked he wasn't leaping at the chance to at least spend a few hours with her.

'I can't,' he said, eventually. 'I'm busy.'

'Oh really?' He could hear what sounded like disappointment in her voice. 'What are you doing?'

'I'm sorry. That was a little insensitive of me. Nothing like that. We're just going out. A few of us. From the office.' He decided not to mention the Anti-Valentine's concept. 'Bowling.'

'Ah, bowling.'

'Your favourite.'

Ellie made a face, then drained the last of her espresso. 'I suppose I should let you get going, then.'

He glanced at his watch. 'I suppose.'

'Nice watch, by the way.'

'Thanks. A friend bought it for me.'

She widened her eyes. 'So we're friends now?'

Nathan nodded, then leaned across the table and kissed her on the cheek, and for the first time in three years, was able to smell her perfume without the usual cloying feeling of nostalgia. 'Friends,' he said.

He walked her to the bus stop, then climbed onto his bike and accelerated away down the street without looking back. While they'd parted as friends, Nathan suspected the truth was he'd never see her again. And while, at one time in his life, the thought of that would have been the worst thing in the world, today, Nathan realised, he was pretty okay with it.

Sophie Jones was sitting in the corridor outside the X-Ray department, patiently waiting for her turn, while simultaneously trying to ignore the drunken advances of a wild-haired old man sitting opposite. She was still wearing the green gown, clutching tightly on to it to make sure she didn't flash her underwear at anyone else, and while her foot was feeling a little better, she still didn't dare try and put her weight on it.

Eventually the radiologist came and wheeled her inside, and gently lifted her foot up onto the machine, then retired behind a thick glass window as he took her X-ray. This was what it had come to, Sophie mused: men hiding from her behind protective screens. Though she suspected where Nathan was concerned, she'd be the one hiding from him at work tomorrow.

Maybe she wouldn't go in. Perhaps she had broken her foot. There was no way she could get into work wearing a plaster cast. so she'd just have to phone in sick... Sophie sighed. Even if she did that, she'd have to face him eventually. And besides, who'd be there to look after her at home?

As the radiologist wheeled her back into the corridor, it occurred to Sophie that maybe she should go *home* home, back to Eastbourne, and stay with her parents while her foot healed. Some time away from London might even do her good. Perhaps Darren would come and visit her. Maybe they could even be friends—in the real world, if not on Facebook. Though the danger of that, she knew, was that she might decide not to come back.

The radiologist reappeared and handed her a brown envelope containing her X-ray, and as the nurse wheeled her back to her cubicle, Sophie couldn't ignore the irony—of all the envelopes to be receiving on Valentine's Day, this was hardly what she'd had in mind. She wondered whether it was safe to get dressed, but didn't want to be caught in her underwear again, so decided to stay as she was. After a few minutes, she heard Doctor Jonesh shout 'knock knock' as before, then he walked tentatively in through the curtain.

'How do you feel?'

Sophie thought for a moment. *Lonely* was the first word that leapt to mind, followed by *desperate*, until she realised he was probably referring to her foot. 'A bit better. Still a little sore, though.'

He nodded at the envelope. 'Is that for me?'

'It's my X-ray.'

'I didn't think it was a birthday card.'

'No.' Sophie handed it over. 'Of course.'

Doctor Jonesh slipped the X-ray out from the envelope, then stuck it up on the lightbox on the wall. 'So, what had you been doing?' he said, studying the black and white image.

'Bowling.'

'On Valentine's Day? That's not very romantic.'

Sophie shrugged. 'It was kind of an office thing.'

'Was that your boyfriend who brought you in?'

'No. Just a friend.' Sophie held her breath and watched Doctor Jonesh closely, waiting for a response to what she'd just said, though at the same time, she knew she couldn't count on Nathan still being her friend after today. Not that he'd really been her friend beforehand.

'That's good,' he said, after a pause so long Sophie worried she was turning blue.

She gulped in a lungful of air. 'It is?' she said, hopefully. Maybe the lingerie had worked its magic after all. Just on a different person.

'Yes. If you look here, at the metatarsals...' Doctor Jonesh was referring to a part of the X-ray, Sophie realised despondently, not expressing an interest in her lack of a boyfriend. 'You'll see there's no break.'

'No break. Right.' Sophie feigned interest in the blurry mono-chrome image, though she was sure the same wouldn't have been true if he'd been examining an X-ray of her heart. 'So what's the diagnosis?'

Doctor Jonesh took the X-ray down from the lightbox and slipped it back inside the envelope. 'Just bruising,' he said. 'I'll give you some anti-inflammatories and painkillers to take for the next few days. Oh, and you should be careful about putting any weight on…'

'You think I should go on a diet?' interrupted Sophie.

'Putting any weight on your foot, I meant. Don't worry. From what I saw…I mean, you look…' Doctor Jonesh blushed again, and Sophie smiled up at him from her wheelchair, and for the brief-est of seconds, wondered if they were perhaps having a moment. Though she knew her judgement wasn't really to be trusted regard-ing that kind of thing.

'Listen, I'm really sorry about earlier,' Doctor Jonesh continued. 'Here.' He reached into his jacket pocket, then handed her his busi-ness card.

'What's this for?' said Sophie, amazed at his forwardness.

'If you want to make a formal complaint, these are my details.' He picked up a clipboard from the bed, and started making some notes on it. 'There are some forms at reception. Just fill one in and give it back to the receptionist.'

'Oh.' Sophie's heart sank again. 'That's okay. No harm done. And besides, how could I, when it's your birthday?'

Doctor Jonesh smiled gratefully. 'Only for another few hours, thank goodness.'

'You don't like birthdays?'

'Not when I have to work on them.'

Sophie turned the card over in her hand, and something occurred to her. If this was the only card she was going to get this Valentine's Day, then she wasn't going to let the opportunity pass her by. This, she suspected, was one of those 'scruff of the neck' moments, and she knew she had to grab it.

'Well, in that case…' Sophie took a deep breath. 'What time do you finish work?'

Doctor Jonesh glanced up at the clock on the wall. 'In about half an hour. Why?'

'Because I thought you might let me buy you a birthday drink, if you don't have any other plans. And if it wouldn't be, you know, hypocritical.'

Doctor Jonesh looked puzzled. 'Oh,' he said. 'You mean if it's not against my Hippocratic oath?'

Sophie shrugged. 'Something like that.'

Doctor Jonesh regarded her for a moment, and then he nodded. 'That would be lovely,' he said, breaking into a smile.

As he backed out of the cubicle, Sophie cleared her throat. 'Can I get dressed now?' she said.

Doctor Jonesh hesitated for a millisecond, then nodded. 'Well, we can hardly go for a drink with you looking like that, can we? And you won't be getting plastered.'

'That depends how many drinks we…' Sophie stopped, mid-sentence. 'You meant my foot, didn't you?'

He smiled again. 'I'll get the nurse to put a support bandage on for you. It should be easier for you when you want to, you know…'

'Take it off?'

'Exactly.'

Their eyes met again, but this time Doctor Jonesh didn't look away, and somehow at that moment, Sophie knew Nathan had been right that morning. Tonight was going to be the start of something special.

～

To her shame, Julie Marshall's first reaction when she spotted Mark Webster walking along the pavement towards her was to hide, or rather, her first reaction was to swear under her breath, and then she'd looked around for a place to hide. But hiding would have been immature, she told herself, and although she hadn't behaved particularly like a responsible adult where Mark was concerned, she'd been hiding from him ever since the Christmas party, and to duck behind the nearest parked car now would be taking that a little too far. Besides, by the way Mark seemed to be staring dejectedly at his feet as he made his way back towards the station, she could have stood right where she was and he'd probably have walked straight past. And things having reached the point they evidently had, Julie knew she couldn't let that happen.

'Mark,' she said, as he drew near, then 'Mark,' a little louder.

As he looked up, she could see the pain in his eyes, but he didn't stop walking, so after a second Julie hurried to catch Mark up, then fell into step beside him. She couldn't think what to say, so decided not to say anything, but as they neared the station, she realised this tactic wasn't working.

'Can I explain?'

'No need.' Mark couldn't bring himself to look at her. 'Your husband's already told me everything I need to know.'

Julie swore to herself again. 'Mark, he's... I mean... Philip and I... We're...' She shook her head. Until she knew what Philip had said, she wasn't sure what her approach should be.

'Seriously. Don't bother.'

Mark kept his eyes fixed on the pavement, still wondering how he could have got it so wrong, and did his best to ignore Julie as he considered his options. There was nothing for him here now, that was clear, and while going back home to his empty flat wasn't particularly appealing, he didn't think he had anywhere else to go.

Deciding he needed some distance, he broke into a jog, forgetting for a moment that Julie had been training for the marathon. In a matter of seconds, she was at his shoulder.

'I can keep this up all day,' she said, eventually.

Mark couldn't. He was already breathing heavily, but fortunately they'd nearly reached the station, so after a few more desperate yards, he fished in his pocket for his Oyster card and then turned to face her. 'Enjoy the rest of your Valentine's Day,' he puffed, then swiped himself through the barrier without looking back.

Julie stood there for a moment, then pulled her purse out and fumbled for her own card, dropping it onto the floor in the process. 'Shit!' she said, out loud this time, and then bent down and scrabbled around to find it. 'Mark!' she called, swiping the barrier open and following him onto the platform. 'Hold on.'

The waiting train was about to leave, and Mark had already got on, so she sprinted towards it and jumped on through the rapidly closing doors, then realised they were on different carriages, so she made her way to the connecting door and peered through the window. Mark was several seats away, so she pulled the dirty glass panel down and knocked loudly on the corresponding window. After a few moments, a large Rastafarian got out of his seat and pulled it open.

'Yes?'

'I need to speak to him,' said Julie, pointing to where Mark was sitting, staring vacantly out of the window.

'Hey,' called the man, making Mark jump. 'She wants to speak to you.'

Mark followed the direction of the Rastafarian's pointing finger, then almost recoiled in shock. 'Are you following me?'

'No, Mark. I often ride the District Line for fun of an evening.'

'What do you want?'

'I...' Julie looked around. The carriage was quite busy, and the last thing she wanted was to play this scene out in public. 'Could you come here? Please?'

Mark puffed air out of his cheeks resignedly, then stood up and moved obediently towards the window, the fight all but knocked out of him. 'Why didn't you tell me?'

'I'm sorry.' Julie sighed. 'It's...complicated.'

'It didn't look that complicated to me.'

'We're separated.'

'It didn't look that separate to me either.'

With the windows open, a breeze was rushing through the carriages, ruffling their hair as if they were standing on top of some windswept moor. 'Mark, it's a long story,' said Julie, pushing her fringe out of her eyes. 'But please believe me. We haven't been...' She reddened slightly. '...husband and wife for a long time.'

'Since Christmas?'

'Especially since Christmas,' she said, and Mark's heart skipped a beat. 'We just live together. But not, you know, in the Biblical sense.'

'The Biblical sense? What does that mean, exactly? Is it where you get stoned for adultery?'

Julie winced. 'Mark, it's not like that.'

'Did you tell him what happened between us?'

'God no. But only because I didn't want to hurt him. He's been going through a bad time, and I...'

'And what about hurting me? You mercilessly kissed me, and then...' He stopped himself, realising how pathetic that sounded.

'I'm sorry. I know how it must have seemed.'

'So why did you do it? Kiss me, I mean.'

'Because I...' Julie felt herself blush even deeper. 'Because I wanted to. And I thought you wanted to kiss me too. Then when we did…I hadn't been kissed for such a long time, and certainly not like that. And afterwards, all I could think about was doing it again.'

'So why didn't you?'

'Where, exactly? In the stationery cupboard?' She threw her hands in the air. 'And how could I? Given…'

'Your husband?'

'My soon to be ex-husband,' said Julie, then she caught herself. It was the first time she'd said it out loud, and it surprised her how easily the words had come out. 'At least, he will be, when I do tell him about us.'

'Us?' said Mark. Despite how he was feeling, he still loved the way the word sounded. 'Is there an "us"?'

'I hope there can be,' said Julie, as the tube rattled into the next station. 'But I need to tell Philip first. Then, once I have, we can work out where we are.'

Mark peered out of the window. 'Turnham Green?'

'I don't care how jealous it makes him.'

'No.' he pointed at the sign on the platform. 'Where we are. It's Turnham Green.'

'Oh, I thought you meant…'

Julie half-smiled, and Mark reached though the window and touched the side of her face. 'I'm sorry, Julie. I just felt—feel—like such an idiot.'

Julie took his hand. 'I'm the idiot. For not trying to explain.'

'Why didn't you?'

'I didn't think you'd understand.'

'Why not?'

'Because I'm not sure I do.'

Mark shook his head. 'Try me.'

'I want to. But like I said. It's…complicated.'

'So is accountancy. But I understand that.'

As Julie stared at him, wondering where to start, the tube came to a halt, and as the doors opened, she squeezed his fingers, then turned and ran out of the carriage. Mark stood at the window, wondering whether he should follow her, but suspected she probably needed her space—and he needed to think things through himself. A beeping sound signified the doors were closing, and he realised it was too late anyway, until he felt someone standing behind him, and he wheeled around.

'Hi,' he said, unable to keep the smile from his face. 'Fancy seeing you here.'

'I could say the same thing to you,' said Julie, and as the tube jolted forward suddenly, she lost her balance and fell straight into his arms. For a moment, they just looked at each other, and Julie held her breath—they hadn't been this close since that night in the taxi. And then, before she could stop herself, she stood on tiptoe and kissed him.

'Can you wait until I get this sorted out?' she said eventually, breathlessly, and Mark nodded. The truth was, he'd been waiting for Julie for all of his life, so what were a few more weeks?

And although the rush-hour tube didn't quite have the privacy of their post-Christmas-party taxi, they kissed again. Though perhaps because it was Valentine's Day, nobody in the carriage seemed to mind.

∽

Nathan Field piloted his bike along Frith Street, a smile on his face. Meeting Ellie had been great. Fantastic, even. No longer did he feel a fool or a mug—he'd just done what most other people did, and had a mismatch in expectations. And in actual fact, he could now see she'd done him a favour by turning down his proposal.

At the same time, he realised he'd been stupid, and that Mark had been right. For the last three years, he'd put Ellie up on a pedestal, assumed she'd been this perfect woman, and yet he'd been so wrong. She'd cheated on him. Misled him. Deceived him, even—someone perfect would hardly behave like that. And if he needed further proof, someone else had dumped her. And as sad as that was, the relief he'd felt upon hearing it was like a huge weight being lifted from his shoulders.

He realised something else too. He shouldn't be holding out for the perfect woman, but like Mark had said, just someone who was perfect for him, and the only way to find her was to start looking. Of course, round the corner from Old Compton Street was perhaps the wrong place to have that revelation, but Nathan didn't care.

For a moment, he wondered how many opportunities he'd missed, or passed up, over the last few years. Then just as quickly, he decided they weren't important. What mattered was what he did from now on in, so no more would he avoid eye contact, or not respond to flirting, in a pointless attempt to be faithful to the memory of someone who'd been unfaithful to him. He would be a number-collector. A street-flirt. And he was going to start right now.

He steered the Vespa into Bateman Street and stopped outside the office. The lights were blazing—the cleaners, probably—so he nipped inside, nodded hello to the man noisily Hoovering the reception area, then headed downstairs and fired up his laptop. Sixteen messages—half of them from everyone at SuperBowl, wondering where he was.

With a couple of mouse-clicks, he reset his clock, then wondered what Mark was up to, and thought about giving him a call, but swapped-phone issues aside, Mark might be busy with Julie, and the last thing Nathan wanted was to interrupt that, so instead he logged off from Outlook and strolled back outside. Soho was still buzzing, the pub on the corner had drinkers spilling out onto the street, and, for a moment, Nathan felt perhaps Valentine's Day wasn't so bad after all, even if you were single.

He supposed he could head back to SuperBowl and join everyone for a drink or two, though thanks to his diversion with Ellie, they'd be even drunker than when he'd considered meeting them before. Besides, his turning up now would only mean there'd be an odd number. And Nathan didn't want to be the odd man out.

He walked round the corner, passing the bored-looking girls smoking outside Spank-o-rama. It probably wasn't the most popular venue on Valentine's night, and he wondered where they'd rather be this evening, whether they all had someone at home, waiting for them to finish dancing nearly naked in front of complete strangers—and to think he'd been worried about his choice of career.

The thought reminded him of Ellie, and he looked at his watch. She'd probably be sitting at home on her own by now, and for the first time in three years, he felt a little of something he recognised as pity. It hadn't been her fault he wasn't what she wanted. It wasn't his fault either. It simply was what it was. And like she'd said, would it really have been better for her to have accepted his engagement half-heartedly in the spirit of Valentine's Day, then spent the next few months thinking how to get out of it? And while the affair was still something he couldn't forgive, perhaps he could understand it. After all, people dealt with things in different ways, or had their own perspectives of what was normal where relationships were concerned, their own methods of dealing with loneliness, and of trying to meet someone new. Look at Sophie. Look at Mark and Julie. And look at Calum.

Old Amsterdam was just round the corner and, on a whim, Nathan headed towards it, thinking he might just peek in through the window and see how Calum was getting on. As he turned into Charlotte Street, he spotted what looked like Mia-Rose, a single red rose in her hand, being escorted out of the restaurant, and realised that must have been embarrassing for Calum, until he saw it was actually Calum who was holding the door open for her.

Nathan wondered if he'd had been stood up, and whether Mia-Rose had come to his rescue, but by the blissful look on his face, Calum didn't care. They hadn't seen him, so he ducked into a nearby doorway and watched as the two of them made their way along the pavement, walking that walk where, were they any closer, they'd be touching, and any further apart, they'd just be two people heading in the same direction. The difference, Nathan noted, though tiny, was in fact huge.

Just before they crossed the road, Calum leaned in and whispered something in Mia-Rose's ear, and in response, she threw her head back and laughed, then gently linked her arm with his. And Nathan didn't know if it was a trick of the light, or whether the pavement perhaps rose a little at that point, but he'd swear Calum seemed to grow a couple of inches taller.

He turned and made his way back to where he'd parked his bike, and found himself outside Poles Apart. The lights were still on, so he pushed the door open and walked inside—despite his earlier pronouncement, a coffee was all he really felt like picking up this evening—and while he didn't expect to find Kasia still working, the sight of her behind the counter was a pleasant surprise.

'Evening,' he said, and she looked up suspiciously, smiling broadly when she recognised him.

'Hello, Nathan. And how is my favourite customer?'

Nathan looked around the empty café. From what he could see, he was her only customer.

'I bet you say that to everyone who comes in here.'

'I do,' said Kasia, matter-of-factly. 'It is good for tips. But I only mean it with one of them.'

Nathan laughed. 'Well, I'm fine; thanks for asking,' he said. 'Tired, though. It's been a long day. Which is why I'm in need of one of your coffees.'

'I thought you would have a date tonight?'

Nathan shook his head. 'No. I'm not the biggest fan of Valentine's Day.'

'No?' Kasia raised both eyebrows. 'Then you would like it in Poland. There, we don't celebrate it so much.'

'Why not?'

Kasia shrugged, and then without asking what he wanted, began to make him a latte. 'For us, Valentine is the saint of, how do you say, people who have fit?'

Nathan laughed. 'People who are fit. Good-looking people. It's kind of the same here.'

'No.' Kasia shook her head. 'People who have fit.' She pulled her phone out of her pocket and jabbed at the screen. 'Wait. I have Google Translate.'

Nathan loved the way she said 'Google Translate.' It made her sound like a sexy vampire, and he was just considering telling her that when she turned her phone round so he could see the screen.

'Epileptics?'

Kasia nodded. 'Like I said. People who have fit.'

'Ah. So it's not quite the romantic day it is here, then?'

'Well, we have some romance.'

'Such as?'

'We also have a custom of throwing a sugar cube into...' She consulted Google Translate again. 'How do you say these words?'

'"Eligible bachelor."'

'...into eligible bachelor's drink.'

'Well, that is romantic,' he said, sarcastically.

Kasia smiled. 'You think? Because we must keep the sugar in our armpit for nine days first. That way, they will fall in love with us. Like I say, it's tradition.'

Nathan grimaced. 'And does it work?' he said, eyeing the sugar bowl on the counter suspiciously.

'Did your coffee taste funny this morning?'

He laughed again. 'I'm back here for another one, aren't I?'

'Good. Then it works.'

She laughed too, and as she passed him his latte, a couple walked in holding hands, the girl grinning from ear to ear while admiring the ring she was wearing, and Nathan didn't have to be a genius to work out what had just happened. He blew on his coffee as he peered at them over the rim of his cup. They were giggling, and as the girl looked at her boyfriend adoringly, for the first time in a long time, Nathan noted to his surprise that something was different. He didn't feel cynical.

He sipped his latte, wondering whether this was the result of his earlier clear-the-air meeting with Ellie, or even something to do with seeing Calum and Mia-Rose. Perhaps it was even due to what had happened with him and Sophie—Nathan wasn't sure—but he hoped it was progress. He leant against the wall, sipping his latte as Kasia served the couple, strangely reluctant to leave. Once they'd gone, he walked back towards the counter.

'So...'

Kasia glanced round at him as she finished wiping the coffee machine down. 'So?'

Nathan's heart was beating faster than normal, and he didn't think it was from the caffeine. 'I was wondering...'

'Wondering what?'

He cleared his throat, then shook his head slowly. 'I was going to ask if you wanted to go out for a coffee sometime, but I doubt that's the most tempting offer for someone who works in a place like this.'

Kasia walked over to the door, turned the sign round so it read 'closed,' then slid the bolt across. 'Not really,' she said, then helped herself to a fruit juice from the refrigerator and sat down at the nearest table.

'"Not really" as in it's not a tempting offer, or "not really" as in you don't want to do it with me?' said Nathan, nervously.

'The first one,' said Kasia, indicating the seat opposite.

Nathan sat down as instructed. 'So what would you like to do?'

'With you?' Kasia pulled the plastic straw from the side of her juice carton, carefully punctured the foil seal with the pointy end, then took a sip. 'I think, most things,' she said.

She smiled briefly, then shyly looked down at the table, and though Nathan wouldn't realise it for a couple of months, that was the precise moment he fell in love.

FROM THE AUTHOR

Thank you for buying (and reading!) *A Day at the Office* – I hope you enjoyed it. If you did, I'd really appreciate if you could:

Tell your friends.

Post a review on Amazon.

Give it a mention on any book forums you might subscribe to.

If you're interested, you can find out about my other books on my website: www.mattdunn.co.uk

You can also:

Email me on matt@mattdunn.co.uk

Tweet (or even follow) me on twitter—I'm @mattdunnwrites

Friend me on Facebook—you'll find me at www.facebook.com/mattdunnwrites

Either way, it'd be great to hear from you!

Thanks again, and best wishes,

Matt

BY THE SAME AUTHOR

Best Man
The Ex-Boyfriend's Handbook
From Here To Paternity
Ex-Girlfriends United
The Good Bride Guide
The Accidental Proposal

ABOUT THE AUTHOR

British writer Matt Dunn is the author of seven (and counting) romantic comedy novels, including the bestselling *The Ex-Boyfriend's Handbook*, which was shortlisted for both the Romantic Novel Of The Year Award and the Melissa Nathan Award for Comedy Romance. He's also written about life, love, and relationships for various publications including *The Times*, the *Guardian, Glamour, Cosmopolitan, Company, Elle,* and *The Sun.* Before becoming a full-time writer, Matt worked as a lifeguard, a fitness-equipment salesman, and an I.T. head-hunter.

His website and blog can be found at http://www.mattdunn.co.uk/.